BUCKLIN FAMILY REUNION SERIES

·HIGH COTTON·

a novel by
Debby Mayne

GILEAD
PUBLISHING

Grand Rapids, Michigan

High Cotton by Debby Mayne
Published by Gilead Publishing, Grand Rapids, Michigan 49546
www.gileadpublishing.com

gp GILEAD PUBLISHING

ISBN: 978-1-68370-1-309 (paper)
ISBN: 978-1-68370-1-316 (ebook)

High Cotton
Copyright © 2018 by Debby Mayne

Published in the United States by Gilead Publishing, Grand Rapids, Michigan.

This is a work of fiction. Names, characters, places, and incidents are products of the author's imagination or are used fictitiously. Any similarity to actual people, organizations, and/or events is purely coincidental.

Edited by Susan Brower
Cover designed by Laura Mason
Interior design/typesetting by Amy Shock

Printed in the United States of America

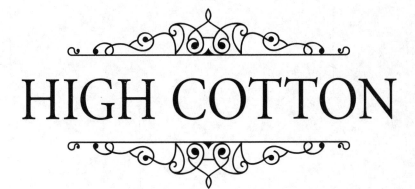

HIGH COTTON

Debby Mayne

"High cotton" originated in the South when an abundance of tall cotton plants and high prices earned by these crops made farmers wealthy. It's still used today to mean that a person is financially successful.

1

Shay Henke

When someone mentions family, I think of unconditional love, hearth, home, and all things safe and wonderful. That is, until the word "reunion" is added to it.

Family reunions serve one purpose as far as I can tell—to remind us that we're only one step away from Crazy Town, no matter how hard we've worked to stay sane and make something of ourselves. And I've worked mighty hard to get where I am, regardless of what Aunt Faye says about my being an old maid.

So when I get the message on the family email loop that the next family reunion is coming up in two months, I stare at it and try to figure out a way to *unsee* it. Unfortunately, as soon as I open the email, the person who sent it knows, making me long for the days when technology wasn't so smart and we didn't have everyone on the same service to see when the email was picked up.

I stare out the window and try to come up with a reason I shouldn't go. It's on a Saturday, and I hardly ever have to work on weekends. I'm not dating anyone, and I have very few friends outside my family, so I can't claim to have other plans. I can't think of a thing to keep me away, unless I lie, and I've never been very good at that, so I quit trying when I was a teenager. Mama used to tell me she got into so much trouble as a kid that she knows all the excuses. And she's not kidding. I've never been able to pull anything over on her.

I turn back to the announcement on the computer screen. We used to get a couple weeks' notice about these events, but that changed to a couple of months when people started overusing the excuse that they had plans. Now there are no excuses—not even when someone has moved away from Pinewood, the small town near Hattiesburg, Mississippi, where my grandparents have lived all their lives. If the people who have to travel don't want to stay with someone who still lives here, there's always the Hilltop Family Inn, or they can stay in one of the chain hotels in Hattiesburg.

I'm about to get up to get a drink of water when my phone rings. It's my brother, Digger, who feels the same way I do about these reunion things.

"I'm not sure we'll be able to attend," Digger says. "It's Jeremy's third birthday, and Puddin' wants to do it up big for him, seein' as it's our last child and all."

"What better way to do it up big than to bring him to the family reunion where you'll have scores of aunts, uncles, and cousins twice removed to give him more attention than he'll ever need?"

"Shay. Seriously."

"Just sayin'."

"What are you going to do?" Digger sounds condescending, and his voice annoys me.

"I thought I'd rent a husband and a Cadillac for the day just to get everyone off my back."

He laughs. "I know you're not going to rent a husband because no one will ever measure up to Elliot."

"Digger." I hope he gets my tone of finality. Digger is the only person who knew about my crush on Elliot Stevens back in high school.

"Okay, let's start over." He clears his throat. "Really, Shay? A Cadillac? Can't you at least get a Beemer?"

"No, Digger, not really. I'm not planning to rent a car or a husband. Are you too dense to recognize sarcasm?"

"I knew what you were doing."

"Sure you did. At any rate, if I go, I think you should, too." I pause. "You know how Mama will be if you don't show up. Besides, she'll want to brag on Jeremy and show him off, he's so cute."

"True. I'll talk to Puddin'." I hear commotion over the phone. "I gotta go, Shay. Puddin' needs me to help put Jeremy to bed. He's been givin' us fits lately."

"Give Puddin' my love." How hard can it be to put a pint-sized person to bed? I laugh. Digger is like a loaf of French bread—crusty and macho on the outside but soft in the middle.

After we hang up, I read the email again. It says to RSVP, but I don't have to do it right this minute. Not normally one to procrastinate, I figure I'm okay just this one time.

I've barely stood up from my computer chair when my phone rings again. This time it's Mama.

"Why haven't you responded?"

"Um . . ."

"I know you saw the message. It says right here that you read it almost twenty minutes ago."

"Mama! Are you the one planning this?"

"Not exactly. There's a group of us—"

"Why didn't you warn me?" I pause to try to get the shriek out of my voice. "You know how I feel about these things."

"And that's precisely why you need to go. Everyone cares about you, even though you keep pushing us away."

Do I hear a sniffle on the other end of the line? I clear my throat.

"I'm sure they do care, but last time they showed me how much they cared, a week later I got a half dozen phone calls from guys those caring folks gave my number to."

"They're just trying to help, sweetie. You need to get out there and meet some men."

"I meet plenty of men at work."

"Yeah," she agrees. "They're all stuffy types who have no idea where you come from. Don't you forget for one minute who you are, Shay."

"I know, I know." I find it amusing that Mama thinks the men I meet at work are stuffy. If anyone's stuffy, it's me.

I don't say what I'm thinking—that I've worked hard to hide the redneck in my bloodline. It's one thing to be a redneck and another to be a geek. But being both . . . well, it's all a matter of perception. It'll always be there, and I'm not saying it's always a bad thing. I just don't think being a redneck helps encourage respect from the people I manage. Or date.

"So are you going or not?"

"I don't think—"

"If you decide not to go, there's no tellin' what everyone will say about you." Mama blows out a breath. "You know how some of our kinfolk can talk behind people's backs."

"I don't care what—"

"But I do. I care a lot. You're my little girl, and I love you to pieces, and it just kills me when I hear—"

"All right, Mama. I'll go." I'm not in the mood to hear Mama's diatribe about how she suffered the whole nine and a half months she was pregnant with me, how much she worried about the fact that I was a clumsy kid and lived in fear that I'd break my neck doing some daredevil stunt, how late she'd stayed up waiting for me the two times I went out when I was a teenager, and how she feared for my life when I left for college. I mean, isn't that all a part of parenting? It's expected.

"Good girl. Now don't forget to bring something. You don't have to cook anything. We always need potato chips at these things."

"I can cook now. I'll make something good, like maybe deviled eggs," I say before clicking the Off button. I might have agreed to go, but I'm still a rebel. Now let Mama worry that I'll leave the mayonnaise out on the counter too long and give everyone food poisoning. I've tried explaining that it's not the mayo that makes people sick, but she's not one to take lessons from her young'uns.

I plop back down in front of my computer, accept the invitation, and type the dish I plan to bring. My attitude is rotten, and it probably comes through. I haven't figured out why it takes so little these days to annoy me, but I'm praying the Lord will show me so I can do something about it.

I take a deep breath and blow it out. *Forgive me, Lord. You know how I struggle with family stuff. I'll try to do better.*

This wouldn't be so difficult if I had a man in my life, more because of what other people think than what I need. Although, I have to admit, I wouldn't mind someone to cuddle with on a cold night. Some of my aunts, uncles, and cousins will say something to me about the fact that I'm in my late thirties and still single. The ones who don't will talk behind my back. It always happens. Mama's right about my not showing up. People will assume the worst, and I'll hear about it after the gossip has made the rounds.

An overwhelming urge to find an award-winning deviled egg recipe washes over me. I might be an old maid in some people's minds, but one thing they can't call me is a slacker. When I do something, I do it right.

I turn back to the computer and Google "deviled egg recipes." Most of them are the same—boiled eggs sliced in half, a dollop of mayonnaise, a smidge of mustard, a spoonful of pickle relish, and something colorful to dash them with after they're on the platter. Too common. I want something to wow 'em.

For the next couple of hours, I search recipe after recipe until I finally find the perfect one. It has one secret ingredient that no one will be able to resist. Bacon bits. And who doesn't love bacon?

2
Puddin' Henke

"I don't care what they say about Shay, I think she's a smart girl," Digger says.

I look at him from above my reading glasses. "Men don't care about smart," I remind him.

"What are you talkin' about? I'm a man. I know what men like." He gives me a scowl. "She's pretty, too."

"In a harsh, corporate-executive, hair-pulled-back-so-tight-her-eyes-are-squinty sort of way. I've told her more than once that she might want to loosen her hair a tad." I put down the book I've been reading, get up out of my La-Z-Boy recliner, and walk over to the man I've been married to for near 'bout twenty years. "Face it, Digger. Your sister has no idea how pretty she is or all the wonderful things she has to offer. I love her to death, but she chose her path in life, and it's not exactly one that'll keep her warm at night."

Digger sighs. "I just don't want her feelin' like she has to apologize for everything she does or chooses."

"She doesn't, sweetheart. Shay will always have us. She's your sister, and that makes her my sister, too." I give him a half-smile. "Besides, I really do care about her. Did you know she's the most trustworthy person I know?"

Digger casts a dubious half-smile in my direction before giving me a clipped nod. "I appreciate that, Puddin'." He lifts the newspaper that he's been trying to read since morning. "Did you see there's a sale on riding lawn mowers over at Jackie's Farm Store?"

I snort. "What on earth would you do with a riding lawn mower?"

"Mow the lawn." He gives me a disapproving glance. "What else would I do?"

The look of desire on his face is something I haven't seen in a while, and even though it's for a lawn mower, I can't resist. "Okay, Digger, if that's what you really want, I don't see why you can't have it."

"Do you mean that?" He gets up out of his chair and walks toward me.

"Of course I do. After all, I'm finally in my dream house, so who am I to deny you something you want?"

He reaches for my hand. I give it, and he pulls me to my feet. I love when Digger shows me some love, and if it takes a lawn mower, well, so be it.

"You know, Puddin', me and you make a great team."

I look up into his eyes and smile. "We do."

My heart aches when he doesn't smile back. He lets go of my hand and shakes his head. "You'd think that between the two of us we'd be able to figure out how to get out of my family reunion that's coming up. I don't get why they keep havin' 'em so close together. Didn't we just have one a few months ago?"

I nod, and as he backs away, I practically throw myself at him. "I think we should go to this one. After all, we finally have something to brag on."

"Jeremy?" he asks.

"Well, yeah, we can brag on him, too. But I'm talkin' about this house. We can take a bunch of pictures and pass 'em around to everyone. They'll all be so impressed that we finally have a brick, ranch-style house with big ol' shutters and a two-car garage."

In spite of Digger's feelings about going to the reunion, he snorts. "I don't know that anyone in my family will be as impressed as you think they'll be."

"Oh, they'll be impressed, all right, even if they don't show it. I know your family near 'bout as well as I know my own."

He lets out a groan. "Well, since you didn't give me any flak about the ridin' lawn mower, I'll think about it."

"You'll think about it?"

"Okay, Puddin', I reckon we'll go."

"And you'll go with a good attitude?" I lift one eyebrow—a skill I've recently learned after countless hours practicing in front of the bathroom mirror.

He grimaces and nods. "If it's that important to you." He yawns and stretches. "I best be headin' off to bed. Mornin' comes mighty early around here during the week."

"I'll be there shortly."

Out of the corner of my eye, I see Digger shaking his head and his mouth moving as he mumbles something about my need to be accepted. As much as I hate to admit it, he knows me all too well.

All my life, I've felt like the poor kid. I remember from a very early age when folks would drop off big bags of clothes that Mama would sort and stack for all six of us young'uns. "This might not fit you now, but you'll grow into it," became her mantra.

Daddy used to say we were too poor to paint and too proud to white-wash, when he talked about the sorry excuse for the crumbling wood house we grew up in. Something was always broken, but we managed to find ways to do what it took to get through life.

Mama tried to put on a positive face when we went out as a family, but I could see her shame behind the facade. It hurt me as much as I'm sure it did her, but there wasn't a thing any of us could do about it. At least not until we became adults.

All of us are doin' just fine now, and we're able to send Mama some money every month to supplement her little social security check. Daddy took sick about ten years ago, and he was finally able to meet his Maker, knowing everything would be just fine with his family, now that we're all grown up and able to tend to Mama.

Every single, solitary one of us is much better off than my parents ever were. My siblings all have jobs and nice homes. My Digger has a great job with UPS, and he gets to wear that cute little brown uniform that makes me tingle all over. I've always loved men in uniform.

My brother Billy Ray is a hauler with his own fleet of trucks that take cargo coast to coast. Mason started out going to college but quickly learned that he was a better salesman than student. Now he sells used cars up in North Carolina, so we don't see much of him since he works seven days a week. Here in Mississippi, most of them close on Sunday, but apparently where he lives now, people never stop shopping for cars. Mason has never been one to miss out on making an extra dime. Once he started making money, he became addicted. Too bad he doesn't take some time off to enjoy it, but at least his young'uns are livin' in high cotton. Tyrell is a maintenance supervisor in a hospital down in Biloxi. My only living sister, Patricia, became a bank teller, married the branch manager, and eventually became a stay-at-home mama just like me. The oldest of us young'uns, Sue Ellen, didn't go to the doctor when she found a lump in her breast, so it spread until she wasn't treatable. We lost her several years ago, shortly after Daddy passed. It still makes me sad, but at least we all have comfort in knowing she loved the Lord. I figure she's up in heaven with Daddy, scopin' the place out for the rest of us.

So now I want to show off what me and Digger have accomplished through hard work, determination, and the desire to pull out of our lower-than-humble beginnings. Digger was better off growing up than I was, but not by much. He still talks about how they wouldn't have had much on their plates if it weren't for his mama bein' such a good gardener and havin' the ability to squeeze a quarter so tight he could hear the eagle scream. When he tells me I can't buy something I want, I accuse him of takin' after his mama. Sometimes it works. Sometimes it doesn't. All depends on the last conversation he and his mama had.

Since we bought this house before the builder put the final touches on it, I still have brochures, swatches, and samples of everything we got to pick out. I open the bottom drawer of the buffet table in the dining room and pull out the box of memorabilia from the pickin'-out stage of our home-buying experience.

I lovingly stroke the square piece of carpet that I'm still in love with. It's not the highest end, but it's not the cheap, not-enough-yarn-to-cover-the-backing quality either. It's much better than what we had in the rental house. Some folks say we should have gone with hardwood, but we couldn't afford that option.

Before I head to my room, I jot down my to-do list for tomorrow, which includes taking pictures of all the rooms in the house so I can pass my phone around at Digger's family reunion. For once, I'll have something besides the kids to brag on.

We were still in the buying stage during the last reunion, so I promised Digger I'd keep quiet about it in case something went wrong. I don't think he believed it would actually happen until it did.

I put the box back in the drawer and let out a deep sigh of satisfaction. I imagine the sounds of Digger's aunts and cousins as they ooh and ahh over our beautiful home with country décor straight out of *Southern Living,* and I can't help but smile.

3

Missy Wright Montague

"And the winner of this year's chili cook-off is ..." Everyone holds their breath as the announcer looks around, his eyes gleaming, a wicked grin playing on his lips. He finally settles his gaze on me as his smile widens. "Missy Montague, for her delectable chicken chili." He starts clapping his hands and adds, "Let's give Ms. Montague a nice round of applause."

Only a few people clap, but the sound of groaning from the other contestants hums in my ears as I feel more joy than I ever imagined bubbling up inside me. I look around at all the disappointed folks—most of them women about my mama's age, along with a few men who use cheap beer as their "secret ingredient."

I have to admit, I don't get all that fancy with mine. I use white beans, shredded chicken, and a boatload of spices. If I had to name one of them a "secret," I reckon it would be the cinnamon. Oh, and Mama once taught me that a dash of sugar makes everything better, so I dump in a palmful. It might not be as nutritious as it would be without the sugar, but no one judges chili for its health benefits. Whatever the case, it works. Everyone loves my chicken chili.

As I wait for the next competition to be over so the judges can give us our awards at the same time, I stand by the front table and look around at the other contenders. They're all caught up in their own lives, hoping for a shred of validation from the judges. I already have mine, so I'm able to relax as I smile.

It takes a while for the rest of the competitions in the slow-cooker category to be done. One thing I notice is that everyone else has a family member nearby to share the glory. By the time they give us our ribbons and shake our hands, some of the joy has faded, and my thoughts are on who I can impress next, which isn't too difficult since the next Bucklin family reunion has just been announced.

Most families have reunions once a year, if that. But not mine. We do it every time someone has a new baby or graduates from college or manages to make it through high school or whatever any of my aunts can think of, even if the reason is simply to bring everyone together. It's not usually as terrible as some of my kinfolk make it out to be, but I can think of other places I'd rather go on a warm summer day. Like shopping.

At least I'll have a dish people will want to eat. The first time I brought something to one of the reunions, there were only a couple of spoonfuls of it missing when I went to get my dish. Mama had told me everyone likes ambrosia. She was wrong. They hate it.

"You should have left out the coconut," she said when I whined about it. Of course, this is coming from someone who thinks tomato aspic is the bomb. No one likes that either, but there's always at least one on the salad table.

But my chicken chili is different. I started working on it immediately after the last reunion, and I've finally managed to perfect it to please even the most discriminating palate, namely these judges. I don't have to think too hard to imagine my uncles and cousins all lined up to get a scoop of this hearty delight, which is what the judges are calling it as they congratulate me.

"Way to go, Missy."

I smile at one of my competitors. "Why thank you, Ms. Dunbar. Maybe next year you'll do better with your meatless chili."

Her expression turns sour. "Those judges wouldn't know good chili if it bit 'em in the—"

"Edna!" The sound of her husband's voice stops her. "Be nice, okay? There are other competitions."

She rolls her eyes and shakes her head. "Okay, then I'll just say them judges don't have much taste in their slimy little mouths."

Mr. Dunbar gives me an apologetic look. "Sorry, Missy. My wife worked mighty hard on her chili."

"I understand." It's easy to be understandin' when you're the winner. I try to show sympathy. "We all work hard. Too bad we can't all go home winners."

He picks up his wife's Crock-Pot, gives me a nod, and heads toward the exit, his wife following right behind him, her face all puckered up like she's been eating persimmons.

I turn back around and face my personal reality. I might have won the chili competition, but no one but me cares.

Yeah, most of the folks had someone behind them to support them throughout the contest, but not me. My husband, Foster, is out on a bass boat with some of his buddies from church, and our daughter is off somewhere with her friends. It doesn't take long for the tent to completely clear out, leaving me and one other contestant standing there, trying to figure out what to do next.

"Wanna swap a bowl of chili?" the man I've never seen before asks, a flirty smile tweaking the corners of his mouth.

"No, thank you." I brush the hair from my face, making sure my wedding ring shows to let him know I'm not available. "I'm not hungry." Before he has a chance to say another word, I pick up my slow cooker and first-place ribbon and leave.

All the way home, I try to relish what I'd accomplished, but it's difficult since no one I care about was there to witness it. I let out a sigh of resignation. Now I know what Mama was talking about when she said she spent so much time carin' for her young'uns, there wasn't anything left for her. I send a prayer up for Mama, and then I add myself.

I pull into the driveway and open my car door, still praying. Before I get out of the car, I finish my prayer, glance over at the almost empty slow cooker, and decide it's high time I start living life for myself. Foster won't be home until tomorrow, and Wendy is eighteen, so why not?

The pot seems heavier when I get it out of the car, carry it inside, and put it on the kitchen counter. It's awful quiet in the house, with Foster on his fishin' trip and Wendy who knows where.

I wiggle the mouse on the kitchen computer to bring the screen to life. The first thing I do is email Aunt Irma and let her know I'll be at the reunion. She and a couple of my other aunts have taken it upon themselves to help coordinate this one, which means it'll be good. Last time we had a reunion, it was Uncle Bubba's turn, and he turned it over to his wife, Aunt Lady, who forgot to assign casseroles, so we wound up with a half dozen lasagnas and no bread. Everyone knows you gotta have bread with your lasagna.

Next, I click around to see what movies are playing in Pinewood. It doesn't look like anything that would interest me, so I change gears and decide to head over to Walmart. I don't need anything, but I'm sure I'll find something interesting.

The Walmart parking lot is huge, and there are no empty spots near the entrance. I find one close to a light, get out of my car, and look around to get my bearings so I can find my car when I come out. I've parked in aisle four, so I repeat that in my head several times to commit it to memory. I can't tell you how many times in the past I've wandered around, looking for my vehicle, wishing I had established a point of reference.

The store is buzzing with activity as usual, and there are long lines populated by weary people who would rather be anywhere but here. I notice a girl with her buggy filled with diapers, thumbing through coupons, her eyebrows knit with worry. That girl was me nearly eighteen years ago. Times were tough back then, and without coupons and a little goodwill from Mama and a couple other people who took pity, I'm not sure what would've happened to us. I'd just married Foster and given birth to Wendy six months later. Mama was furious with me. She kept talking about her premature grandbaby to everyone else, but we didn't fool anyone.

I turn my buggy toward the electronics department. Maybe they have those smartphones everyone's been talking about. They've been out for a number of years, but Foster doesn't believe in replacing anything that's not broken. My flip phone keeps cutting out on me, so I have every reason to get a new one. If Foster and I had even a fraction of my cousin Bucky and Marybeth's money, I'd have me a brand spankin' new phone every time one comes out. I'd love to be one of those folks who can shop for groceries, watch movies, and check my email, all while sittin' at the beauty shop, waitin' for the color to take.

I let out a sigh. All that material stuff sounds good, but deep down, I know what I really want is more attention from my husband, who seems less interested in me now than ever. I'd give up just about anything if Foster would give me more of his time.

4
Sally Wright

My identical twin sister, Sara, annoys me to no end. She not only borrows my eyeliner whenever she wants, she expects me to know where to find her stuff. And it's never anywhere I'd put it.

People think we're alike in every single way, but we couldn't be more different. She's a slob, and I'm OCD when it comes to putting things away. She's left-handed, and I'd poke out my eyeball if I tried to feed myself with my left hand. Don't get me wrong, I love Sara and can't imagine life without her. But sometimes . . . well, maybe it's just a twin thing.

"What did you do with my lipstick?" she hollers from her room in the two-bedroom apartment we share.

"I didn't do anything with it."

"Then where is it?"

"Right where you left it," I holler back. It takes every ounce of self-restraint to keep from growling at her. She growls back, and since we're identical twins, I can tell it's not a great look for either of us.

"It's not in my makeup drawer." She storms into my room and stands at the door glaring at me.

"Are you sure you put it there?"

A flicker of doubt flashes across her face. "I'm pretty sure."

"Why don't you look under your vanity? Sometimes things roll and, you know, gravity happens."

She opens her mouth then quickly closes it as she shakes her head but remains standing there, watching me do my hair. I let out a sigh of relief that this hasn't turned into a full-blown argument. We've been fighting a lot lately, and I hate it. But I'm not about to let her get away with accusing me of something I have nothing to do with.

Even though we've been out of our parents' house for almost a year, I still can't get over the fact that I finally have my own room. Mama and Daddy said that since we were twins, there was no reason to move out of the family's perfectly adequate house and into a bigger one just so Sara and I could have our own rooms.

I lift another section of hair and wrap it around the active-ion brush that's supposed to smooth out my frizzy hair in seconds. Before I hit it with the blow dryer, I look at my sister, whose shoulder-length blond hair forms a halo around her head.

"You really should get one of these," I say.

She shrugs. "I don't see why. You already have one. I can just use yours."

Annoyance once again floods my veins. Still holding the handle of my brush, I slowly turn to face her and narrow my eyes. "You may *not* use mine."

She smirks, the look that, even though I make it, too, bugs me to no end. "You'll never know. We have the same color hair."

"Oh, I'll know. You never put anything back where it belongs."

We both pause and widen our eyes, glaring at each other, waiting for someone to yell for us to stop bickering. Then it dawns on me that there isn't anyone else to interfere, so I start back up as I smooth out the section of hair I've been working on.

"And you'll probably break it. I had to watch a lot of YouTube videos to learn how to do it right."

She rolls her eyes. "How do you know I haven't been watching YouTube videos?"

Once again, I turn to face her. "Have you?"

"Maybe." Without another word, Sara turns and goes back to her room.

"That Sara." I shake my head and chuckle.

She reappears at my door. "What do you mean, *that Sara*?"

I see her annoyed expression, and somehow that tickles my funny bone. I start to laugh, and after she gets past whatever's bothering her, she laughs, too. Then we both stop at the same time, and she leaves my room shaking her head. "That Sally."

I go deep inside my own head while I finish getting ready. Although I love my sister, I often have mixed feelings about being with her so much. Not only are we twins and roommates, but we also own an Etsy business together. It has its positives, but the negatives sometimes make me want to give up and start my own business without her. We had no idea how big it would become when we first signed up on Etsy.

It all started as a side job when we worked as tellers at two different banks. Neither one of us could imagine counting money all our lives. In fact, I wasn't even good at it, and I suspect she wasn't either. Every evening during supper, we spent the first half hour complaining about work.

"I think I'll go back to college," she said one evening before we turned on the TV.

"And major in what?"

"Elementary education."

I laughed. "You hated the thought of teaching when you found out you'd have to work with kids."

She shrugged. "I don't know, then. Something that pays a lot and I don't have to deal with annoying people."

"Good luck with that."

After six months of misery, she came up with a plan to make hair bows for little girls. "Remember when Mama used to go to craft shows and come home with all those gaudy things she stuck in our hair?"

"Why would someone buy a hair bow from us when they can go to Walmart and get one really cheap?"

Sara gave me a closed-mouth grin. "Because we'll make 'em bigger and better than the ones they have at Walmart. Ours will be different, and they'll stand out."

That was the start of the business we now own and run full time. It never dawned on us that we'd ever make more than pocket change. But we do. Much more. In fact, each of us makes more than double what we earned in our former teller jobs, and it appears from the upward trend that we'll soon be doubling our income again over the next year or so. We figured out that the bigger the bows, the more people wanted them, and we could charge a fortune for them.

As soon as we're both ready for the day, we meet in the kitchen for coffee. "There's a sale on ribbon at the craft store, so I'm thinking it's time to stock up," she says as she fills two mugs and hands one to me.

"That is, if they have any decent ribbon left." I take a sip of my coffee. "Didn't the sale start last week?"

She shrugs. "We can look around." She glances at her phone. "Mama's texting us."

My phone is still in my room, so I walk over and look at her phone. "What does she want?"

Sara groans. "There's another family reunion."

"That's crazy. Didn't we just have one?"

"I know, right?" Sara stares at her phone again. "We're supposed to RSVP."

"Of course."

"But why? We all know who'll be there and who won't."

I tip my head back and laugh. "Sara, I don't know how you can say that since we don't even know if *we're* going."

"I think we should go."

"Now that's a first." I take a deep breath and slowly let it out. "If I go, I'm not staying long. It gets old—"

"Having people think we're the same person just because we're twins, right?"

"Yeah, just because we finish each other's sentences..." I look her in the eyes. "I guess we should probably go to make Mama happy."

"Yes, for Mama," she agrees.

We both grow quiet for a few seconds. I can tell she's thinking the same thing as me when she shudders. The very thought of what Mama will do if we don't show up gives me chills up and down my spine. Granted, all southern mamas know how to use guilt, but ours is the master at it. I won't be surprised to hear that she gives classes in guilting your young'uns.

She breaks the silence. "What should we bring?"

"We never bring anything." I shrug. "I don't see why we should start now."

"We don't live with Mama and Daddy anymore, so that makes us adults. We have to bring something. Adults bring stuff to these things."

Memories of the dessert tables at the family reunions pop into my mind, and I get excited. "Hey, how about some pies?"

She gives me an incredulous look. "Pies?"

"Yeah, like apple, blueberry, sweet potato, or pecan."

"You're kidding, right?" She shakes her head. "We're not even good at heating up frozen pies. How do you think we'll manage that?"

"Don't be so dense, Sara. All we have to do is go to the Blossom Bakery and pick them up."

"People will know."

I grin as a plan hatches in my head. "Not if we buy some matching pie pans with our initials and get Rosemary to bake the pies in them."

"You're brilliant, Sally."

"I know."

5

Shay

I glance at the time on my cell phone as I wait for the light to turn green. I'm getting to the office early, but that's exactly what I want to do. It's not easy juggling all the demands I face each and every single day as general manager of a major food distributor. As busy as I am, I've done everything so many times, the challenges have become busywork. But it still has to get done.

A company that wants us to represent them is sending some people over to tout their attributes. Sometimes this aspect of the job gets old because we can't take on everyone. We're the premier food distributor in South Mississippi, so we're generally the first place people start. If I could give any of them advice—and I typically do after they finish their presentation—it would be to start with the smaller distributors where there's not as much competition. Once they reach a level of success that they can sustain, they can work their way up to my company, Southern Foods.

My phone rings, but the traffic light has turned green, so I decide to wait until I'm in the office parking lot to answer since the only person who calls me this early is Mama. No doubt it has something to do with the reunion.

Once I pull into my designated parking spot, I call Mama back. She doesn't waste a second before letting me have it. "What took you so long?"

"I don't like to talk on the phone while I'm driving."

Mama makes a guttural sound with her throat. "You're probably the only person in Pinewood who feels that way."

She and I have always had a frustrating relationship, but I love her, and I know she loves me. In fact, I suspect that all her pushiness is to help me remember where I come from.

"So what's up?" I ask. "I have a meeting in a little while, so I don't have long."

"I thought you didn't have to be at work until nine."

"I have to get ready for this meeting. If you want me to call you back later, I will."

"No," Mama says. "I just need to know if you're bringing someone to the reunion."

"Bringing someone? Like who?"

"I don't know. A date, maybe?"

I don't even have to think about this. "I doubt it."

"Shay." Mama's voice is soft but deep, reminding me of what I used to think was a tone of disapproval when I was a teenager. Now I hear it more as concern and desperation. "You can't keep this up. Everyone in the family is worried about you being . . . well, staying single."

"You mean being an old maid?" I hate the sound of that, even coming from my own mouth. "Look, Mama, I'm happy with my life. I have a nice job, a comfortable condo, and lots of friends."

"Yes, I realize that, but—"

"Like I said, I'm happy. I'm in the office parking lot, and I need to go in."

"Okay, Shay, but you have so much to offer the right man, and I'd really like for you to at least give this dating thing some thought."

"I'll think about it."

"That's all I can ask."

After I click the Off button, I sit and stare straight ahead for a few minutes. I told Mama that I'm happy, but am I really? I'm content . . . most of the time. Yet there are moments that make me think it might be nice to have someone by my side. Someone to lean on. Someone to laugh with. Someone to share life's difficult moments. Someone to gripe to after a bad day at the office. Truth be told, I'm not always happy with my job. In fact, even though I have a ton of stuff to do, lately I've been bored to tears. And of course that makes me feel guilty as all get-out since I know dozens of people who would love to be in my shoes.

I lift my chin, square my shoulders, and get out of my car. I have a meeting that deserves some preparation. It wouldn't be right to give this new company anything but all my attention.

Easier said than done, as Mama has always said.

Throughout the sweet little company's presentation about why they would revolutionize the condiments industry with their variety of flavors in 3-in-1 packs that go from dinner table to tailgate party, I picture the product on a picnic table ... at my family reunion.

"There's enough for a party of twelve to season their hamburgers and hot dogs at a tailgate party and still have some left over," the main woman whose name I can't remember says. She's trying to show confidence, but I can see the redness of her nervousness creeping up her chest and starting to reach her face. Her hands shake as she gestures.

Her sidekick speaks up. "Or you can serve all your friends and neighbors at your backyard party without having to tote a whole bunch of bottles of stuff." She turns to the first woman. "Right, Doris?"

Okay, good. Now I remember her name.

"We use only top-of-the-line ingredients in our condiments, so they should make even the pickiest eater happy."

After the people finish touting their condiments, the Southern Foods marketing manager opens the meeting to questions. I've already instructed the team to go easy on these people since this is their first attempt to get into the big leagues.

Doris wrings her hands as she nervously glances around the room at the Southern Foods executives. I notice how she has to keep swallowing before she speaks, and my heart goes out to her. Finally, one of them lifts a finger and speaks.

"I've seen similar products on the market already. Have you researched the competition?"

Doris's eyes widen, and she slowly shakes her head. "I ... I didn't know anyone else had this. I thought I invented it."

A few more people on my team come up with some lame questions, letting me know that they're just trying to appear interested, when all they're doing is placating the nervous prospective vendors. There are three people here to do the presentation, but once the rehearsed part is over, the only one speaking is Doris, the inventor of the product.

My heart goes out to this sweet little lady with the accent that is not only southern but country as well. The urge to put her at ease washes over me.

"I'm not sure we're ready to make a decision on this just yet," I say. "Let us discuss it, and we'll get back to you."

She turns to her people, who both nod, then looks back at us. "Would y'all like to have some samples to help you make the decision?"

Since I happen to know that this company started on a shoestring, and these people invested their life savings in getting it up and running, I nod. "That would be nice, but I'll be happy to pay you for them."

"You don't have to." The look of desperation on her face nearly cracks my businesslike facade.

"I insist." I turn to my assistant. "Please have the bookkeeper cut a check for this case of samples."

After they gather their presentation materials, my assistant escorts them to the door. Doris stops, turns to face everyone still seated at the table, and manages a shaky smile. "Thank y'all so much for agreeing to see us. It would be such a pleasure for us to do business with a great company like Southern Foods."

Once we're alone, I turn to my team and, fighting the emotions that have welled up in my chest, force a smile. "Well? What do y'all think?"

The marketing manager lets out a chuckle, then clears his throat when he realizes I'm not laughing. "It is rather naïve for them to think this would be a success."

"Why?" I tilt my head and fold my arms as I hold his gaze, making him squirm. "Have you even tried their product?"

He frowns. "No, of course not. They didn't give us anything to try." He gestures over the empty table. "Most of the vendors bring us food."

"Really? Are you willing to sit here and eat condiments right out of the package?" I give him a look that makes him drop his gaze and shift in his seat.

"Well, no, but they could have brought—" He cuts himself off and lets out a breath, his nostrils flaring in the process.

"Actually, they're leaving plenty of samples for us to try later. I don't think it would be fair to make a decision before we know what the product tastes like and how it works in a real-life situation."

One of the reasons I'm successful is that I don't make rash decisions unless I'm one hundred percent sure of something. Although I suspect my marketing guy is right, I want to make sure we do the right thing by the vendor.

When my assistant returns to the meeting room, I ask, "Did you get the case of samples?"

She nods. "Two cases, and they're paid for. There's enough for all of us to take some home."

"Good." The image of the condiments at my family reunion returns, and I let out a sigh of satisfaction. What better way to know if this product will be a success than to run it by my very picky, very opinionated family?

6

Puddin'

Digger stands in front of the coffee pot, his legs peeking out from beneath his brown shorts, giving me that familiar tingly sensation all over. I know he's thinking about that ridin' lawn mower, but I'm not.

"I thought I'd go on over to Jackie's on my way home from work and take a look at those lawn mowers." Yeah, I'm right.

So I pull out the big guns. "I'm cookin' a pot roast for supper, so don't stay there browsin' too long."

I obviously said the right words, if his eyes rollin' back and his soft moan mean anything. And I know they do. Me and Digger went to a married-couples retreat where we learned about love languages. His is obviously food, even though that's not officially one of them. It should be.

He downs the last of his coffee, grabs another biscuit from the basket, takes a bite, chews a couple of times, swallows, and gives me a quick hug and kiss on the cheek. "Any chance you can make a lemon meringue pie for dessert?" His look of love is definitely melting me from the inside out.

I grin back at him. "Of course I can."

"That's my girl." He shoves the entire rest of the biscuit into his mouth and leaves the house with his cheeks bulging. I lean over and look out the window to watch his backside until he slides into his truck. I sure do love that man.

Digger and I were awful young when we got married, so we had no idea what we were doing. One thing I know now that would have made me want to wait is the amount of debt we managed to amass in such a short time after high school. His cool set of wheels with the killer stereo system set us back quite a bit and took forever to pay off. Then three babies …

I don't ever want him to worry about providing for us, so rather than go back into debt, I work that part-time job that he doesn't know about. Keeping quiet about it isn't something I'd choose if I had my druthers, but since Digger is so proud, I keep it a secret, and my boss is willing to go along.

If he ever finds out about my job, hoo-boy, he'll be so upset. And his pride will be in the gutter. He loves to brag about how he's able to support his family and I'm able to stay home for the young'uns. Our little "oops," Jeremy, goes to a preschool program at the church, so I don't have to feel guilty about my job.

I'm fortunate that one of my old high school pals is doing so well with her boutique, La Chic, that she can't keep up with the customers *and* the books. So I go in several days every week and do her bookkeeping. It's fairly easy, and I get to sit in the back room where no one can see me. She gives me an employee discount, but I don't even have enough money to take advantage of it. Truth be told, I don't need what she sells—mostly high-end designer clothes and overpriced fashion jewelry, most of which is way too flashy for my taste. But there are a few things I might indulge in if…

Oh, who am I kidding? I love the stuff. All of it. *Especially* the flashy pieces. Okay, I can't think about that now, or I might get all weepy about the things I want but can't have.

We have always loved our family more than anything, which is good since our first young'un came almost exactly nine months after we got married, and then the next two came two years apart. My mother-in-law made a few snide remarks about my being a baby factory, but she quickly got over it when she saw what a good mother I was.

I finish cleaning the kitchen as I ponder what to do next. My boss, Amanda, doesn't need me for a couple more hours.

"Mama!" The blood-curdling scream startles me, but it shouldn't.

Jeremy has always been a late sleeper, and since he's still in his crib, he can't get out until I go get him. Our other young'uns were climbers, but not Jeremy. That might be on account of his low center of gravity since he's so stocky.

"Mama's comin'," I holler back. I wipe off my hands on the dish towel, toss it onto the counter, and run back to his room.

His little grin sends that familiar warmth all through me, and when he opens his arms wide for me to pick him up, I almost fall apart right there in his room. That boy has me wrapped around his little finger, sometimes to Digger's dismay, since I've been known to drop whatever I was doing to answer Jeremy's call. God knew what He was doing when he plopped our little unexpected bundle of pleasure into our lives.

"Banana." Jeremy grins. "Banana?"

"Do you want a banana?" I sure hope we're not out of them. He loves bananas, but that's not something I can buy in bulk since they go bad so fast.

His whole body wiggles in my arms as he nods with enthusiasm, and then he stops, lifts his chubby little hands to my cheeks, and turns my face toward his. "Toast?"

We definitely have bread, so I can make him some toast. Jeremy has never liked biscuits, which is why Digger jokes we have a Yankee baby in the family.

I'm relieved to see a banana in the fruit bowl. It's covered with brown spots, which is just the way Jeremy likes it—and probably why it's still there, because no one else does.

I put him in the booster seat and set his place with a Sesame Street place mat I picked up at a garage sale on the other side of town, where Digger's rich cousin Bucky lives. Jeremy watches me as I prepare his sippy cup with half apple juice and half water, then peel the banana. I drop a slice of bread in the toaster before I sit down with my coffee.

"School?" he asks.

"Yes, you have school today."

Jeremy grins and takes a sip of his juice. He loves the church preschool where he gets to hang out with other kids his age and actually be the big kid for a change. He's big for his age, but at home, he's still the baby.

He downs the last of his juice and thrusts his cup toward me. "Mo'."

Digger is concerned about how Jeremy only speaks in single words, mostly commands. All three of our other kids made sentences by the time they were three. I'm pretty sure it has something to do with the amount of time I had to spend with them, but with this job, I'm doing well to keep his mouth fed and his bottom dry. Oh, that's another thing.

He's not potty trained yet, and he doesn't show any signs of interest in using the potty.

I spend the next half hour feeding and dressing Jeremy. On the way to the church where he goes to preschool, we listen to kids' worship songs and I attempt to sing along. Singing has never been my strong suit, but Jeremy doesn't seem to mind. He even chimes in with unrecognizable words and tunes every once in a while. Our pitiful attempt at harmony makes my heart happy.

After I deliver him to his classroom, I rush out to my car and speed toward La Chic, where Amanda awaits.

"You're a little late. I was worried about you, Puddin'. Is everything okay?"

I nod. "Digger took forever getting out the door, and then I burned Jeremy's first piece of toast, so I had to fix him another one."

Amanda gives me a sympathetic smile. "I totally understand. I've had more than my share of days like that." She pauses. "Hey, I have an idea. Why don't you pick out something from the clearance jewelry case? I know when I'm havin' a rough day, it always cheers me up to get a new bracelet or pair of earrings."

I glance longingly toward the case but shake my head. "I'd better not. If I come home with something new, Digger will wonder, and I don't feel like answering questions."

"Don't you think Digger will understand?"

"Maybe so, maybe not. I'm just worried about bruising his pride." I leave out the part about how I love his swagger, and he might lose some of it if he thinks I'm having to work.

She giggles. "I can't believe you've been able to keep this job a secret for so long."

"I'm not sure how much longer I can. It's getting increasingly difficult."

Amanda's smile quickly fades. "I hope you're not plannin' on quittin'. I don't think I could ever find anyone to replace you."

That little bit of encouragement makes me smile. "Maybe I won't have to. Digger's softening up about a lot of stuff lately, so maybe he'll understand why this job is so important to me. I just can't mention the fact that we need the money."

She knows all about Digger's old-fashioned sensibilities. "He'll probably be happy about it if you tell him you're doing it because you enjoy it." She pauses and gives me a look of concern. "You do enjoy working here, don't you?"

More than she'll ever know. "Yes, of course. Speaking of working, I'd better get to it so I can pick Jeremy up when preschool is over. I can't be late again, or they'll start fining me."

7

Shay

I leave the office early on Friday afternoon feeling, as Mama would say, plum tuckered out. It's difficult enough to deal with hiring a new store set coordinator after the one who's been with me since I got promoted decided to "find herself" in a cross-country motorcycle trip with some guy she's been seeing all of two months. Now I have to start hunting for someone to fill her position, as well as a sales manager to replace the one I trusted but who went off and accepted a position with our chief competitor.

I've always been loyal, so I expect those around me to be the same way. Unfortunately, I'm often disappointed when I find out how little I know about someone.

The only thing that'll make me feel better today is a new head-to-toe outfit, and the best place to find one of those is La Chic. I usually wind up with an extra-nice bonus since I wear the sample size of most of their shoes, and they almost always have something they're taking off the display that I can pick up for a steal. I've asked Amanda about how that always happens when I visit her boutique, and she says I have great timing.

I pull up in front of the store, get out of my car, and walk toward the front door. To my surprise, as soon as I step inside, my brother's wife, Puddin', is standing there talking to the owner.

Puddin' looks like she just spotted a ghost. Before I can say something nice, which I always do when I see her because she's so sweet, she starts babbling about how little time she has to shop, since she has to leave and pick up the baby from his church program. Her hand flies up to her mouth as though she might have let something slip. "I hope you don't think I'm a spendthrift," she adds with a shaky smile. "I almost never spend money on myself."

Amanda freezes and appears awkward momentarily, which also surprises me since she's always so confident and self-assured. Then she reaches over behind the counter, picks up a bracelet, and holds it out toward Puddin'. "Don't forget this bracelet that you bought *from the clearance case.*"

She puts so much emphasis on where the bracelet came from, the situation goes from awkward to suspicious. Puddin' stops in her tracks and accepts the bracelet. "Gotta run or I'll be late." She lifts a hand and smiles at Amanda. "See you—" She stops mid-sentence and runs out the door.

I turn to Amanda, who makes a show of moving something from one side of the case to the other. It appears she's trying to avoid looking at me.

"What's going on?"

She shrugs. "Not much here. How about with you?" She says it so quickly she sounds even more suspicious, and I can't help but wonder if she's trying to hide something.

"I didn't expect to see my sister-in-law here."

Amanda glances away. "I have a lot of customers." She slowly turns her gaze back to me as she swings her arms forward, clasps her hands, and smiles. "We just got a new line of casual wear that I think will look great on you."

I spend the next hour pulling things from the rack and trying them on. To my delight, all of the things in her new line are so reasonable I'm able to buy more than I expected.

As I pay, I think about Puddin' again. "Did my sister-in-law see this new line? I can totally see her in that green outfit."

"I'm not sure." She pulls some tissue out from beneath the counter and starts wrapping my purchases. "How about this necklace to go with the tone-on-tone crop pants and top? The gold will really jazz it up."

It looks perfect for the family reunion, so I nod. "Yes, I'll take that, too."

Amanda is clearly not going to say anything about Puddin', so I decide to do a little investigating on my own. After I leave the shop, I drive toward her and Digger's house that they just bought on the edge of town. It's in a brand-new, sweet, quiet, unpretentious little tree-lined neighborhood with sidewalks and matching mailboxes. I can't help but smile when the image of her joy over the house pops into my mind. She is so stinkin' proud of her new place, even though it's just a normal house. Too bad everyone isn't that easy to please.

When I pull into the driveway, I see the curtains part in the front window. Next thing I know, little Jeremy has opened the front door. According to the chatter, the rest of the family is worried about the fact that he only uses single words, but I think he's a smart little dude. Some of the smartest people I know are the quiet types, so I'm not worried about him in the least.

"Jeremy, what on earth are you doing? Get back inside." Puddin's voice is screechy until she spots me standing on the front porch.

A slow smile creeps across her face. "Oh, hi, Shay. Come on in. Want some tea?"

"Sure."

"What brings you here?" She glances up at the wall clock on the living room wall. "I thought maybe you were taking a late lunch when I saw you earlier. Is everything okay at work?"

"Rough week, so I knocked off early."

Her gaze darts off to something behind me. "Jeremy! Get back in here. How many times do I have to tell you not to bring your squeezy box into the living room?" She gives me an apologetic look. "Those squeezy juice boxes are as messy as an open cup. It doesn't take much pressure for all that liquid to squirt out the straw."

"I understand." I glance over at the kitchen table that still has open boxes of cereal lined up from breakfast. "Mind if I sit down?"

"Oh, sorry, I should have offered. Let me clear off a spot for your tea." She frantically starts clearing a place for me, letting me know she's more nervous than she wants me to know.

I want to help her, but last time I did that, she fussed at me, so I just sit and watch her scurry around her kitchen as though her child's life depends on getting everything put away in record time. After she has all the cereal put away, she opens the cabinet and pulls out a glass. "This one okay?"

I nod. It's a jelly jar, but that's fine as long as it's clean.

She pours both of us some tea then joins me at the table. Before I have a chance to ask her what she was doing at La Chic, she starts rattling off questions. "What's going on with you? Did something terrible happen at the office?" Her eyes widen as though something just dawned on her. "Did you get fired?"

I hold up my hands and let out a chuckle. "No, but that might not be a bad thing if I did."

"I thought you loved your job."

"I used to, but now I find myself caught up in the same whirlwind every single day. I can almost always predict what's going to happen based on the day of the week. I probably shouldn't admit this, and I know I sound ungrateful, but I'm bored."

"I'm sorry to hear that. So what do you think about the family reunion?"

"What's there to think?" I pause. "We have them so often, it's almost like they don't mean anything anymore."

"I think it's sweet," she says.

This is a first. The last couple of reunions had Puddin' nearly in tears. "'Sweet' isn't how I would describe some of our relatives."

Puddin' crinkles her nose. "I hear ya, but I'm sure they mean well."

"So what were you doing at La Chic?"

"Um ..." Puddin's face scrunches, then her eyes light up. "I like to stop by every now and then to see what they have on clearance."

She's a terrible liar. "You don't have to explain anything, Puddin'. There's absolutely nothing wrong with buying yourself something nice every now and then."

"I know. It's just that—" She cuts herself off and glances at something behind me before letting out a sigh and looking me squarely in the eyes. "Can you keep a secret, Shay?"

"Of course I can. You know that."

"I mean a deep, dark secret that you can't tell a single, solitary soul." She grimaces. "*Especially* Digger. He'll be so hurt if he finds out."

I swallow hard. I don't mind keeping secrets, but this sounds like a doozy, and I certainly don't want to upset any of my blood relatives, especially my brother. As much as I want to know the secret, I'm not sure it's such a good idea to hear it now.

Before I tell her to stop, she blurts, "I work at La Chic. I have for more than a year."

"You what?" I think back to all the times I've been there over the past year, and I can't think of a time when I saw her there. "Why is that a secret? Why don't you want my brother to know?"

"Digger doesn't want me to work. He says a woman's place is in the home." She takes a swig of her tea and places it on the soggy napkin in front of her. "That sounds good and all, but it's just not practical."

It doesn't sound good at all to me, but I don't want to make Puddin' feel even worse than she already does. "Can't you at least talk to him about it?"

She shakes her head. "I've tried, but every time I bring up the very notion of me getting a job, he puts his foot down. And I mean literally lifts his foot and puts it down. Hard."

"But—"

"He tells me no wife of his will ever have to have a job."

"When was the last time y'all talked about it?"

Puddin' taps her chin for a moment as she looks away to think before meeting my gaze again. "It's been a while, but I'm sure he still feels the same way."

"But don't you enjoy it?" I can't imagine not loving a job at La Chic, working for Amanda. I'd do it if I didn't need to maintain a level of income to support myself. Besides, sometimes I think it's better to be bored on my job than to disappoint Mama. One of the few things she seems proud of me for is what she calls my "important job."

"I love it." Her eyes get all dreamy. Puddin' has never been one who could hide how she feels about anything. "I even dream about it."

"Then why don't you tell Digger that it's something you *want* to do, even if you don't *have* to?"

"I don't think that'll make a difference with Digger."

"Did someone say my name?" My brother appears in the doorway, a wide smile on his face. "I got my route done, so I was able to knock off early. I stopped by Jackie's. Those ridin' lawn mowers are nice, but I can't bring myself to—" He stops talking when he sees me. "What are you doin' here, Shay?"

8

Missy

I'm loading the dishwasher when I hear Foster's truck pull into the driveway. I send up a silent prayer that his fishing trip was a success so he'll be in a good mood. I don't feel like dealing with a sulky husband.

"Hey, how was fishing?"

He walks over to the stove then turns back to me with a half-smile. "What's for supper?"

I narrow my eyes and glare at him, wishing he wouldn't keep on ignoring me. He's been doing it for a while. "We can either have a frozen lasagna, or you can take me out to dinner to celebrate."

"Celebrate?" He tilts his head. "Did one of the other wives call you?"

"No, but I won the competition."

"You what?"

I purse my lips to bite back what comes to mind. I speak slowly as he stares directly at me. "I won the competition," I repeat.

"What competition?" He moves over to the pantry and pulls out a bag of pretzels that he rips open. He sticks his hand inside and pulls out a mess of them, sending crumbs flying all over the place.

I grab the broom and hand it to him. "The chili contest. I won for my chicken chili."

"That's nice. Where do you want to go?" He holds the broom handle and leans on it without making a move to sweep.

We've been married long enough that I don't expect much more from my husband. Anyone else would be proud of his wife, but Foster isn't fazed by this kind of thing, and he's never been effusive with praise. "How about the Rib Shack?"

He rubs his belly. "I'm thinkin' a burger sounds pretty good. It's been a while since I've had a burger with all the fixin's."

I want to scream. Why does he even bother to ask me what I want? But again, I realize that yelling my head off won't do a bit of good. So I sigh and nod. "That's fine."

"Aren't you going to ask me about my fishing trip?" He rests the broom against the wall, grabs another handful of pretzels, rolls up the bag, snaps a clip on it, and tosses it onto the counter.

"But I—" I grab the broom and do what he should be doing, fuming as I go. I've argued with him in the past, but it got me nowhere really fast. "Okay. How was your trip?"

"You don't sound interested."

I close my eyes for a few seconds as I count to ten. "Just tell me, Foster. Did you catch any fish?"

He squints and gives me one of his clueless looks. "What?"

I raise my voice a little, knowing that my annoyance is coming through loud and clear. "Did you catch a fish?"

Without hesitation, he holds his hands out about a foot apart. "Not only did I catch the most fish, I got the biggest. I swear, Missy, you shoulda seen the looks on the other guys' faces when I reeled it in."

"Where's the fish?"

"Huh?"

"I said, *where's the fish*?"

"Oh." He gives me an incredulous look. "We ate all of it."

I tighten my jaw to keep from saying the first thing that comes to mind. It's hard to believe that the passionate beginning to our marriage has fizzled to this. He's never been all that attentive, but now he doesn't even pretend to listen to me.

"It was good, too. Larry did a great job with the batter."

Is he trying to drive the nail in the coffin so hard it pierces my heart again? I feel like turning around and giving him the what-for, but last time I did that, it took weeks to heal the hurt from what we both said to each other. He even thought I said some things I didn't say. So I've learned to keep my mouth shut until the queasy feeling in my stomach subsides.

"Are you mad at me?" he asks as he approaches with extended arms.

I look directly at him then blink as I turn away. "Not exactly mad. It's just that—" The words are right there on the tip of my tongue, ready to be spewed, but I know I need to exercise caution.

Before I can decide whether or not to tell him how I feel, he glances at the wall clock and blurts, "We'd better get going. Last time we ate late, neither one of us could go to sleep."

That was because we had huge pieces of chocolate cake for dessert. I'm not sure if it was the sugar or the chocolate, but whatever the case, it doesn't matter. Not now. Maybe never. This is my life, and unless I can gather the courage to do something about it, it's my life until I die. What a depressing thought. I grew up believing marriage is forever, but sometimes I'm not so sure it always has to be that way.

Throughout our meal, Foster ignores everything I say. He goes on and on about the antics of his buddies in the boat, in the cabin, and on the way home. Every time I open my mouth, he talks over me. "You'd think they'd never gone fishin' before." He lets out a snort then grows silent while he shoves his burger into his mouth and chomps down.

I take advantage of his full mouth to talk about my time while he was gone. "The chili cook-off had quite a few more entries this year." I pause and wait for a reaction, but I don't get one. "There was this guy who stuck around. I think he wanted to talk to me, if you know what I mean."

Foster swallows and nods. "Yeah, it's always fun to talk to folks."

He still doesn't get it, so I decide to make it clearer. I raise my voice as I continue. "He wasn't a bad-looking guy either."

"What guy?"

"The guy I talked to at the chili competition."

"You didn't say ..." His voice drifts off as he looks confused. "Did you taste his chili?"

I close my eyes and shake my head. What's the use of taking this conversation any further? Nothing happened between that guy and me, and nothing ever will. Even though my marriage isn't in a good place at the moment, I took a vow twenty years ago, and I fully plan to keep it. It's just that sometimes—

"What's the matter, Missy? Are you feelin' sick?"

I open my eyes and force a half-smile. "Not exactly sick ..."

"That's good. I hear there's something going around, and it's pretty miserable."

Yeah, there's something going around. It's called an inattentive husband.

He finally finishes his food and stands up. "I'm done. Ready to go home?"

Half of my burger and most of my fries are still on the plate. I look up at him and nod. "Sure."

He reaches over, picks up my burger, and takes a huge bite. With his mouth still full, he says, "I hate seein' all that good food go to waste."

After we get home, Foster heads straight for our bedroom. I follow behind. As soon as I get to the door, he turns around and smiles at me.

"Missy, I want you to know how much I appreciate you. The other guys told me how much grief their wives gave them about going on the trip." He pauses, and his smile grows wider as he opens his arms. "I told them I have the best wife in Pinewood because you not only let me go without fuss, you actually want me to have a good time."

9
Shay

My heart goes out to Puddin'. Although my brother is one of the sweetest guys I know, he also has more pride than any man I've ever seen. We were both raised by the same old-fashioned parents, and I'm the one who rebelled by going to college and becoming what Mama calls a "career woman." Sometimes she brags about my job, like when she's trying to impress friends, but other times, like when she needs to make a point, she says that as if it's a bad thing. Digger might have been more influenced by our parents than I was, but he's still a sweet guy who wants his wife to be happy.

I sure hope Puddin' can figure out a way to tell Digger about her job so she doesn't have to continue with the secret that no doubt is eating away at her. It's been almost a week since I last saw her, so I think it might be time to pay her a visit … but not at home.

After a busy morning, I tell the receptionist that I'm taking a long lunch. Naturally, she assumes that I'm meeting clients or prospects, as I rarely go out to lunch just for fun. I don't do anything to quell that.

I practically run out of the office toward my car. There have been way too many times when someone has called, and the receptionist has run out to catch me before I leave.

Amanda glances up when I walk into La Chic. Her eyes widen, and she swallows hard like she's nervous about something.

"Is Puddin' here?" I ask as though it's the most natural thing in the world.

"Um …" She glances over her shoulder and grimaces as she turns back to face me. "I don't—"

"That's okay, Amanda," Puddin' says from behind her. "She knows."

Amanda's shoulders drop as she blows out a breath. "I wasn't sure, and I didn't want to get you in trouble."

I look back and forth between them before my gaze settles on Puddin'. "Can we talk for a few minutes?"

She turns to Amanda, who nods, then she smiles at me. "Only for a few minutes, though, because I have to finish up here and pick Jeremy up from preschool." She gestures toward the back room. "Why don't you come on back to my office?"

I'm not sure what to expect, but it isn't what I see. Although Puddin's "office" is the size of a closet, it is neat and orderly to a fault. There are colorful file boxes on the shelves toward the back of the space. The tiny desk has a full-size blotter and a laptop computer that takes up most of the top surface. A file cabinet that appears to have been covered in contact paper sits beside the clerical chair on wheels. She smiles with pride as she looks at me, but she doesn't say anything right away.

"This is a nice office, Puddin'."

She doesn't speak as she picks up a folding chair that rests against the wall, opens it, and gestures for me to sit. Then she goes behind her desk and plops into the chair. "So what's up, Shay?"

"I ... I just wondered if you've told Digger about your job yet?"

Without hesitation, she shakes her head. "There's really no reason to. Not at this point." An odd expression that appears to be a mix of fear and trepidation washes over her face. "You're not planning on telling him, are you?"

"No, I don't plan to tell him, but I really think you should. My brother is a very sweet, understanding man who might give you some flak at first, but ..." I let my voice wander off to let my words sink in. "Once he knows how much this job means to you, I'm sure he'll come around."

"Don't you understand, Shay? As long as he doesn't know about this job, it's all mine." She clears her throat. "It's the only thing I have that belongs to me and only me."

The desperation in her voice touches my heart. Even though Puddin' and I have been friends for decades, there's something here that I don't understand and maybe never will.

As much as I would like to understand what she's saying, I can't. But then again, I've never had to share every minute of my life with a husband and three children.

"Any money I make goes into a small account for vacations, extra treats, and a rainy-day fund." She shrugs. "And for those times when we come up short with the family budget, I have enough to cover it without stressing Digger about finances. I see too many couples fighting over money, and I don't want to do that."

"But the fighting isn't really about the money." I speak slowly, trying to find the right words that won't come across as an insult to my sister-in-law. "I think it's more about trust, which is—" As soon as I start this sentence, I realize it might hurt Puddin's feelings. "It's just that if he knows, the two of you can talk about it and plan as a team."

"No." Puddin's single word comes out so strongly I'm shocked. I've never seen her like this.

"No?"

"You heard me. Everything else in my life is a team effort." She starts to giggle but quickly covers her mouth with her hand until she recovers. "Shay, you've known me long enough to know I never played sports or got involved with any kind of team before. Even though I've always had friends, I'm still more of a loner. You're really the only person I feel that close to, outside the family that lives here."

"Yes, I did know that."

She tips her head forward and gives me a long look that lets me know she means business, and she's not budging. "Which is why I need this."

"Okay, but why can't you tell Digger what you just told me? You can say—"

"Don't tell me what to say, Shay."

"I didn't mean to tell you what to say. It's just that—"

"I like things just the way they are, and I intend to keep them this way."

I let out a sigh as I stand. "Okay. I just thought I'd try to help."

"I appreciate your concern, but this isn't about you one single, solitary iota. To be honest, it really isn't any of your business either, or I would have said something before now." She gives me an apologetic look.

"If you didn't just happen to come in here that day when I was leaving, you'd never know about my working here."

I tilt my head as our gazes lock. "You probably wish I still didn't know."

She glances away, sighs, turns back to me with an apologetic look, nods, and rises to her feet. "Probably."

"Okay, then, I best be leavin'." I stand up and slowly walk toward the door. The air is thick with tension, which I know I'm partly responsible for. But I still think Puddin' needs to come clean with Digger. I can't imagine him being anything but thrilled about her feeling fulfilled with this job. Plus, I'm willing to help if she needs support. She knows that.

Amanda's eyes are still open wide as we walk past her, but she doesn't say a word. I notice a look passed between her and Puddin', as though there is some silent communication that I'll never understand. Amanda quickly glances down at whatever she's doing at the counter.

"Maybe we can have lunch soon," Puddin' says as we approach the door of the shop. "Like on a Wednesday when I leave here early, but before I have to pick up Jeremy."

"Sounds good." I smile at her before turning to leave.

"Oh, and when we get together for lunch, we'll pretend that you don't know anything about my working here. It'll be much easier if it never comes up again."

"Okay." I'm not sure I'll be able to do that, but Puddin' couldn't have made things any more clear than she already has.

Well, that was a bust, I think as I slide behind the wheel. All of my good intentions have been shot down, and now that I know how much this means to her, I vow to keep her secret. It's hard, considering the fact that my brother will be furious not only with her but with me if he ever finds out I know. But sometimes women have to stick together, even if they're not blood related.

Guilt continues to hover, so when I'm halfway to the office, I pull over into a parking lot, close my eyes, and ask the Lord to forgive me for keeping such a big secret from my brother. I also ask Him to put it on Puddin's heart to talk to Digger and try to get him to understand how important the job is to her. When I open my eyes, my stomach starts to rumble, reminding me that I still need to eat lunch.

I swing by a drive-thru and order a salad to take back to the office. When I walk in, the receptionist glances at it and grins. "Must be hard to eat when you have a working lunch."

"It is." Without stopping, I head straight back to my office that is at least ten times as big as Puddin's. What amazes me is that she's at least as contented as I am. Maybe even more so.

10
Sally

I am so tired of arguing with Sara about what color ribbons we should use. We always sell a ton of pink and light blue, but she wants to go with orange and green, just because she likes those colors. The problem with that is I don't think mamas will put orange and green bows in their daughters' hair, especially the size of the ones we sell.

"All we ever do is pink and blue," Sara argues. "I'm getting sick and tired of pink and blue."

"We do some black and white, too." I sigh. Maybe I should give in, as always, and agree to a few in the colors she likes. "Oh, all right. But why don't we go with the mint green and the peachy orange?"

"Mint green is fine, but I like bright orange."

I have to put my foot down since I'm not into losing a boatload of time and money. "The only time pumpkin-orange bows sell is in October."

Her forehead crinkles as she gives me one of those practiced looks to make me feel bad. "Bright orange is my favorite color."

"I thought yellow was your favorite color."

"That was last year." Her lips form a pout, taking the sad face to a whole new level. I can do those faces too, but she's actually better at it. Maybe that's because she practices.

I remember what happened last year with the yellow bows. We made dozens and dozens of yellow bows that didn't sell, so we wound up giving most of them to charity.

I finally nod. "Okay, we can make a *few* bright orange bows to display on Etsy, and when the orders come in, we'll make more."

She opens her mouth but quickly clamps it shut and nods. "Okay, I suppose that's fair."

When we arrive at the craft store, there's a line at the register. Sara leans into me, whispering, "It's obviously one of the better sales."

I nod. "Obviously."

We head straight to the ribbon aisle and start loading up our handheld baskets with the colors we know will sell. Sara walks over to the next aisle and lets out a huge groan.

"What happened?"

"We got here too late. The orange is all gone."

Some woman wearing a smock with the store's logo rounds the corner. "I couldn't help but overhear what you said about the orange ribbon. We can't keep that color in this season, it's so popular."

Sara widens her eyes, bobs her head, and glares at me. "See? I told you it would sell."

I sigh as I turn to face the saleslady. "When will you get more in?"

The woman grimaces as she shakes her head. "There's a huge back order on it, so there's no tellin'." She points to the yellow ribbon. "We have plenty of yellow left from last year. It was supposed to take off, but it was nowhere near as popular as orange is this year."

Sara and I do our best to get a little more variety before we finally get in line. I find some peachy orange and hold it up for her approval. She starts to shake her head but changes her mind and shrugs. "I reckon we can try that."

There are times when my sister and I think alike, but that doesn't happen as much as it used to. And I hate being on the wrong end of the decision.

After a half hour of waiting in line, we pay and head to my car. Neither of us is in a talkative mood, so we don't say a word until we get to the parking lot of our apartment complex. We're so close that sometimes our silence speaks louder than our words, and I'm hearing her loud and clear. Sara is the first to finally say something.

"Ya know, our place is too small for us and our business. We ought to start looking for a house or something."

I shake my head. "I don't want to rent a house. That's an awful lot of work to maintain someone else's property."

"Who said anything about renting? I was thinking we could buy a house. We make enough money, and we've been doing this long enough that I think we could get a mortgage company to lend us the money."

"I don't know. Let's talk about this later, okay?"

She stops and turns to face me. "You always do that, Sally, and quite frankly, I'm sick of it. I want to talk about it now."

"Then talk about it now. Just don't expect me to contribute to your lame-brained ideas."

"Lame-brained? Are you serious?" The shrill sound of her voice goes all through me. "Is it any more lame-brained than my idea to do this business that got us both out of jobs we absolutely hated?"

"Who came up with the idea?" Now my voice is just as shrill as hers. "As I recall …" My voice trails off as I think back and remember that she truly was the one who thought of it. "Okay, so you said it first, but I'm sure we would have thought of something."

"That's just it. When we think of something, we need to act on it like we did our business." She pauses. "I know you're worried that one of us will find a man and want to get married, and that'll leave the other one of us with a house."

I actually hadn't thought of that, but now that she's mentioned it, I know we need to discuss it. "So what are your thoughts about that?" I ask.

She gives me a sheepish smile and shrugs. "I figure we can come up with a plan later."

"Tell you what, Sara. As soon as you have some ideas for all the possibilities and what-ifs, we can discuss it. But for now, let's table this discussion."

She gestures toward the dining room table covered in ribbons and hair clips. "I'm sick of living like this. We can't even eat at our own table."

"We have TV trays that are perfectly fine."

"I hate eating on TV trays," Sara argues. "And so do you."

I bob my head, trying to come up with something. She's right. I'd much rather eat at the dining room table, but I don't see that we have much of a choice now.

"We're doing it as a means to reach our goals." I heard someone say that recently, and it sounds very grown up and businesslike.

Her entire face scrunches up. "Why are you doing that?"

"What?"

"Acting like you're in charge of our business," she replies. "It's supposed to be a partnership. We've never talked about *our* goals. You just like to call the shots and tell me where we should take this business."

I plant my fists on my hips and glare at her. "It *is* a partnership, which means that we have to agree on any changes we make, and I'm perfectly happy with things the way they are. If you can figure out a way to make things better without the risk, I'll listen."

"But I'm not happy with how things are."

"Then that should motivate you to come up with a plan." I give her a sarcastic grin. "If it's good, I'll go along with it, but if it's not, then we'll continue as we have been."

"Sally, you and I both know that things are going to change, no matter what we do. So I think we should force the change and not let it just happen to us."

My sister makes sense, but I'm starting to get the feeling that the change she's talking about involves something different between us. We've been inseparable the whole almost–twenty-two years we've been alive, and the thought of that changing makes my stomach hurt. Sure, she gets on my nerves, but I love her so much the very thought of not having her by my side through the rest of our lives is unfathomable.

She places her hand on my shoulder. "This is supposed to be a fifty-fifty partnership."

I shrug. "And that's exactly what it is."

"Then why won't you let me have half the say?"

"You've always had half the say." I pause. "Look, Sara, we make joint decisions all the time, and what you're proposing is such a major change, we both need to be on board for something this big."

"Or one of us could move out or buy the other one out."

"No." I can't believe my sister would even suggest such a thing.

"Okay, then we can do it together. Just think, Sally. If we buy a three-bedroom house, we can make one of the rooms into an office with a table and lots of storage cabinets so we can really stock up on ribbons and not have to depend on sales at the craft store and—"

I hold up my hand to shush her. "Whoa there, sis. I'd like to have the space, too, but we can't do anything stupid."

She gives me an incredulous look. "Are you saying I'm stupid?"

11

Shay

I can't help but smile when I see the Wright twins in the produce section at the Winn-Dixie. They always look so pulled together and joyful, but as I get closer, I see pinched looks on both of their faces.

"Hey, girls. How's the hair-bow business?"

One of them turns to the other, then they both give me a blank look. "Okay," they say in unison.

I can't put my finger on exactly what, but something is obviously going on. And even though they're my cousins, I don't see them often since they're so much younger than me. And to be honest, I don't know them very well, and what I do know is only stuff I've heard through the family grapevine. I rack my brain for something to say, when I notice the big hand-printed sign in front of a display. "Looks like the eggplant is on sale. I think I'll get one."

They glance at each other and walk away. It's strange that I've known them since they were born, yet still I can't tell them apart. But I know I'm not the only one, which is why a lot of our cousins just call them "Twins."

I meander up and down the aisles looking for things on my list. When I reach the cereal section, I hear them on the other side. "It's insane to even think about buying a house. I can picture it now. We close on a house and get it all set up, and then boom! You come home all starry-eyed because your Prince Charming has asked you to marry him. Then what will I do?"

"That won't happen, but let's say it does. All you'd have to do is buy out my half of the house."

"You just made my case."

Okay, so what I witnessed in the produce section was two sisters disagreeing over whether or not they should buy a house. That makes sense, and it's something I know a little bit about since I've bought and sold a couple of houses and purchased a condo that I now live in.

I grab the box of cereal on my list and push my buggy around toward the twins. They both look up at me at the same time.

"Girls, I couldn't help but overhear you talking about buying a house." I pause and think about how it's none of my business, but I can't help myself. "That's not a bad idea, but it is a huge commitment."

"See?" One of the girls gives the other one a mock smile before turning back to me. "That's what I keep telling Sara."

Okay, so now I know Sara is the one in the animal-print top. I continue. "But if it's set up properly, it can pay off."

Now it's Sara's turn to gloat. "I'm willing to set everything up."

"It's not that easy," Sally says as she bobs her head at her sister. "What do you know about real estate?"

I hold up my hands. "Why don't y'all finish up here, take your groceries home, put them away, and come over to my condo when you're done? I'll fix dinner and we can discuss it from a business perspective."

They glance at each other and then nod in unison. Sara smiles as she nudges Sally. "That sure beats heating up a frozen dinner."

Sally frowns at her and turns to me. "That's a lot of trouble. Are you sure?"

"It's no trouble at all," I say. "I was going to cook for myself anyway. And it'll be fun to share my own real estate experiences with you two."

Sara nods. "I have total confidence in you, Shay. Everyone knows you have one of the best business minds in the family."

I blink. I have never known that people think this about me.

I still have some shopping to do, but the twins appear to be finished. "See y'all in a little while," I say, "like maybe in an hour?"

Still smiling, I push my buggy toward the seafood counter. I'm almost there when I hear, "Hey, Shay. I haven't seen you in a while."

I spin around and find myself face to face with Elliot Stevens, my former crush back in high school. Instinctively, I glance at his left hand.

To my delight, it's ringless. I look up at his face and realize he's aware of what I just did.

"Oh, hi, Elliot." My face flames and I want to hide, but there's nowhere to go. He continues watching me, and my face gets even hotter. I finally manage to speak. "I thought you got married and moved away."

"I did, but I'm back. After my divorce, I realized I needed to move back here to regroup and figure out what to do with my life."

So he's divorced. He still looks as good as ever, and I feel that old attraction edging its way back into my heart. But my mind says, *Hold your horses, Shay.*

"It's hard to talk here," he says. "Hey, I have an idea. Why don't we get together tonight—that is, if you're free for dinner?"

I let out a sigh and give him an apologetic look. "Sorry, Elliot, but I just made plans with a couple of my cousins. Maybe some other time?"

He nods. "What's your number? I'll call later and we can make plans."

I give him my number, finish my shopping, and nearly float out of the store. Ever since Elliot and I were partners in tenth-grade biology class, I've dreamed of dating him. But he was on the high school football team, while I was president of our school's chapter of Future Business Leaders of America. He had girls flocking to date him, while I had guys calling me for homework answers.

One afternoon when we were finishing up our biology project toward the end of the school year, he gave me one of those heart-stopping smiles. I remember how my lips quivered when I smiled back. And then he asked me if I'd like to go to the movies with him. As my heart thudded, my mind went into automatic pilot. I knew who I was then—just as I know who I am now—so I turned him down.

No way was I about to make a fool of myself over a guy. Guys like him simply didn't date girls like me unless they needed help with homework or answers on tests. There have been times since then that I've wished I'd gone out with him just once to see if he was as different as he seemed. I once thought that I had to make a choice between college and personal happiness. Now I know I possibly could have had both.

As soon as I arrive at my condo, I put everything away and pull out the rotisserie chicken and potato salad from the deli and put them in my own serving dishes. I slice a couple of tomatoes and arrange them on a bed of lettuce just like Mama always did.

The twins arrive a few minutes later. "Come on in, girls. I have supper ready."

"Nice condo," one of them says. Since they changed clothes, I'm not sure which one is talking, so I need to find some way to tell them apart.

Now the other one speaks up. "How many bedrooms do you have?"

"Three." I gesture toward the living room. "Would y'all like to take a look around before we eat?"

They both nod with enthusiasm. I can almost see the wheels turning in their heads, and I get it. Before I looked at this condo, I could only see myself living in a single-family house. Until now, they haven't thought about a condo. However, I suspect my place is way out of their price range, since I know they just started a little mail-order craft business a year and a half ago. I don't think they make enough money to swing a place this expensive. It took me a dozen years and several houses to work up to it.

After they see the third bedroom that I've converted to an office, they glance at each other, smile, and turn to me. "This is what we need to do. A condo will be perfect."

I offer a motherly smile and lead them to the kitchen. It won't be easy, but I can see that I'll need to give them a basic economics lesson while they're here. Maybe I can even help them come up with a plan to purchase a smaller house and work up to something this big and expensive.

One of them speaks up as we get to the kitchen table. "Thanks for not calling us 'Twins,' Shay." She glances at her sister, who nods. "Most people think we're the same person, just because we look alike."

"To be honest, I still can't tell y'all apart."

The more outspoken one speaks up. "I'm the pretty one."

The other twin rolls her eyes. "Sally's the obnoxious one. I'm the sweet one."

I love this playful banter between the girls. I never realized how much fun they are. "I'm starting to get some clues."

Sally points to a tiny scar beside her eye. "When you're in front of us, just look here. I fell when we were three, and I had to have stitches."

Sara nudges her and wiggles her eyebrows. "She's still the clumsy one."

When we sit down, I bow my head to say the blessing. Before I open my mouth, one of them starts the prayer. After we all say, "Amen," the twin to my left begins to chatter.

"I can't believe we didn't think of buying a condo before, but this will be perfect for what we need."

Sara nods vigorously. "Sally was concerned that one of us would be stuck with a house and all the hassles of maintaining it if the other one got married and left."

I tilt my head and give her a curious look. "Why would it be any different with a condo?"

Sally speaks up. "You don't have to mow the lawn or do any of that stuff, do you?"

I shake my head. "No, but I pay dearly for it. We're charged an association fee."

"How much is that?"

I expect her to be stunned by the amount, but she isn't. She just looks at her sister, who leans forward on her elbows and tells me how much money they've saved. My chin drops. They actually have enough to pay cash for a condo, if they want to.

As soon as I gather my wits, I blink. "But I thought y'all just had a little mail-order craft business."

"We sell little girls' accessories and we have a few stores that buy in larger quantities." She grins and holds up her hands. "And we're making more than we ever made as bank tellers."

Then she tells me how much they pull in each month, and I'm shocked speechless. They can afford to buy two condos with what they're making.

12
Puddin'

I certainly hope my sister-in-law can keep our secret. Even though she thinks Digger will understand and accept what I'm doing, I know better. The few times I've tested his pride, hoo-boy, it was bad. It's not that he hollers or threatens me or anything, but I think what he does is just as bad. He goes into a blue funk so deep that I can't even get him up to go anywhere, including church, which is terrible since he loves spending Sunday mornings in Sunday school and church.

Amanda hasn't said much, but I know she's itchin' to find out what Shay and I discussed. She keeps giving me those looks that have question marks all over them.

After several days of her odd behavior, I finally decide it's time to bring it up. "Shay and I talked about how important it is to keep our little secret."

"You don't think she'll say anything?" Amanda's eyes light up with eager anticipation, and then she pauses. "After all, Digger is her brother, and there is bound to be some kind of loyalty there."

"I know, and that's what I'm countin' on. Her loyalty makes her want him to be happy." When I see that Amanda's confused, I explain. "I told her all about the pride thing and how it upsets him to think he can't provide for his family."

She shrugs. "I suppose that makes sense on some level, but you do realize you can't keep this a secret forever, don't you? In fact, I'm surprised you've kept it under wraps for as long as you have. I mean, it's not like Pinewood is all that big, and people know people."

"It's not a tiny town either. Besides, I'm usually tucked away in the back where no one sees me."

"Oh, that's something else I need to discuss with you. I have a few things coming up when I can't be here, and neither of the part-timers can fill in for me." She makes a face like she's scared to continue, but she does anyway. "Would you mind …"

"Are you asking me to wait on customers?" I've always thought it would be fun to help women pick out their clothes, but it is awful risky, since everyone who is anyone shops at La Chic.

Amanda nods as she gives me an apologetic look. "The times I need to be away aren't typically busy, so you should be fine."

I take a deep breath, trying to control my hammering heart. "Like what time?"

"Tomorrow morning for about an hour after we open, then next Monday right after the lunch rush."

I don't see a problem since I know for a fact that those are definitely not high-volume times. "I'll do it. In fact, I'll even work on the books from the checkout desk so I'm not standin' here idle."

A big old honkin' smile spreads across her face. "Thank you so much, Puddin'! I was worried you wouldn't do it, and I didn't know where else to turn."

Momentarily, I'm annoyed that she just let me know I'm her last choice, but reality sets in, and I know it's because I've made it clear that no one else is to know I work here. Whatever the case, I'm ecstatic.

We talk for a few minutes about what I'm supposed to do. "Are you comfortable running the cash register?" she asks.

"Yes, but why don't I practice a little before I'm here alone?"

"Good idea." She pulls out her purse and extracts a twenty-dollar bill. "Here. I'd like to buy that scarf that I just marked down."

"You just marked down a scarf?"

She holds it up, picks up the red pen, crosses through the price, and puts a new, much lower number on it. "I have now."

I laugh as I ring up the sale without any trouble. I've watched her enough times I think I know the whole process by heart.

"Excellent." She yanks off the tag and wraps the scarf around my neck. "You're good to go."

I start to take it off, but she holds up her hands to stop me. I grin. "Thank you."

All I can think about while doing the books that day is how much fun it will be to be in the actual boutique. I know I'll be living dangerously, but this is one of those times that the fun factor outweighs the risk.

Digger gets home at his usual time that evening, walks up behind me as I flip the chicken-fried steak in the skillet, and gives me a kiss on the neck. I turn around and grin at him.

"You're lookin' mighty chipper." He unbuttons his shirt, making my breath catch in my throat. "Havin' a good day?"

I try my best to tamp down my excitement and bob my head in a half-nod. "I've had worse."

He laughs. "The way you were dancin' when I walked in, I thought you might be havin' a party." He glances around. "Without music or people."

"I wasn't dancin'. I'm just cookin'."

Digger looks at the food in the skillet and gives me a sideways glance. "I've never seen you cook to a beat before."

"That's because you don't normally get here until it's done." It's time to get the subject off of me, or I might spill the beans. "Digger, honey, would you mind setting the table?"

"Sure, but let me go put on some jeans. Be right back."

As soon as he leaves the kitchen, I take a couple of deep breaths and slowly blow them out. My excitement is getting harder to contain, but I need to get a grip so Digger won't be suspicious.

He comes back wearing some ragged jeans and a very old Petra T-shirt that we got at a concert when we were kids. But he still looks just as good as he did back then—at least to me he does. But my feelings for him are deeper than the physical attraction. He's such a kindhearted man who wholeheartedly loves his family. His only flaw that I can gripe about is his old-fashioned ideas, but that's one of the things I've always found attractive about him. Our gazes meet, and my tummy does a flippy thing. He gives me one of his too-charming grins, letting me know that he is fully aware of how I'm feelin'.

"Mom, I'm starving!" Brett walks in through the back door, bouncin' his basketball like he's still on the court.

"Take that thing outside, young man." Digger points to the door. "And while you're at it, leave your shoes in the mudroom. I don't want you trackin' mud all over the floors your mama works so hard to keep clean."

I slink down in my chair as I notice a dust bunny float across the floor and feel guilty as all get-out. It's been more than a week since I've had time to mop. Fortunately, if Digger's shoes don't stick to the floor when he walks across it, he doesn't notice the dirt.

Supper is yummy, and I'm delighted that Digger and the boys have so much to say they can't possibly notice that my mind is elsewhere. Life couldn't be better for me at the moment, even though Hallie is actin' a mite moody.

"What's going on with you, girlie?" Digger asks her.

She shrugs and shoves another bite of mashed potatoes into her mouth. Everyone grows silent, but that only lasts a few seconds before Jeremy shrieks.

We all jump and turn to face him. A humongous blob of mashed potatoes sits smack-dab in the middle of the top of his head, and he's trying to add gravy. Digger starts laughing, and in spite of the mess I know I'll have to clean up, I laugh, too. Even Hallie cracks a smile.

After supper, everyone carries their plates to the sink while I pick Jeremy up from his booster seat and carry him straight to the bathtub. He's such a happy child, always laughing and making funny faces, that I never get too mad at him no matter what he does.

To my delight, when Jeremy and I return to the kitchen, the entire mashed-potato-and-gravy mess is cleaned up. I glance at Digger, who gestures toward Hallie. "She took care of it."

I close the distance between me and our only daughter, but after a brief instant of leaning into me, she pulls away. "Don't worry about it. I couldn't very well leave the mess for you," she says. "I gotta go finish my homework." Then she leaves.

An hour later, after Jeremy is in bed and the other two young'uns who are still at home are in their rooms, Digger and I sit at the kitchen table to chat. "What are you doin' tomorrow?" he asks. "I was thinkin' about going in late so me and you can do something, just the two of us."

My heart stops as my brain goes numb. "I ..." I don't want to lie, so I smile and shrug. "What do you have in mind?"

13

Shay

"Slow down, Puddin'. Take a deep breath and start at the beginning." I sit up in bed and glance at the clock. It must be pretty bad for her to call me after ten o'clock because I know she and Digger go to bed early. He has to get up at dawn to start his route.

"It's Digger—no, it's La Chic." She loudly exhales. "No, it's me and my insane secret. I promised Amanda I'd help her out at the shop tomorrow morning, and now Digger says he's goin' in late because he wants to spend some time with me. What can I do?"

"Be honest with him."

"You know good and well I can't do that. Not now, anyway. I need your help, Shay."

This is hard. I love and appreciate my sister-in-law, but she is asking me to get involved with something that would hurt my brother deeply, if he knew we were in cahoots in a secret plot that involves him.

"Please do something, or at least tell me what to do." The panic in her voice lets me know she's worried sick about this.

"Have you asked him to go in late on another day?" I ask. "You could have said you have to do something at one of the kids' schools."

"But that would be lyin'."

"Puddin'." I swing my legs over the side of the bed, slide into my slippers, and get up. "Keeping your job a secret is a form of lying."

I hear her take a quick, shallow breath. "Don't lecture me now, Shay. I'm in panic mode, and I can't think straight."

She's not kidding. I think as hard as I can, but the only thing I can come up with is pretty conniving. Still, I can't let Puddin' suffer like this, so I finally say, "Let's hang up so I can call Digger. I have an idea."

Feeling like a disloyal monster of a sister, I speed-dial Digger's cell phone. He picks up on the third ring and answers with a sleepy voice. "Whaddya want, Shay?"

I sniffle. "I need to talk to you."

"It's way past bedtime. Can't it wait?"

"I don't know." I pretend to blow my nose. "I really need to talk to you."

"It's late." I hear him shift his position. "Are you cryin'?"

"Digger . . ." Like Puddin', I don't want to lie, so I don't answer. "Please, can we talk?"

"I reckon. What's it about?"

"I can't talk about it over the phone. Can you come to my office sometime tomorrow?"

There's a long pause before he makes a clicking sound with his tongue. "I promised Puddin' I'd hang out here with her in the morning, but if it's important enough for you to call me in the middle of the night, I'm sure she'll understand."

"I know she will. Puddin' is a very understanding woman." *If he only knew.* "When's the earliest you can be at my office?"

"Sometime in the mornin'."

"Can you get there around nine?"

He lets out a sigh of resignation. "Yeah, I'll be there."

After we hang up, I stand and stare at the wall. Puddin' and I need to have another serious, heart-to-heart talk because I can't keep deceiving my brother like this. It's just wrong.

I toss and turn half the night thinking about what to say to Digger, and the only thing I can come up with is the fact that I saw Elliot Stevens at the Winn-Dixie. Digger has always teased me about Elliot, so he might understand my excitement. However, he might not understand why I would need his support . . . or he might. I'm not sure.

Early the next morning, I get a call from Puddin'. "You're plum brilliant, Shay. And thank you so much! I owe you one."

"I want you to talk to Digger about your job soon. He needs to know, and you can't keep this up." And I mean it, too. My involvement in Puddin's scheme kept me up all night, and it takes twice as much concealer as normal to get rid of the dark circles.

As soon as Digger walks into my office, he takes one look at me and lets out a low whistle. "You look rough, Shay. What's going on? What's got you in such a dither?"

"So I guess the cover stick isn't working."

He gives me a curious look. "Huh?"

I shake my head. "Never mind. Have a seat. Want some coffee?"

"Yeah, I'll take some."

I get up and walk around from behind my desk. "I'll be right back." I'll do anything I can to prolong having the lame conversation and semi-lying to my brother.

When I come back, he's on his phone, texting someone. I sit down behind the desk and stare at the numbers on my computer screen.

He glances up and notices the coffee. "Oh, thanks, Shay. I don't know why Puddin' isn't answering my text messages."

"Maybe she doesn't have her phone on her."

"I hope that's the case. She seemed mighty disappointed that I wouldn't be able to stick around the house this morning. I hope she's not mad at me about that."

"Mad?" I think about how overjoyed Puddin' sounded. "No, I don't think she'll be mad. This is Puddin' we're talking about."

"Yeah, you're right. It takes a lot to make her mad. I do have me a sweet wife, don't I?" He shoves his phone in his shirt pocket, takes a sip of his coffee, and sets it on the edge of my desk. "So why did you need to see me?"

I swallow hard and wait for the tension in my gut to subside before looking my brother in the eyes. "Remember Elliot Stevens?"

Digger nods. "How can I forget him? He was the football player who led Pinewood High School to the state championship, and you were googly-eyed over him. Why?"

"I saw him at the Winn-Dixie. He wants to get together for dinner."

Digger's eyes widen. "He's married, Shay. You know how I feel about that."

"No, he's divorced."

"I didn't know that." He scrunches his forehead. "Then what's the problem?"

I chew on my bottom lip for a few seconds. "Do you remember the crush I used to have on him?"

Digger laughs but quickly regains his composure. "You know I do."

"He was way out of my league back then, and now I'm afraid ..." I let my voice trail off as I try to think of something powerful to say. Something that will justify calling him to come here.

Without hesitation, Digger gets up out of his chair and comes around to my side of the desk. He puts his hand beneath my chin and lifts my face to his. "I don't want you to worry about how things were in high school. You've made something of yourself, and he's a fortunate guy if you have it in you to give him the time of day."

"That's so sweet of you, Digger." Tears form in my eyes as I realize how comforting my brother can be.

"I'm trying to make it up to you for how mean I was when we were kids." He offers a half-smile. "I shoulda been whupped for how I behaved."

"No, you were just being a normal kid, I'm sure."

He shakes his head and gives me a sympathetic smile that digs even deeper into my heart, compounding my guilt. "I never realized how difficult a time you had back then, or I woulda tried to be a better brother. I always thought everything was hunky-dory for you, but now I realize you studied so hard because you never went out much." He winces. "That didn't come out right. What I mean to say is you're the best sister a guy could possibly have."

"Thank you." I glance down at my desk. "I try to be." *Lord, please forgive me for this.*

"I mean it, Shay."

My chin quivers as I open my mouth to thank him. But the guilt is so powerful, nothing will come out.

"If Elliot Stevens asks you out, and you want to go, you have my blessing. I'm not crazy about the fact that he's divorced, because you know how Mama and the rest of our family can be, but I see how much this means to you."

I nod. "It means a lot to me."

He lets go of my chin and widens his smile. "If he does anything to hurt my sweet sister …" Digger shoves a fist into his other palm. "He'll have to answer to me."

Could the guilt get any worse? I look up at my brother who is acting all … well, brotherly.

14

Missy

Granny Marge has always been one of my favorite people. Even in her eighties, she's active and fun, and I don't dare call her spry on account of that's what you say about old people, and she will never be old. Another thing that makes her extra special is that she has never cared what people think of her. She says she follows where the Lord leads, and as long as He is happy with her, she figures she'll be just fine.

Throughout my childhood, she made sure she was there for the important moments of all of her grandkids. And when I needed someone to talk to, she listened.

And is she ever funny! She is one of the funniest people on the planet, especially when she's not trying to be.

Those are some of the reasons I don't want to miss any of the family get-togethers. As long as she's alive, I want to be there for her. And to be honest, I want to see her reaction to other family members and some of their shenanigans.

Now I have to find a way to convince Foster to go with me. He missed the last one, so I went alone, leaving everyone speculating on the state of our marriage and placing bets on when we'd be announcing our divorce. I can't honestly say I haven't thought about it, but truth be told, I love my husband, and I know he hasn't done anything that the Lord would see as a good reason for me to call it quits. Besides, I think there might still be something special between us, and I keep praying that it'll eventually spring back up.

I think about the fact that I still have a hundred-dollar bill Foster gave me a few days after his fishing trip. He said he wants me to spend it any way I see fit, but he sure does like it when I wear red. Yeah, that's a hint that he wants me to go buy a new red dress, since my old one is beyond snug on my halfway-between-forty-and-fifty-year-old body. Dieting doesn't work for me since Foster's favorite part of any meal is dessert. I've tried eating low-fat, sugar-free pudding while he has cake, but that only lasted about a week.

I have a few days off from my job as assistant activities director at the senior center, so I decide it might be fun to go look around at La Chic. The owner, Amanda, always has cute things, and she's the best at helping me pull together outfits I wouldn't even think of. I'm just not sure a hundred dollars will go very far. Not in that place, anyway.

As soon as I walk into the boutique, Amanda's eyes start darting around like a cornered alley cat. "Are you okay?" I ask.

"Oh, I'm just fine and dandy." She lifts a finger. "I need to run to the back for a sec. Take a look around and see if there's anything you like. I just got some really cute accessories in last week."

Okay, so she probably has to use the ladies' room. I'm always a little jumpy, too, when I wait until the last minute.

I walk around the shop and feel the fabric of dresses I'll never be able to afford. When I'm close to the door leading to the back room, I can hear Amanda whispering. I'm curious about who's back there with her, but it's really none of my business, so I move away from the door and toward the jewelry display case by the cash register.

"Did you see the cocktail rings?"

I glance up at the sound of Amanda's voice and point to the right-hand side of the case. "Is that what those are?"

"Yes, ma'am. We have them in simulated diamonds, emeralds, and rubies." She gazes at them with admiration. "They look real, don't they?"

"They sure do."

"Why don't you try some on? I'm sure we can find one you like."

"They're pretty, but I don't think I can afford one right now. I just need a new red dress, and I can't spend more than a hundred dollars."

Amanda is good at what she does, so I know she's sizing up the situation as she slowly turns and looks around her shop. "We'll find you something. I was just getting ready to put some of last season's dresses on clearance. Maybe if you find one you like, you'll have enough left for one of the smaller rings. One that I'm about to put on clearance."

I cast a dubious look at her. "I don't know . . ."

She quickly glances over her shoulder and then at me. "I have an idea. Why don't I pull a few dresses and start a room for you? I'll keep bringing you stuff until you tell me to stop."

"How much are you putting on clearance?" I ask.

"A lot. We have to make room for new things, so it's a never-ending cycle."

Something doesn't ring true, but who am I to argue about getting a good deal? So when she grabs a dress and heads for the fitting room area, I follow right behind her.

Over the next hour or so, I try on just about every single red dress in my size in the shop. I can tell she's eager for me to make a decision, but it's hard since several of them have won my heart. I wish I knew how much she's marking them down to.

"Well, what do you think?" She stands back and gives me a once-over after I slip into the last dress. "It looks great on you. How does it feel?"

"I like it, but then I like the ones over there, too." I point toward the hook where I've hung my favorites. "It might be tacky for me to ask this, but how much are they?" I looked at the price tags, and the retail prices are all way over what I have in my pocketbook, some by as much as double.

"You said you have a hundred dollars?" She looks through the dresses and pulls a couple of them out. "You can buy either of these or the one you have on and the small simulated ruby ring." She gestures toward the remaining dresses. "Or you can get one of these without the ring."

"Are you sure? I don't remember any of these dresses from last time I came in here. It seems too early to put them on clearance."

"Positive," she says way too quickly. "I have to admit, though, that I'm partial to the one you're wearing."

"Me, too." I turn and look in the mirror again. "Okay, I'll take this one and the ring, if you have it in a size seven."

I change back into my slacks and top and head for the cash register. To my surprise, she has already rung up the sale and has the bag waiting for the dress.

"You don't waste any time, do you?" I hand her the money, and she gives me back a couple dollars change.

"I know you have a lot to do on your day off, so I don't want you to have to stand around while I ring up your sale." She takes the dress, puts it on a hanger, carefully places a plastic bag over it, and hands it to me. Then she drops the ring box into a bag. "Have a very nice day and enjoy the dress." And then she walks me to the door, something I don't remember her ever doing before.

Once I'm in my car, I hold up the dress and stare at the price tag. It's hard to believe this dress was on clearance for less than half the original price. And the ring! It is absolutely stunning, with two large simulated rubies in a nest of smaller simulated diamonds. The price on the ring box is as much as I paid for both items. I can't get over how great my timing is. If she'd already put the dress on clearance, it would surely have been snapped up by one of her more regular customers. But then again, most of her customers can afford to go in and purchase whatever they want, regardless of whether or not it's on clearance, so they don't even bother looking at the price tags.

I go straight home and try the dress on again, this time with some body-shaping underwear, the shoes my daughter Wendy gave me when she decided to stop trying to shove her size-eight feet into size-seven-and-a-half shoes, and the ring. I turn this way and that, looking at my reflection, feeling like I can conquer the world in this outfit. I look that good.

A strong urge to go out tonight washes over me, so I pick up my phone and call Foster. "Hey, honey," he says. "I'm glad you called. I told some of the guys we'd meet them and their wives at the bowling alley after supper tonight."

"But I thought—"

"I figured you'd like getting out." He continues talking over me, as though I haven't said a thing. "I'm dying for a rematch. That Elmore Barker and his wife, Miranda, they're not as good as they bowled last time. You're much better than she is." He pauses. "In fact, you're actually a pretty good bowler for a girl."

I turn back to see my reflection once more before I sigh. "Okay. I'll have supper waiting for you when you get home."

I have to remind myself that I truly love my husband. But this is one of those times when I'd like to ...

I squeeze my eyes shut and send up a prayer for patience and under-standing. Being married to Foster has never been easy, and it might never be. But I still hold out hope that one of these days he'll understand how I feel.

15

Shay

Families are such interesting and complex institutions. Not only do they show you how you can you love and hate the same person at the same time, but they have the ability to make you feel as though you're the only sane person in the world. At least that's the way it is in my family, and I assume we're not the only ones.

Then again, I'm dealing with a lot of craziness in my life right now. My brother's charming pig-headedness and his wife's determination to keep a secret from him. My younger twin cousins coming to me as the voice of reason even though their little craft business is shockingly successful. My high school crush who is socially light years ahead of me finally asking me out after all these years. To say nothing of the crazy number of family reunions the Bucklin family has, even though I don't know a single cousin who wants to go but we all show up anyway.

I feel as though all of my sanity has been sucked out of me. And maybe it has. Or maybe it was never there to begin with.

The only thing that remains on an even keel is work. As crazy busy as it is, nothing much changes there. We sell a wide variety of processed food to grocery stores, vet people who want us to represent their companies, and try to maintain the perfect balance of inventory. Every day I go into work, I know I'll be dealing with one or more of those issues, with the only differences being in the ratio and number of fires that need to be put out. We're not talking forest fires. It's more like the fire on the end of a match when you first strike it. In other words, that's all a piece of cake compared to the personal stuff happening in my family.

I still find it hard to believe that Puddin' has been able to keep her job a secret from my brother for as long as she has. I can't get past the niggling feeling that there's something not quite right about why she's doing it, though. Yes, I realize he has a very old-fashioned notion about providing for the family, but I've known Digger all my life. He'll kick up a fuss for a little while, but when he realizes how much she enjoys having her own thing, he'll eventually come around, and he'll do it joyfully. In fact, he might actually like it when he realizes that not only will she be a happier wife, but she'll be able to take some of the financial pressure off him. I know he's proud of his job, and it's a good job. But I also know his income is limited, and he only gets a small raise once a year.

I turn back to my work. Everything I need to sign is in a nice, neat stack on the corner of my desk. All of my appointments send me little reminder dings a few minutes before they begin, so I'm never late. Occasionally, I have to get creative when an issue arises, but it's not the norm.

Fortunately, most of my schedule for the day is filled with routine tasks, so I don't have to do much thinking outside the box. After quitting time, I call Mama to check on her.

"I'm worried about your brother," she says. "Can you come over now, or do you have plans?"

"I'll be there in a little while. Let me go home and change into something comfortable first."

I have one leg in my jeans when my cell phone rings. It's Elliot, so as I answer, I sit down on the edge of my bed to keep from falling.

"Hey, Shay. How about dinner tomorrow night?"

My heart hammers nearly out of control. "Tomorrow night?"

"Yes, but if that doesn't work for you, I'm open. That is, unless I misread the situation and you're not interested."

"Tomorrow night is fine. What time?"

We decide on a time, and I jot it down to put on my phone calendar later. Then after I tell him my address, I finish getting dressed. I'm excited, but I don't want to be, so I take a few deep breaths and turn my thoughts back to Digger and Puddin'.

A half hour later, I pull into Mama's driveway. Daddy passed away when I was in college, so she lives alone in the house where Digger and I were raised. The lawn is huge, and the trees shed more leaves than any one woman can rake. The house itself needs work. Digger does as much as he has time for, and I send plumbers and electricians over when she needs them. I've tried to talk her into moving into a condo, but she insists that she's comfortable here.

"I've been here so long," she says, "I can find my way around the kitchen with my eyes closed."

By the time I close my car door and turn around, I see her standing at the front door, waiting for me. She offers a shaky smile, letting me know she's deeply disturbed about something.

"I made meatloaf," she says. "It's already on the table."

I follow her through the living room, down the long, narrow hall toward the back of the house, and into the kitchen. When we stop, I take a deep breath and inhale the aroma of fresh-baked meatloaf, one of my favorite foods Mama makes.

My eyes pop wide open when I see the spread on the kitchen table. "That's a lot of food for two people. Is anyone else coming?"

"No." She shrugs. "At least I'll have leftovers. Sit down and say the blessing."

I do as she says. After I say, "Amen," I start filling my plate with meatloaf, mashed potatoes, peas, and tomato slices. Then I look directly at Mama. "What did you want to tell me about Digger?"

She shakes her head. "It's not really about Digger. Something isn't right with Puddin'."

I hold my breath. "What happened?"

"Well, you know I've never been all that happy about them putting Jeremy in preschool at such a young age, but they insisted it would help him socially since he's the youngest one in the family."

"Yes, I do know that."

"He still can't talk."

I tilt my head as I try my best to give her a reassuring look. "I think it's pretty normal for the baby of the family to be a late talker."

Mama stares at her empty plate, then she looks up at me with sadness in her eyes. "And she's never home in the mornings."

My throat constricts. "I'm sure she has places to go." Puddin' sure has put me in a predicament with my family. I wish she hadn't told me about her job.

"Like where?" Mama asks.

"The grocery store?" I think hard to come up with more. "The bank?" I shove a bite of meatloaf into my mouth.

"I don't know about that. There's only so much grocery shopping and banking a person can do. I would think she'd want to go home and putter around the house, like I did when you and Digger were little." A beatific look washes over her face as she sighs. "Those were the days. Your daddy was still alive, and I had the house to myself to do whatever I wanted. And then you all came home, and we sat down to dinner together. I want that for Digger."

"Puddin' always cooks and has dinner waiting for him when he gets home."

Mama tips her head forward and gives me one of her looks. "Maybe so, but she doesn't cook everything from scratch like she used to."

I snort. "I'm sure everything is fine with them."

"I'm not." Mama sniffles. "Do you think ... I mean, you don't think she's seeing another man, do you?"

"No, of course not. This is Puddin' we're talking about, not some hussy."

Mama shrugs. "Sometimes things happen. Puddin' might have put on a few pounds since she had Jeremy, but she's still a pretty woman."

"I know she's pretty, but that has nothing to do with it. She loves Digger, and she'd never ..." My voice trails off as I think about Puddin's job. It's tempting to tell Mama, but if I do, my sister-in-law will never trust me again. She and I need to have another chat so I can talk some sense into her. I hate having to keep this secret that seems senseless to me and keeps me on edge.

"Maybe you're right." Mama looks around the table and points. "Can you pass me the peas?" Before I have a chance to say another word, she blurts, "I hear you ran into Elliot at the Winn-Dixie. Is it true?"

"Yes, Mama, it's true."

"I hope you don't go gettin' all mixed up with him." She makes a sad-mama face. "That boy is way too charmin' for his own good, and I don't want my baby girl getting hurt. I love you too much to sit back and watch your heart get broken." She pauses before adding, "He's a divorced man, you know."

16
Sally

"I never thought we'd go condo."

Sara rolls her eyes. "Go condo? That's something Daddy would say."

"I know." I look at the real estate listings on my computer screen and pull up one that looks interesting. "Look at this one. It overlooks the pool and has soft-close drawers in the kitchen."

"What's that?" Sara leans over and glances at the pictures.

"I have no idea, but it sounds good." I read some more of the listing. "It also has dimmable canned lighting and a subway-tile backsplash."

"I know what dimmable is, and I'm pretty sure I know what a backsplash is." Sara backs up and makes a face. "But I don't understand the canned part of the lighting or the subway tile."

I try to envision it, but I'm not sure either. "It's probably a really good thing to have, or they wouldn't list it here."

Sara buries her face in her hands for a few seconds before lifting her head and looking at me with frustration. "I'm not sure we're ready for this."

"You were the one who wanted to buy a house."

"Yeah, but this is a condo. It's different. A house is something I understand."

"But you said it first, and the more I think about it, the more I see the value of having a place we own."

She makes a face. "I know."

"We need to do something. After I thought about it, I realized I'm getting sick of living in a warehouse. If we find a condo or house that has a third bedroom, we'll get our dining room back. And if we buy instead of rent, we'll start building equity." As soon as the words come out of my mouth, I think back to the fact that buying our own place started out being Sara's idea.

"That does sound good."

I click on the contact button to request a viewing of the condo. After I press Send, I turn to my sister. "We'll probably get a call in a few days, so—"

My cell phone rings before I finish my sentence. Since it's a number I don't recognize, I answer in my most businesslike voice. It's the Realtor I just contacted.

"Just a minute," I say. "I need to find out when we're available." I cover the mouthpiece and ask my sister if she'd like to look at the condo tomorrow.

Her eyes bug out. "Are you kidding? Already?"

I nod. "Yeah, just answer me, please. Can we look tomorrow?"

She makes a face and nods. "I guess so."

After I make arrangements with the Realtor to see the condo, I spin around in my chair and grin at Sara. "Can you believe this? We're actually going to look at a condo." I squeal. "To buy!"

"Isn't that what we want?"

"I guess. I mean, absolutely. Like I said just a little while ago, we have to do something, or one or both of us might lose our minds."

Sara lets out a snicker. "You'd have to find yours to lose it."

"Stop talking like that, or I might have to smack you upside the head."

She feigns fear. "I wouldn't want you to do that."

We both turn away from each other, smiling. That's how we express our love, but a lot of people don't understand. Being twins, we can say whatever's on our minds because, more likely than not, the other one is thinking pretty close to the same thing.

Mama used to get all worked up when she heard us talking about smacking, pulling, pushing, or whatever else we threatened the other one with. And that just made us do it more because she was so funny when she worried about us. Her face would sweat and turn red, and she'd get this crazy, wild-eyed look. So funny it makes me chuckle to even think about it.

"Are you thinking about Mama?" Sara asks.

Oh yeah, we're definitely twins. "Nah."

"Liar."

Again, we laugh. It might not be funny to anyone else, but we think we're hilarious.

I get off the real estate site and pull up our Etsy page. "Man, oh man, we just got a boatload of orders. Look at this, will ya?"

"I'm looking, and do you know what I see?" She gives me a look of self-satisfaction. "Orange bows." She clamps her mouth shut and gives me a head bob, causing her blond hair to shake around her face. "Most of those orders are for the orange bows we made with that new ribbon." She gives me a gloating look. "And you said they wouldn't sell."

"Not most of them." I run my finger down the list of orders on the screen. "I only see a couple orders for orange. Most of them are pink."

"Whatever." She twirls her chair around toward the rows of ribbon on the rod above our desk. "Let's get these things done so we can go look at furniture for our new condo."

Even though I know she's jumping the gun, I agree. We had a blast decorating our first apartment. Doing up a condo that we own will be even better.

As we work on looping the bows and attaching them to clips, we talk about what colors we want to paint the walls. I tease her and say I'll help her paint her bedroom orange.

She lifts her face, curls her lip, and sniffs. "I'll paint my own room, thank you very much."

"Orange?" I cast a sarcastic grin in her direction.

She gives me the look right back, and we both laugh. "Maybe."

It takes us every bit of two hours to get all of our bows made for the day. I still have to pinch myself when I think about how blessed we are to have such an easy business. Sure, it gets boring sometimes, but I'd much rather be bored silly than have to listen to all the drama that went on around the bank. Sara's bank didn't have as much drama, but she had a boss who didn't allow employees to fraternize. That sounds even more boring than making hair bows, but as much as I hate to admit it, his policy probably prevented the drama that I dealt with.

But, oh well, that's not our problem now. The worst things we have to deal with are deciding what to put on our site and what colors to make our bows.

"I've been thinking about adding charm bracelets to our lineup," I say.

"Not a bad idea. I think we're close to being ready for expansion." She looks at me over her shoulder and grins. "Once we have a third bedroom, we'll have room to do that."

Sara's cell phone rings. She glances at it then looks at me. "It's Mama."

I tip my head in the direction of her phone. "Answer it."

She lets out a long-suffering sigh. "Hey, Mama."

Her eyes roll as she gives me a look, and I stifle a laugh. She says a few words that let me know Mama's still all worried about the fact that we haven't purchased health insurance yet. But why should we? We work out and eat well, and we're both healthy as a couple of horses.

"Okay, Mama, we'll be there at six . . . love you, too." Sara presses the Off button, closes her eyes, and shakes her head.

"We're not goin' there for supper."

Her eyes pop open. "Oh, yes, we are. You're not getting off the hook that easy."

"I don't get the big deal about health insurance. We had it at the banks, and as far as I'm concerned, it was a huge waste of money. Neither one of us ever went to the doctor."

"I know, right?" She pushes away from the desk and stands. "Let's get these bows wrapped and in the mail so we don't have to think about it."

"Work, work, work. That's all we ever do." I laugh. "Can you believe this? How can life get any better?"

"Well, for one thing, I wouldn't mind some Prince Charming riding up on his steed and sweeping me off my feet."

I roll my eyes. "Oh, right, as if that ever happens."

Sara frowns. "It does happen. I really want to find a nice man, settle down, and maybe have a couple of children."

"But why?" Every once in a while, when she says something like this, I get a crazy painful ache in my heart. If she's off with some guy, who will I tease?

Her expression droops. "Don't you ever get lonely?"

"How can I get lonely when you're always around?" When I see that my attempt at a joke isn't working, I just shake my head. "No, I really don't get lonely. Do you?"

She nods. "Yes. I think it might be my biological clock ticking. I want a husband and kids."

"What if you have twins?" I give my eyebrows a cartoon wiggle. "Remember the grief we gave Mama?"

"I know, but I'll know how to deal with that." She makes a duck face and laughs.

"And tell me, sweet sister, how would you deal with that?"

"I'd call my evil twin." Her expression lightens as she flashes a closed-mouth grin. "Where did you put the address labels?"

17

Shay

My nerves are a jangled mess as I wait for Elliot to pick me up. I told him I could meet him somewhere, and he insisted on coming to my place. "I'm sort of old-fashioned that way," he said. "My ex hated the fact that I like being a gentleman, and I expected her to act like a lady."

He shows up right on time. The evening is nice and very calm, after I get over my case of nerves. Elliot talks about normal things, like work and the weather. And then he brings up his ex. A lot. Once that conversation starts and goes on and on, I want to pound the table and insist on equal time with the woman who supposedly isn't even in his life anymore.

After an hour of that, he finally stops and shakes his head. "I am so sorry, Shay. It's just still so fresh, and it's hard for me to forget what I just went through."

"How fresh?" I tilt my head forward and narrow my eyes. *Please, Lord, let his divorce be final.* It didn't dawn on me to ask if all the paperwork had been signed. If it hasn't, this is the last time I'll go anywhere with him until it's final.

He clears his throat. "It was just final a couple months ago."

I let out a huge sigh of relief. "Well, I'm sure it'll just take time for you to get over her."

"Oh, trust me, I'm over her."

"Then why do you talk about her so much?"

He makes a face. "I don't know."

"I don't know that you're ready to go out with someone else yet." It pains me to continue, but I have to protect my own heart. "Regardless of what happened, I don't want to be your sounding board about all the things that happened in your marriage, all the things that went wrong."

"I'm afraid you're right, but I don't want to take any chances on losing you again."

Losing me? Again? What on earth is he talking about? I give him a curious look.

He grins. "I've wanted to ask you out since high school, but you always seemed so smart and sure of yourself. I think I did ask you out once, but you turned me down, and I don't think you took me seriously."

"If that's the case, why didn't you try again and let me know you meant it?"

He shrugs. "I was afraid of rejection."

I tilt my head forward in disbelief. "*You* were afraid of rejection?"

With a smile, he nods. "I can handle it now, but back in high school, that would have destroyed my ego."

"So you didn't really lose me," I remind him.

"True." He chuckles. "You can't lose what you don't have, right?"

He manages to stay off the subject of his ex for the remainder of dinner, but he keeps starting sentences that he doesn't finish. I can tell it's a conscious effort. In some weird way, I'm flattered that he'd go to that much trouble for me.

After dinner, he pulls up in front of my condo. "I'm glad you agreed to go out with me. You're everything I ever dreamed you'd be."

"Really?" I smile at him. The evening was nothing special, but since my life is so boring, it was one of my better nights—unlike most of his, I'm sure.

He nods. "And on top of everything else, you're even smarter and prettier than you were back in high school."

Heat rises to my face. "You're very sweet, Elliot."

"Now I'm hoping you'll go out with me again." He clears his throat. "I'll understand if you say no since I acted like such an idiot about my ex, but please give me another chance."

I sigh. "I want to see you again, but why don't we wait until you're ready?"

"I think I am ready. Or at least I can be."

"Maybe so, but it won't hurt to wait just a tad longer." I'm proud of the fact that my head is winning this battle with my heart.

He sucks in a bunch of air and slowly blows it out as he nods. "I understand. Maybe in a couple of weeks?"

"Do you think that's long enough?"

"I do. It's not my ex I have to get over. It's my habit of talking about her." He glances away as if deep in thought before turning back to me. "Can we at least meet for coffee sometime?"

Before I respond, he gets out of the car, comes around to my side, and opens the door. "I'll walk you to the door."

I feel like I'm living my high school fantasy, complete with the nerves about the goodnight kiss. Will he or won't he? I giggle at the silly girlish thought.

Before I have a chance to pull out my house key, he places his hands on my shoulders and slowly turns me around to face him. I lick my lips in anticipation of a kiss. He smiles and slowly closes the distance between us before dropping a kiss—a very brief kiss—on my lips.

And then he tweaks my nose with his fingertip. "Good night, Shay. I'll call you soon."

"Before you leave . . ."

He stops and turns to face me. "Did you need something?"

"We can meet for coffee, if you want to."

He smiles and gives me a thumbs-up. Then he turns and walks quickly to his car.

As I let myself into the condo, I try to block out the massive quaking going on inside my body. Between my belly doing that roller-coaster thing and my pounding heart, I'm sure I look absolutely ridiculous.

❧

I can't believe my twin cousins are looking at a condo across the lake from mine. Sally called late last night and said they have an appointment today. When she asked if they could stop by my place afterward, I reminded her that I have a job.

Now I'm sitting here at my desk at work, trying to come up with a reason to knock off early. I've finished everything important, and there's nothing pressing on my afternoon schedule. But I don't want to set a bad example for the office staff. They all work so hard, and if I leave, they might resent me. Folks have always told me I worry too much about what other people think, and they're right. But it's how I'm wired.

I press a key on my computer to bring it back to life. Since I'm here, I might as well do some busywork. There are a few vendors that need to be prodded every month to send their shipments, so I write a generic email, copy it, and paste it into emails to each of them. After I send it to all of them, I pull up the shipment docket. Even when I'm caught up, there's always something else I can do.

Half an hour before I can leave without raising eyebrows, my phone rings. It's Sara.

Before I can say a word, she starts talking. "We absolutely love the floor plan, but it seriously needs some work. I mean, how on earth can people live like that?"

"Live like what?" I envision holes in the walls, ripped—or worse, burned—carpet, appliances that don't work, and broken or dirty windows.

"It has beige appliances. Can you believe that? And all the drawer handles are a hideous fake wood. It's awful. That place needs to be completely gutted before we can even consider moving into it."

I have to hold back the laughter. "They were built in the nineties, so what did you expect?"

"Don't those people ever watch HGTV?" The serious tone in her voice lets me know she's devastated. "And I just scratched the surface."

"You mean there's more?" I ask half jokingly.

"Oh, believe me, it just gets worse." I listen as she goes on and on about the stark-white walls that look like a government office, the basic builder's beige carpet, and the ceiling fans with rattan blades. "There's not even a dimmer switch on the lighting. We expected to have to do some work, but that place is a total disaster. I'm afraid we'll need to put a lot of money into it if we decide to buy it."

"Actually . . ." I let my voice trail off as I try to decide whether or not it's a good idea for my cousins to live in the same neighborhood. Then I sigh. I have to share my wisdom, or I'll never be able to live with myself.

"Actually, Sara, those are all minor cosmetic issues. It sounds to me like the only big expenses will be replacing the appliances and carpet."

"We hate carpet."

"Then you can replace it with wood or tile. The home-improvement stores have sales all the time."

"How do you know all this stuff, Shay?" She pauses. "Oh, that's right. You're old."

I hear Sally fussing at her in the background. She covers the mouthpiece and says something that comes across muffled before getting back with me.

"I'm sorry, Shay. I wasn't thinking. You're not old, just seasoned and experienced."

I laugh. "Yes, I have bought and sold a place or two. Would you like some help with this?"

"That's what we were hoping you'd say." I can practically hear her smiling. "What do we do next?"

"How many places have y'all looked at?"

"Just the one. Why? How many are we supposed to look at?"

I remember last time I went looking at real estate, I must have seen several dozen places. "Don't you want to look some more before you settle on something?"

"But what if someone else buys the condo?"

They have so much to learn about business. Then again, looking at their success, I realize they obviously know some things that I've missed.

"Have y'all talked to your parents about this?" Their mama and daddy will be furious with me for advising their daughters if they don't agree with what I tell them.

"Are you kidding? No way."

"Maybe you should before you do anything rash."

"They'll just try to talk us out of it."

Maybe that's what I should do, but I can't. If those girls are determined to buy their own place, nothing will stop them. Besides, I actually agree with them.

"Will you please tell us what to do next?" Sara's begging voice stabs me right in the heart. "If you don't, we'll wind up making a humongous mistake, and that would be terrible."

"Of course I'll help you. What do you want me to do?"

"We have an appointment to see the condo again in about an hour and a half." Her tone is much lighter and more cheerful now. "Sally told her that we need our aunt to look at it."

"Your aunt?" It takes me a moment to realize she's talking about me. I suppose I am old enough to be their aunt, since their daddy is my first cousin. "Oh, okay. Why don't y'all come to my place first, and we can walk over there."

After I hang up, I think about the big old mess I'm about to get myself into. It's not like I can hide after helping them. Not only do their parents still live in the Pinewood area, I won't be able to avoid them at the upcoming reunion.

I arrive at my place mere moments before they pull into my driveway. Both girls hop out of the car with energy that I don't ever remember having. This makes me feel as old as they think I am, but they rush to me for hugs.

"Thank you so much for doing this, Shay." Sally's voice is tight with nervous excitement. "We'd be completely lost without your help."

Now Sara speaks up. "Hey, Sally, remember what Mama said about too much gushing." Sara turns to me. "Mama says we gush way too much and it makes people uncomfortable."

Sally gives me an apologetic look. "Yeah, I don't want to make you uncomfortable, especially when you're being so good to us. But you're being such a huge help, and—"

Sara groans. "There you go again."

I smile at both of them. "Let's go inside for a minute before we look at the place you want to show me."

Twenty minutes later, we're on our way to the condo that's for sale. As soon as we round the corner, Sally points to it. "That's it, right there." She turns to me with a smile. "The one with the sign in the window."

"You'll be directly across the lake from me."

Before any of us can say another word, the door opens, and I see the grinning face of Conrad Fulton, one of my former classmates. "Hey, ladies."

Sally steps up. "Where's Jolene?"

"She couldn't make it, so she sent me instead." Conrad tips his head toward me. "So how's the food business treating you, Shay?"

"Just fine."

Conrad is one of those geeky guys none of the girls wanted to date in high school, but after he got out and started his real estate empire, he suddenly became the hottest catch in town. He wound up with the girl who won all the beauty pageants, and last I heard, they had three stair-stepper children, two years apart. Fortunately for them, they got their looks from their mama.

He steps out onto the porch and gestures toward the entryway. "After you, ladies."

As I walk through, I notice a lot of extra touches that my place doesn't have, including wainscoting, crown molding, and a kitchen that opens to the great room. If I were looking for myself, I wouldn't hesitate to put a contract on it.

"See what we're talking about?" Sally says. "It's a huge mess, isn't it?"

I glance over at Conrad, who appears amused, so I turn to Sally. "I wouldn't call it a huge mess, but it could use a bit of updating, I suppose." I stop in the middle of the front room and take in all the detail. "It's really nice for a starter home."

"Starter home?" Sara gives me a curious look. "What's that?"

I glance at Conrad and notice that he has to stifle his laughter. I don't respond. Instead, I shake my head.

"Does it have good bones?" Sally asks.

"Good what?" I look at Conrad, and he laughs.

"That's what the Realtors on HGTV say if all the updates a place needs are cosmetic." Sally gives him one of her *duh* looks.

Conrad nods. "Oh. Yes, I think it has excellent bones." That sounds strange, but I get it.

We walk into the kitchen, where I'm stunned by all the cabinets. This is a gourmet cook's paradise.

"Aren't those the most hideous appliances you've ever seen?"

I remember when this bisque color was the rage. "They're not hideous, but stainless steel would probably be more to your liking."

Sally nods, but Sara shakes her head. "I like black appliances."

"Stainless looks better." Sally flutters her hands around. "It's all shiny and pretty."

"But black looks sleeker."

I glance in Conrad's direction and see that his arms are folded as he studies the appliances. "Have you girls seen the black-and-stainless combination? You'll get both sleek and shiny with that combination."

"Ooh." Sara's face lights up. "I think we might like that."

"Now that we have that settled, let's look at the rest of the place." Conrad leads the way through the entire downstairs and toward the screened-in area that overlooks the lake. "This is one of the few units with a wraparound back porch. Over here, you have a Jacuzzi, and over here …" He walks around the corner and gestures. "Here you have a gas grill. It's built in, so it stays."

"Why would we want someone else's used grill?" Sally makes a face. "That would be disgusting."

I'm practically drooling over this place. "Can we see the bedrooms?" I ask.

"Sure, come on back inside. I think you'll like some of the things the current owners did when they first moved in."

Once we're upstairs in the loft area, I look around at the wall-to-wall bookshelves. "Those would totally have to come out," Sara says. "They're taking up too much wall space."

"I think it's perfect." An idea flits through my head. I quickly clamp my mouth shut, but I can see that Conrad is aware of my reaction. In fact, from the look on his face, I suspect he's reading my mind.

"I have an idea." He turns to the twins. "What do you think of Shay's condo?"

"We love it." Sara turns to Sally, and they both nod. "That's the kind of place we're looking for."

He smiles at me. "What you could do is sell them your place, and you can buy this one."

Now I know why Conrad is so successful. He is able to read people during their weakest moments.

18

Puddin'

Ever since that morning when I worked on the sales floor and Digger went to Shay's office, he's felt guilty as all get-out. He keeps trying to make it up to me. I reckon I should be happy, but I feel guilty—probably even more than he does.

"What's wrong with you, Puddin'? Haven't I said I was sorry enough? I told you I won't ever do that to you again."

"No, it's not that. It's just that—" I almost blurt what's really bugging me, but I quickly come to my senses. This doesn't seem like the right time to spring the fact that I have a job on him. "I have a lot on my mind."

The wrinkles in his forehead grow deeper as he looks at me with more concern than I deserve. "Do you think you might have that disease women get after their babies are born?"

"Disease?"

"What's it called? Postpartum depression?"

I shake my head. "No, the only time I had that was after Trey. After that, I was too busy to even think about myself." I scrunch up my face. "Besides, postpartum depression doesn't usually last three years."

"Then what's going on?" The concerned look on his face continues to deepen.

I can't continue letting him worry, so I take his hands in mine as I conjure up something he might believe. It's not that I'm lying to be mean. *Forgive me, Lord, but I have no choice.* "I've been thinking about what school Jeremy will go to. There's a waiting list for the new charter school."

"What on earth is a charter school?" Digger looks at me like I just sprouted a new head.

Since I'm not sure what a charter school is, I sigh. "Kids get better educations at those places."

"Says who?"

I shrug. "I saw it on the news."

"I don't know about that. The other kids did just fine without charter schools. Besides, why are you so fired up about that now? He still has a couple more years of preschool before we have to worry about getting him into the fancy school." He pauses. "How much do these charter schools cost?"

"I'm not sure, but I think they're free." Not only am I not sure about that, I'm not sure about anything. In fact, I'm not even sure Pinewood has charter schools. But I did see something on the news about them.

"Tell you what, Puddin'. If it makes you feel any better, I'll look into this tomorrow."

I smile at my husband who clearly loves me, even after all these years and all the pounds I've put on around my hips. "That would be nice."

"Okay, so now that we've settled that, why don't we cheer up and try to enjoy the evening?" Without waiting for me to say something, he asks, "What are we having for dessert?"

Sometimes I worry about Digger. Before he deals with any kind of conflict, he wants something sweet, like a big old piece of pie or cake. And if it's a big problem, it has to be topped with ice cream or whipped cream.

After a heaping helping of cherry cobbler with a plop of ice cream on top, Digger sits down in front of the TV to catch up on some of the shows he's recorded, while I go to our bedroom and figure out what I'm going to wear to work for the rest of the week. I'd love to buy something new, but I don't want to alarm Digger by bringing something home. Maybe if he thinks he's the one buying me a new outfit . . .

After I have my work wardrobe laid out, I march right out to the living room to talk to my husband about gettin' me something new to wear. Digger's eyes are closed, and his mouth is hanging open, while a soft, rhythmic snore floats through the air. I reach for the remote and press the Off button, knowing that'll wake him up.

He jumps. "What'd you go and do that for?" he asks. "I was watching something."

"What were you watching?" I hold the remote just out of his reach. "Do you even know what was on?"

He scrunches his face, then slowly shakes his head. "I've had a long day, Puddin'. I'm exhausted."

I'm thinkin' this isn't the best time to bring it up, but I still want that outfit. "Please just focus for a minute—I'd really like some new clothes."

"Then get them. It's not like you go out and buy everything your little heart desires. If you need something new to wear, just write a check for it."

My heart melts. I don't know why I thought he'd say anything different. Perhaps it's my own guilt that's kicking in. "That's okay. I don't really *need* anything."

"No, Puddin'. You deserve something new. So please get yourself something." He leans over enough to get his wallet out of his back pocket, pulls out a twenty-dollar bill, and hands it to me. "Get yourself something pretty."

For a moment, I wonder what planet my husband's been living on for the past twenty years. But I quickly remember that this is the best outcome I can expect. There's no reason for him to know the price of women's clothes—especially the prices at La Chic, which is where I plan to shop. I'll add a little of my own money and use my employee discount on something Amanda will have on the clearance rack.

I've managed to save about forty dollars, five at a time, and I've put it in a special corner of my billfold. With this twenty from Digger, I can get one of the clearance print tops and some earrings or a sundress that I can wear with last year's purple shrug.

I go back to our room to put the money in my billfold, but before I get there, the house phone rings. It's Trey, who moved into a two-bedroom apartment with three of his buddies from high school. At first, they were all enrolled in the community college, but living with three other guys proved to be too difficult for any of them. So one by one, they dropped out of college and increased their hours at their jobs.

"Hey, son, what's up?"

"Mama, I'm starvin'."

"I bought you groceries last week."

"I know, but the guys are a bunch of pigs, and they ate it all up."

I can tell there's something else he's afraid to tell me, and I suspect I know what it is. "Do you want to move back home?"

He makes a few grunting sounds, letting me know his pride is getting in the way.

"Trey, answer me now. Do you want to move back home or not?" I hate the fact that I've gotten used to him not living at home and enjoy not having his mess all over the place.

"Yeah."

My mind races with all the things I'll need to do to get his room ready. It'll take me at least a couple of days, since I promised Amanda I'd help with inventory this week. "When?"

"Now."

I blow out a breath. "Now?"

"Yeah."

"Do you want your daddy to come help you get your stuff?"

"Nah, I got everything out already."

"All your furniture?"

"No, just my clothes. Look, Mama, I can't talk about it now. I'm tired and hungry, and I don't know what else to do."

How can I say no to my firstborn child? He thinks he's an adult—or at least he did a few months ago—but he's still my baby.

"Okay, you can come tonight, but you'll have to sleep on the couch until I get everything out of your old room."

We barely hang up when I hear the key in the front door. He walks in looking more pitiful than anyone I've ever seen living on the street.

"What happened, Trey?" I rush to my son and put my arms around his stiff shoulders. As the seconds and then minutes pass, he relaxes. I pull him to the sofa. "Tell me all about it."

19

Shay

I'm not sure how it happened, or if it's a good decision, but I'm now under contract for the condo on the other side of the lake, and the twins are buying my place. Since Conrad is handling both deals, and there's no negotiation going on since I offered full price for the one I'm buying, he's cutting his commission in half and splitting it with Jolene.

The whole thing caught me off guard. At first, I had buyer's remorse, but now that I've gotten used to the idea of having a Jacuzzi, built-in grill, wraparound porch, and more kitchen cabinets than I'll ever be able to fill, I'm excited.

And now the twins have to be out of their apartment, and they have no place to go. As much as I value my alone time, what kind of cousin would I be if I didn't ask them to go ahead and move in? Plus, they're going to close on my place before I close on the new one, so I'll need a place to stay for a little while until the sellers get out of the unit I'm purchasing.

Of course, after I give them the go-ahead, they don't hesitate for a single second before hiring a truck, getting a bunch of their pals to help move them, and piling everything into my living room.

It's been a long time since I've lived with anyone, and it's much worse than I remember. Not only do I not have the peace and quiet I'm used to, but the kitchen is always in a state of disarray. I bite my tongue, force a smile, and remind myself that this is temporary.

What amazes me about these girls is their ability to argue one minute and then turn around and act like they never said a cross word to each other. They clearly don't hold grudges, but I'm not sure if that's only between the two of them or how they are with everyone. I don't plan to test them.

"You're the best cook ever," Sara says one night over a spaghetti dinner I prepared from a jar. "Can you give me the recipe?"

"I won't tell Mama you said that." Sally takes another bite and sighs. "But I agree that it's the best I've ever had. This is delicious."

When I tell them how simple it is to cook, they seem astonished. Sara shakes her head. "If we knew how easy it was, we wouldn't have eaten out so much." She twirls some noodles around her fork and holds it in midair. "We would have had this at least every other night."

Flattery is a great motivator for me. "What would you girls like tomorrow night?"

They exchange a glance and shrug in unison. "Surprise us."

"Okay." I finish eating my spaghetti and stand. "Have y'all decided what to do about the family reunion?" I look back and forth between them. "You're both going, right?"

"Yeah." Sally makes a face. "You're going, aren't you?"

"Of course."

They nod. "What are you bringing?"

"I'm bringing deviled eggs, but I haven't decided what else yet." Since I have yet to taste a single thing prepared by them in the kitchen, I assume they're not bringing anything, so I don't even ask.

"We're bringing pies," Sara pipes up.

"Pies?" Now I'm surprised. "What kind?"

Sally shoots Sara a warning glance, but Sara ignores her. "Whatever they have when we go to the bakery."

"Well . . ." I think back to the last reunion. "I imagine there'll be plenty of pecan pies and maybe an apple pie or two. Why don't y'all do peach or maybe even chocolate?"

"Chocolate!" Sara's eyes sparkle. "I didn't even think of that."

"And you know what? You don't even have to go to the bakery. I can teach y'all how to make a chocolate pie that'll knock everyone's socks off."

Sara shakes her head. "We're not very good in the kitchen."

"You don't have to be. My recipe is so easy, you can be the worst cook in the world and it'll still come out perfect."

Again, they look at each other and then at me. "Okay," Sally says. "When can we do it?"

"How about we clean up this mess, go to the store for the ingredients, and make it tonight? It'll be a trial run."

"Can we eat some tonight?"

"I don't see why not. After we stick it in the fridge, it only takes about an hour to set."

"Then let's get this place cleaned up."

Both girls hop up out of their chairs and start clearing the dishes away. I've never seen them so excited about cleaning anything—especially the kitchen. Now I know how to get them to do it.

An hour later, we're back home with all of the ingredients laid out on the counter. "I can't believe you use pudding mix," Sally says. "That seems like cheating."

I widen my eyes and give her a mock warning look. "No one else has to know, okay?"

Sara does a lip-zip with her fingers across her lips. "I'll never tell."

I show them what to do and let them assemble everything. After they pour the pudding mix into the graham-cracker crust, Sally sticks it in the fridge.

She straightens up and stares at the refrigerator door. "If this turns out good, I'll be making chocolate pie every night."

"And you'll get fat," Sara says.

"Correction: *we'll* get fat. I know you, and if there's a chocolate pie in the house, you won't stop eating until it's gone."

I can't help but smile at the playfulness of these girls. Now I know that when I lighten up around them, I might actually enjoy our time together.

My phone rings. When I see that it's Elliot, I take it to my room and answer.

"So how's everything with you?" he asks.

I tell him all about the condo sale and purchase and how the twins are living with me now. He laughs at some of the things I tell him, like how they seem too young to be successful business tycoons who are about to purchase their own condo.

"How old were you when you bought your first place?" he asks.

"Early twenties."

"I was a little older." He pauses. "I'd been married about five years before we bought the house of my ex's dreams. We could barely afford it. I thought that would make her happy, but apparently there's no pleasing someone like her."

A sense of dread washes over me. I'm not sure he'll ever get over talking about his ex. I listen to him rant for another few seconds.

Finally, he stops himself. "I am so sorry, Shay. You're just so easy to talk to, I forgot myself."

"That's okay. I understand."

"You said you'd have coffee with me sometime. Are you still up for that?"

"Sure." I try to tamp down my excitement. "When?"

"How about tomorrow?"

20

Missy

Foster has tried his best to be attentive ever since our bowling fiasco a few days ago. Our team won, but one of the other ladies couldn't accept the win without making a dig about my bowling stance. She was loud, too, which only made it worse because everyone at the bowling alley could hear her. And then Foster joined in on the laughter. I cried all the way home, and that quieted him down.

Now that he realizes I'm not made of Teflon, he's trying his derndest to be nice. And for the most part, he's succeeding with only an occasional slip-up.

So I take advantage of his guilty conscience and let him know it's time we go out someplace nice for dinner. He hates dressing up, but after a tad more prodding, he finally nods and asks where I want to go.

I lift an eyebrow and give him one of my looks. "Are you serious?"

He nods. "I'll take you out to eat anywhere your little heart desires."

"I want to go to Stephen's."

His eyebrows shoot up. "Stephen's? That place'll cost me an arm and a leg."

"No," I say slowly. "Just an arm. I won't order the lobster."

"I don't think we need to go there."

"But you said—" I sigh. "Oh, never mind. I should have known you didn't mean it when you said we could go anywhere I wanted to."

"Why would you want to go to a place where the prices are sky high?"

"Because the food's good, and the service makes me feel special."

"Your cookin' is just as good as theirs. There's no point in making the owner rich when we can eat fancy food here. I'll even throw a towel over my arm and pretend to be your waiter." He turns around and picks up the outdoor magazine he dropped on the table a couple of days ago.

Now I've had it. "Foster, I want..." I swallow hard.

He picks up one of his hunting magazines and starts thumbing through the pages as though I'm not even there. I stare at him in disbelief, clearing my throat and making little sounds to get his attention, but he doesn't even look at me.

"Don't you even care what I want?" I hear the frantic screech in my voice, but at this point, I don't care.

He lowers the magazine and looks at me with concern. "What do you want, Missy?"

"I think we need to see a counselor."

"What?"

I raise my voice. "A marriage counselor."

"Why on earth would we need a marriage counselor?"

"Because I'm not happy, and something around here has to change."

His chin drops, and I fully expect him to make noise. But he doesn't. Instead, he sighs. "I suppose it's about time I take you out someplace nice. You're probably getting sick and tired of fast food, and you do work mighty hard around here." He flinches. "Maybe we should go to that fancy restaurant."

Ya think? I don't say that, but it's obvious enough to me and should be to him. After all, he knows it's been years since we've gone to a restaurant where they don't have paper napkins in a metal container on the table.

"But I still think we should see a—"

He holds up his hands. "Let's discuss that counselor thing later. Right now I want to talk about eatin' at that fancy restaurant."

I know this is his way of avoiding something he has no intention of doing, let alone talking about. So he has chosen the lesser of what he considers two evils, and that means we'll go to Stephen's. And that's fine for now. But I'm not letting go of the counseling idea. There is no doubt in my mind that we need it.

I give him a slow nod. "Okay."

"Then I reckon we'll need to make reservations."

"Absolutely," I agree. "You have to do that at Stephen's."

Since I know he'll forget to call for reservations, I do it. The only times they have available for the next couple of weeks are early evening, which is fine with me. In fact, I don't care what time our reservations are as long as we can go.

On the afternoon of Foster's and my date, I lay his suit, shirt, and tie on the bed. I polish the shoes he only wears to weddings and funerals and put them where he'll see them when he first walks in.

Then I take a long, leisurely bubble bath. By the time Foster gets home, I'm out of the tub and putting on my makeup.

"Why're you puttin' on all that war paint? It's not like I don't know what your face looks like *au naturale*."

I puff some powder over my nose as I look at him in the mirror. I lift my chin and raise my voice to make sure he gets the point. "It's for everyone else. I want them to think you have a pretty wife."

He gives me one of those heart-stopping grins I remember from when I first fell in love with him, then he wraps his arms around me. "It doesn't matter what anyone else thinks, Missy. I know I have the prettiest wife in all of Mississippi."

In spite of the fact that we've been married for more than twenty years, and I've been frustrated as all get-out lately, my insides get all squishy. Before I have a chance to turn around and give him a kiss, he lets go and mumbles something about having to put on his monkey suit.

"You look so handsome in a suit, Foster. I'll feel like the princess out with her prince tonight."

"Are you gonna wear that tight red dress? Last time you had it on, you complained the whole night."

I shake my head. "No, I have something special to wear." I grin and wiggle my eyebrows as he holds my gaze in the mirror. "I think you'll be happy."

He takes a shower while I finish applying my makeup. After he gets out, he walks over to his suit, stares at it for a moment, then starts putting it on. By the time he has his shoes laced, I'm standing by the closet wearing my brand-new red dress and some shoes that kill my feet but make my legs look shapely.

The instant he notices me, his jaw goes slack and his eyes bug out. A grin creeps across his face, and he extends his arms toward me. "C'mere, Missy, and give your man a kiss."

I shake my head. "Not now, big boy. I don't want to mess up my face. It took me almost a half hour to get it like I want it."

"Then let's go get this thing over with so we can come back here and mess up your face."

Most women would probably get upset with his attitude, but I'm used to it. The most important thing is that he has finally listened, and he's taking me someplace nice for dinner.

The maître d' gives me a long look of approval, and I have to force myself not to grin like an idiot. It's been such a long time since a man—any man, besides my husband a little while ago—has looked at me like that.

Foster possessively puts his hand on my shoulder and leads me away from the maître d' stand. As we're waiting to be seated, he leans over and whispers, "You look beautiful, sweetheart, but I don't like those other men gawking at you."

"Foster, you know you have absolutely nothing to worry about. I'm married to you, and I'll stay that way."

He smiles at me with open admiration. "That's what I like to hear. I was beginning to wonder."

As soon as we sit down, I take a sip of water and open my menu. I almost choke on the water when I see how much they're charging for tiny little steaks. Maybe Foster was right. I clear my throat and do my best to regain my composure.

Foster contorts his mouth. "Looks like the prices are a little higher than I thought."

"Do you want to go somewhere else?"

"Not a chance," he says. "I'm in the mood to be treated like royalty, and I reckon if that's what I want, I'll have to pay a pretty penny for it."

We both order the most basic—and cheapest—chicken dish they have on the menu, knowing it'll be better than the most expensive chicken anywhere else. I have no doubt it will probably be a very long time before we're able to return, so I vow to savor every bite and enjoy the experience as much as possible.

To my delight, Foster seems content and downright pleasant

throughout the meal. He gives me all of his attention and compliments me on some of the things I've done recently.

"You've been a good mama and wife," he says. "I don't know how you do it, day in and day out." He shakes his head. "When you decided to go work at the senior center, I thought you'd lost your mind, and to be honest with you, I thought you might not have enough time to keep up with all the things you do at home."

I resist the urge to comment. Sometimes I think the same thing, but I do enjoy having my little job and the regular paycheck, small as it is.

"But you never skip a beat. You're an amazing woman, Missy, and I want you to know how much I appreciate everything about you."

Whoa. Who is this man, and what did he do with my husband?

"I mean it," he continues. "I know I don't say this often enough, but you're the best wife a man could ever ask for."

"Thank you, sweetie. I—"

He holds up his hands to stop me. "Wait. I'm not finished." He takes a sip of his water and sets the glass back on the table. "I want to apologize for not getting all excited about you winning the chili contest."

"I didn't think you heard me."

"I didn't." He gives me a sheepish grin. "Some of the guys at work told me about it."

One of the servers approaches from behind Foster and speaks softly. "Would you like—"

Foster keeps talking as though he can't hear the server. I narrow my eyes and nod in the direction of the server. Foster glances over his shoulder.

"Oh, did you need something?" Foster asks.

"Did you not hear him come up behind you?"

My husband slowly shakes his head. "I didn't hear a thing. In fact, I had no idea he was there until you nodded."

Then it dawns on me. My husband isn't ignoring me. He can't hear me.

21

Shay

"No, absolutely not." I close my eyes and shake my head. I've shown as much patience as I can manage. But no more. "Why can't they be out of the condo before the closing? I want to do a walk-through before I sign the papers, and you know how hard that is with someone's junk in the way."

And I'm talking major junk that has been collected over the years. The first time I saw the place, they had their stuff in a storage unit, but the second time, they'd brought it all back into the condo, and it was a huge mess, with boxes stacked to the ceiling.

"It's a personal thing." Conrad clears his throat. "Something to do with her health. A female problem, I think. It's taking longer than they expected to get everything in order."

"Like what?" I've made the most of living with the twins, and I can honestly say it's been fun—but only because I have assumed that it's for a limited time. "I've never heard of the sellers moving out *after* the closing." Frustration makes my stomach hurt. "A week or two after closing?"

"It happens sometimes." He sniffles and makes a few more sounds with his throat, letting me know how uncomfortable he is discussing this. "Let me talk to them and see if there's anything else we can do."

"Fine. Let me know as soon as possible. I want to move in right after I sign."

After we hang up, I lean back in my office chair and think about the conversation. I'm due to close on my new condo in a few days, so I've made arrangements for movers to take all of my furniture, and I have my personal items already boxed up. I can tell that even the twins are eager to have me out of there.

One of the vendors calls and interrupts my thoughts, which is a good thing. If it weren't for my job, I don't know what I'd do. It's the one thing in my life that is at least somewhat predictable. Even the problems are typically the same ones over and over, so I'm well rehearsed in dealing with them. I get bored, but at least I know what I'm doing in that environment.

The remainder of the afternoon is filled with dealing with warehouse issues, handling shipping problems, and soothing sales reps' anxiety. These are tough times, even for the grocery business, so a lot of what I do involves hand-holding and counseling.

At the end of the day, I head to the condo that I used to call home but now see as an insane asylum. Both twins' cars are in the driveway, but I'm happy to see that they've left the garage for me. We've already closed on the place, so if they want, they can justify taking the garage away from me. I have no room to complain.

I walk into the living room and see one of them in my favorite chair and the other sitting on the couch, both their feet on the coffee table, papers strewn everywhere, talking about their business. I've always been a neatnik, so I have to stifle a low growl.

"You look miserable, Shay." Sally stands and gestures toward the chair. "Why don't you take a load off and I'll fix you some tea?"

I force a smile. "That's really sweet of you, but even tea won't help me now."

Sara glances at Sally, and they both look at me with wide eyes. "Why? What happened?"

I point to the sofa as I lower myself into the chair that's still warm. That annoys me, but I don't mention it since they're being so sweet.

"The owner of the condo I'm buying wants to stay another week or two after we close." I tell her what Conrad said earlier.

Sally splays her hands and gives me one of her looks that shows she doesn't see the problem. "And?"

"That means I can't move until they're out and I get the place cleaned."

"Is that what's got you all upset?" Sally frowns and glances down. "I thought it was something serious. This really is no big deal when you look at the big picture. The week or two will pass, and then you'll be in your new place."

Sara nods her agreement. "Shay, I know you believe in God and everything, so why don't you turn it over to Him?" She makes an apologetic face. "When we get ourselves into a pickle, we pray."

"I agree." I swallow hard. "I know this isn't that big of a deal."

"But you know good and well that Jesus listens to all of our prayers." Sally glances at Sara who nods, and they both smile at me. "Let's pray about it right now."

"Now?" I can only imagine what Jesus is thinking about me right now. He's probably looking at me with pity about how silly I'm acting.

They nod again. "Yes, right this minute."

I slowly lower my head as Sally and Sara take turns praying, first for His timing to show itself on the condo and then for whatever the sellers are experiencing. When I open my eyes, I realize that I've spent more time worrying about this than is necessary. After all, what's a delay of a week or two, besides a slight inconvenience and more opportunity to bond with my cousins?

Although I'm still not happy about having to stay in the condo with all my boxes packed, it's nice to know that the twins care enough to remind me how insignificant this blip is. I can't help but smile when I think about how these girls who are only slightly more than half my age have taught me more than I will ever be able to teach them.

"Can you fix that delicious meatloaf again soon?" Sara asks. "Ever since we had it last week, that's all I can think about."

"I'd be happy to. How about tonight?"

"You can do that?" Sara's face lights up.

I nod. "I almost always have the ingredients on hand, and it's not all that hard to do." I pause. "I've got an idea. Why don't I teach y'all how to make it so you can have it whenever you want, even after I move out? You can watch me."

Sally nods with enthusiasm. "That's a great idea!" She turns to Sara. "It'll be cool to be able to go into the kitchen and whip up a meal whenever we want without having to leave home."

I have to stifle a giggle. Before they moved in with me, their idea of a home-cooked meal was getting carryout and heating it up in the microwave.

The three of us go into the kitchen, where I tell them what to get from the pantry. I pull the ground beef out of the freezer and pop it into the microwave to thaw. I put them to work chopping onions and bell peppers while I mix egg, breadcrumbs, and seasoning in a bowl that we eventually dump it all into. A half hour later, the meatloaf is in the oven, and Sally is working on the mac and cheese. They only know how to make it from a box, which isn't any easier than the way I make it, with packaged shredded cheese and elbow noodles. That's next on my list of cooking lessons, but for now I'll try to tolerate the packaged variety without making a face.

We go into the living room to wait for dinner to finish cooking. Sara plops down on the sofa and sighs. "I can't believe we'll be eating meatloaf that I actually helped make."

"Don't get too excited until you taste it." Sally grins and winks at me. "We've messed up plenty of perfect recipes before, so my expectations aren't all that high for this one."

"Trust me, it'll be good." I oversaw the whole process, so nothing can go wrong. It'll be just as good as any that I've ever made.

When the oven buzzer sounds, we go into the kitchen to prepare our plates. The meatloaf is beautiful, and my mouth waters. It looks like a work of art.

We go into the dining area where they've cleared their ribbons and bows from one side of the table. As soon as we sit down, Sally reaches for our hands for the blessing. After she finishes, we all dig in and take huge bites of meatloaf.

I almost gag. "What happened?"

Sara shakes her head. "I have no idea. I did everything you told me to do."

"How much salt did you put in this?"

"Three tablespoons, just like you said."

I put down my fork. "I said a third of a teaspoon."

"Oh." Sara's face scrunches up. "See? I mess everything up."

"That's okay." I try to keep the disappointment out of my voice. "You'll know next time."

Sara tosses her napkin onto the table as she stands. "You don't understand. Every single thing I try to cook turns out like this. I'll never be able to make a decent meatloaf."

"Yeah, same here." Sally shakes her head. "We both suck in the kitchen."

Now it's my turn to make them feel better. "Do you want to hear about some of my early kitchen disasters?"

22
Sally

"Do you think she actually bought it?" Sara gives me questioning look.

"I think so."

"I can't believe she's so gullible. I mean, why would we be so upset about a stupid meatloaf?"

I glare at her. "Because we made such a big deal of it."

"I know, but it's just meatloaf."

"Don't worry about it, Sara. She believes we're upset about being horrible cooks, and actually thinks we're fine with her staying here."

As much as I adore my cousin, she's really getting on my nerves. I don't know where she got her OCD from, but it's enough to set my teeth on edge. Every stinkin' time I put something on the coffee table, she picks it up and puts it somewhere else. And she acts like the world might end when we forget to use coasters.

"We must be pretty good actresses." It's time to change the subject. "Hey, did you see the last order that just came in? Some momzilla wants a bow in every single color we have, and she wants to know if we can make and send them out right away so she can have them before they go on vacation."

"Yeah, I saw that. I hope she realizes we'll have to charge her for express shipping."

Sara makes a face. "Let's go knock the order out now so we can pack and send it tomorrow."

"I hope she has a separate piece of luggage for the bows." I follow her to the table, where we both sit down and pick up spools of ribbon.

As we work in silence, I think about how challenging it is for Sara and me to deal with Shay's ways. I realize it's not easy for her either, but it would be so much better if she'd relax a little. It's no wonder she hasn't found a man and settled down yet. No one can be as perfect as her. I mean, what man wants to feel like he's not smart enough, clean enough, or whatever she's watching for every minute of every day that she's in the condo?

A pang of guilt shoots straight through my heart. *Jesus, forgive me for thinking such thoughts.* But I feel what I feel, and it's still frustrating as all get-out to deal with someone who is so set in her ways and thinks everyone who doesn't agree with her is wrong.

One thing I'm happy about, though, is being in this condo and knowing it'll always be ours. I don't know how Sara and I would have done in a house. We love everything about this place, or at least we will after Shay moves out. It has two master bedrooms, each with its own bathroom, and a guest room that we'll use for the business. The kitchen is huge, with quartz countertops, nickel hardware, and a combination of track lighting, canned lights, and pendants. The only thing we hope to change is the appliance package. They're stainless but not what we like. We went to the appliance store and found a humongous refrigerator with a drawer between the top French doors and the bottom freezer. It's perfect for storing all the yogurt we eat.

We finish the bows in an hour and a half. "That's a crazy number of bows," Sara says. "I feel sorry for her daughter."

"Me, too."

"Oh, I almost forgot to tell you. I have a date on Friday night." She avoids looking me in the eyes.

"What? Why didn't you tell me?"

"I just accepted this afternoon."

"How did it happen? You've been with me all day."

She grins. "Remember when I went to pick up some supplies a few days ago?" Before I have a chance to reply, she continues. "I ran into Justin Peterson. He is so cute!"

"I still don't see it, but I remember that you've always had the biggest crush on him."

"Well, apparently he has a crush on me, too. All those times he and I used to hang out, apparently he kept watching for a sign that I liked him, too." Her cheeks flush, and she gives me a shy look.

"Really?" I have to bite the insides of my cheeks to keep from laughing. Her crush was so long ago, I can't believe she's acting like this.

I remember the fact that Justin never could tell us apart, so he just called us the Wright Twins. When he saw one of us, he'd say, "How's my favorite Wright Twin doing?" And when we were together, he'd say, "Hey, Wright Twins. How's it going?"

I hate to burst her bubble, but she needs a healthy dose of reality. "Did he actually call you by name?"

Her forehead crinkles as she thinks, and then she slowly shakes her head. "Not exactly. Why?"

"Just wondering." No point in ruining her good mood. I like seeing her smile. "Where are y'all going?"

"He's talking about going to the high school football game, then grabbing a burger afterward at the Goal Line."

Sounds to me like he wants to relive his glory days when he was the co-captain of the football team. "Watch out, girl. He's pulling out all the stops." I roll my eyes.

She picks up a spool of ribbon and throws it at me. "Don't be so negative. I enjoy high school football games."

I shrug and pretend indifference. "Good. I'm glad. You'll have fun. But please be careful and make sure he knows which twin he's with."

She lifts an eyebrow. "Are you saying he thinks I might have been you?"

"All I'm saying is that, in the past, he had a hard time telling us apart." I pause. "But I'm sure everything will be just fine."

Sara glares at me. "You don't have to sound so condescending."

"Look, Sara." I clear my throat and try to come up with some words of wisdom. "That's not my intention. If you enjoy going on dates to football games, then Justin is perfect for you." I don't look at my sister because I hate the feeling I get after I say something she doesn't like.

"I just like Justin. I don't care where we go." Her icy tone lets me know I've said too much.

"Seriously, Sara, if you like Justin, then I hope you have a good time."

"I'm sure I will." She pauses. "If things go well, I might even ask him to go to the reunion with me."

A lump forms in my throat. If she goes with Justin, then I'll have to go by myself. Or even worse, be a third wheel with them.

Lord, help me.

23

Shay

A week later, I get a call from Conrad. "Good news, Shay. The sellers say they'll be out of the condo by closing, so you'll be able to move right in after you sign on the dotted line. The wife's medicine is working, and she doesn't need surgery after all."

If he were standing in front of me, I'd kiss him. But I'm in my office with the sales team leaders sitting across the desk from me.

"That's good news indeed." I try to keep a straight face for the sake of maintaining my business persona, but it's hard.

"Shay?" Conrad's voice goes up. "Are you okay? I thought you'd be over the moon."

"I am." I pause. "I'm in a sales meeting right now. Can I call you back later?"

"Oh, sorry."

"That's quite all right. Thanks for calling." I hang up and smile at the others in the office. "Now, where were we?"

As they give their reports and discuss different sales strategies, I'm half listening and half planning my move. The condo is basically move-in ready as soon as the sellers get their stuff out, but it could use some freshening up, and I plan to get it cleaned first. Fortunately, the cleaning crew can do it quickly with a day's notice.

As soon as I get back to my desk, Puddin' calls, and I hear her hyperventilating. I ask her what's wrong, and she makes some hiccupping sounds.

"Okay, Puddin'. Stop, take a deep breath, and start over."

"I'm at my wit's end."

"What happened?"

"It's Trey. His roommates were involved in partying until the wee hours with who knows what and who, and they disrupted the neighborhood, and the whole group of them got evicted from the apartment, and—"

"Puddin'." I clear my throat to soften my tone. "Is Trey okay?"

"I reckon he is. He's sleeping off his trauma."

"At least you know he's safe . . . for now."

She lets out a shaky breath. "I know, and I'm relieved it wasn't any worse than it is."

"Things will get better. I'm sure he's learned his lesson." I don't know what else to say, so I pray I'm giving her some comfort.

"I sure hope you're right."

I let out a sigh after we hang up. The remainder of the day seems to drag, but quittin' time finally comes. I head home to tell the twins the great news about the condo.

I walk into the living room and see Sally sitting on the sofa, staring at the TV that's playing some mindless talk show with a bunch of women babbling about first world problems. Sally glances up at me. "Hi, Shay."

"Why so glum?" I drop my handbag on the table and sit in my chair. "Where's Sara?"

"She's out with Justin for, like, the third time this week." The sarcasm in her voice lets me know she's not happy about it.

"That's a good thing, right?" I lean forward to try to get a better read on her. "They must really like each other."

"Oh, I'm sure." Sally pushes off the sofa and heads toward the kitchen. "Want some iced tea?"

I'm not really thirsty, but I don't want to turn her down with her acting all pouty. I don't think she can handle the rejection right now. "Sounds good. Do you think Sara will be home for supper?"

She gives an indifferent shrug. "I doubt it."

"Then why don't we go out for sushi?"

"Seriously?" Sally's eyebrows shoot up as she gives me a scrutinizing look. "I thought you didn't like sushi."

"Well, it's not my favorite, but I don't dislike it like Sara does."

Some of the gloom disappears from her expression. "If we go to Mr.

Fuji's, you can get something else, like teriyaki chicken on a stick." She stops in front of the fridge. "I'm really hungry. Can we go now?"

"Okay, let me change into something comfortable and we can go." I grab my purse and head back to my room.

I really don't need to change, but I want some time to decide whether to tell Sally the news or wait until Sara is with us. By the time I buckle my sandals, I decide to fill her in now and tell her sister later. Maybe it'll cheer her up. I've noticed that, although the twins are a lot alike, they're also competitive. With Sara clearly winning in the boyfriend department, I can give Sally the edge on the latest condo development.

As soon as we're seated at Mr. Fuji's, I lean forward. "I have some wonderful news that I think will make you feel better."

She lifts an eyebrow. "News?"

I try hard not to appear as though I'm trying too hard as I give her an enthusiastic nod. "I'm going to be able to move right into the condo after closing next week."

Fear instantly flashes across her face, and her chin quivers. "But you can't."

Okay, now I'm confused. "What? I thought you'd be happy."

"If you move out, I'll be all by myself and ... I've never been alone before."

"Sara's not going anywhere. Or is she?"

"I don't know." Sally grimaces. "She has Justin, and it seems like they're getting pretty serious."

"But they just started dating, right?"

Sally nods. "Yeah, but they've known each other most of their lives, and I've overheard her talking to him on the phone. Something's going on, and I don't like it."

My heart goes out to this young woman who has never been completely on her own before. Until I lived with them, I never realized how close twins can be. They've been together all their lives, from birth, and now the very idea of one of them moving on leaves the other one floundering.

"Well, first of all, I don't think Sara will just take off and leave you." I pause to take a breath and let my words sink in. "And secondly, if you need someone and she's not there, you know I'll be on the other side of the lake."

"What if she and Justin ... what if they ..."

I smile at her. "You and Sara are beautiful, smart, sweet women. I won't be surprised if both of you find nice young men and fall in love."

"But *you* didn't." She swallows hard. "You're pretty and smart, and you didn't find someone to fall in love with."

"I ... uh ... well, I chose a career, and I haven't exactly ..." As I flounder, she studies me with interest. Finally, I just shrug. "The right man hasn't come along for me—at least not yet."

"What if that happens to me? I don't want to be alone."

"It's really not that bad," I say. "In fact, a lot of times it's a good thing."

"Oh yeah?" She tilts her head and gives me a scrutinizing look. "Like when?"

The sincerity in her voice makes me want to answer. The only problem is, I don't have a good answer to give her. I could say it's nice to be able to go wherever I want without having to think about inconveniencing someone else, or eat what I want without worrying about what the other person likes. But in all honesty, at this point in my life, I would love to sacrifice my own desires to share my life with the right someone. And even though I'm okay with my job, I'd like to have someone else to share my frustrations with about how I'm not able to express my creativity in such a cut-and-dry profession.

The server approaches our table, saving me from having to say anything. After she takes our order, I decide to go on the offense.

"Why don't we start a tradition of getting together once a week for our own little potluck? If Sara is available, she can join us. If not, it'll just be you and me."

She blinks and wipes her eyes with the back of her hand. "You'd do that for me?"

I nod. "Not only for you. I've gotten kind of used to having the two of you around, and I enjoy the company. You girls are fun to hang out with."

For the first time that evening, she grins. "I like you, too, Shay. I can't believe we never got together before. I mean, you are quite a bit older than Sara and I are, but we have a lot in common."

I stare back at the gorgeous blond with big blue eyes and more brains than anyone else in the family has ever given her credit for. Since I've gotten to know the twins, I understand why they're successful. They both have drive and determination, and they complement each other in their business.

"There's no time like now to start something new," I remind her. "That's what Sara has done, and you and I can do it, too." I prop my elbow on the table and rest my chin on my fist. "Now what'll happen to me when you meet your prince?"

She snorts. "Like that'll ever happen."

"You never know." I smile.

"Hey, I have an idea." She picks up her handbag, unzips it, and rifles through it before pulling out some familiar-looking gizmo. "I just got a new selfie stick. Let's take some pictures of us eating sushi and"—she gestures toward my plate—"what's left of your chicken on a stick."

I scoot my chair toward hers, and she starts snapping shots. At first, I'm self-conscious, but then she teaches me some poses—like the pouty face and duck lips—that have us both rolling in laughter. Even the server gets in on the action by photobombing us.

After we finish, we head back home. Sara isn't in yet, but Sally seems to be in much better spirits, so I go to my room to pray and meditate. The stress of my upcoming move is starting to sink in.

I'm not sure when I fell asleep, but I'm awakened by shrieking. I hop out of bed, grab my robe, and head out to the living room, where Sally is standing by the door gripping a slip of paper, her face red from crying.

"What happened?" I step closer, and she hands me the note. As soon as I read it, I can't do anything but shake my head.

The note is in Sara's handwriting, and it simply reads, "Justin and I eloped. I'll call you soon. Love, Sara."

24

Puddin'

You'd think someone got shot, the way the family is reacting to Sara's elopement. I pretend to be appalled when Digger's mama calls to tell me, but deep down, I think it's romantic.

I've always thought that Digger's family goes way too overboard with weddings. They spend money most of them don't have—with the exception of Bucky and Marybeth, of course—to have a big blow-out where everyone comes dressed in clothes they're not comfortable in and pretends to have a good time, while all they want is to be home in front of the TV, in their jeans, watching the Saints play football.

"I'm not sure you heard me, Puddin'. She *eloped*." The way she says the last word makes it sound like it's a federal offense. I don't dare tell her about what happened to Trey. No tellin' what she'd say to the family.

She makes a clicking sound with her tongue. "I reckon I don't have to tell you that Sheila is fit to be tied. I just hope Sally doesn't up and do something foolish, now that her twin has gone off and gotten married. I hear she took the news real bad."

I've always thought Sally was the smarter of the two girls. "I don't think she'll do anything stupid, but I bet she's just as upset as her mama."

When I sign on to my email, I see that all of Digger's cousins, aunts, and uncles are buzzing about it on the family loop. It seems the only people who haven't commented are Sally and Shay. So of course, they're the ones I want to talk to. But first, I get supper prepared to make sure no one in my family starves to death, which is what they'll act like if I'm as much as ten minutes late puttin' it on the table.

I plan to discuss the situation with Digger after we finish eating, but

Hallie brings it up. "I can't believe Sara just up and married this guy. I didn't even know they were dating."

"Where did you hear about it?" I ask.

"Justin's sister is a senior, and she's bragging about having Sara for a sister-in-law."

"Oh. I suppose word's bound to get around in such a small town as Pinewood."

Digger starts shoveling food in his face without saying a word. I fold my arms and glare at him.

He gives me a double take, swallows, and narrows his eyes. "What?"

"What do you think about Sara and Justin eloping?"

"I say they saved Sara's mama and daddy a boatload of money. Weddings are expensive these days."

"How would you know?"

"One of the guys at work was talking about how much his daughter's wedding was costing him." Digger turns toward Hallie. "When you start thinking about getting hitched, you might want to consider eloping. If you do that, I'll give you the money to put down on a house. That way you'll have something to show for it."

"Digger!" I reach over and swat him on the arm with my napkin. "Don't you say such a thing. I want to be there to witness the happiest day of Hallie's life."

Brett makes a gagging sound. "That'll be the grossest day in some stupid guy's life."

Hallie's eyes nearly bug out of her head, and I see her body jerk, indicating she has kicked her younger brother under the table. "Moron."

His chin juts. "Ouch!"

She bobs her head and turns the corners of her lips downward in a mocking manner. "That's what you get for saying such stupid stuff."

"I don't think anyone will ever want to marry you," he says. "You're too mean."

"Stop it now." I close my eyes and take a deep breath before turning to Hallie. "When you eventually fall in love and get married, your daddy and I want to share the moment with you."

"Are you tryin' to get rid of me or something?"

Digger laughs. "Maybe your mama is, but I'm not."

I glare at him. I know he's kidding, but I still don't want him to plant those thoughts in our children's minds. "Oh, come on, Digger, you know better than that. I'm not trying to get rid of anyone."

"Certainly sounds like it." Digger winks at me, then looks at Brett. "I used to think my sister was mean, too, until our daddy passed away. Then I realized how much I love everyone in my family. Including my sister." He makes a face that has our young'uns laughing. "Except when she used to pinch me right here." He points to the tender skin on the underside of his arm. "That used to hurt, but now she would never want to hurt me. We have a good relationship now, filled with trust, which is what y'all will have some day when you grow up and stop acting like—"

"That's right, Brett," I say, cutting Digger off. "Listen to your daddy."

A surprised look covers Brett's face. "You're actually agreeing with Daddy?"

Before I have a chance to say a word, Hallie pipes up. "That's a first. Sometimes I wonder how the two of you ever agreed to get married in the first place."

My chin drops. How can she not see the love that flows between her daddy and me? I want to say something, but I'm speechless for the moment.

Digger steps up and responds. "Your mama and I might bicker every now and then, but we do it out of love." He gives me a sideways grin as he reaches out, takes my hand, and kisses the back of it. "And I do love your mama more than you'll ever know."

"I can't watch this." Hallie gets up from the table and carries her plate to the sink. She turns around to face us. "I have tons of homework, so I'm going to my room now."

"Me, too."

Brett tries to follow his sister, but Digger lets go of my hand and stops him. "Get back here, young man, and take your plate to the sink. We don't have cleaning staff to pick up after messy kids."

Since Trey is out with friends, the only child we have left in the kitchen is Jeremy, who is having fun playing with his food. That gives Digger and me a chance to talk.

"Do you think we need to stop bickering so much?" I ask.

He shakes his head. "We really don't bicker all that much. You should hear some of my buddies from work. The way they tell it, most of them are only a few steps away from divorce court."

I shudder to think of going through a divorce. Digger is my first and only love, and I don't have any desire to change that.

He closes the distance between us and wraps his arms around me. "As long as we get along most of the time and we're honest with each other, I don't think we'll ever have a serious problem. And truth be told, I enjoy a little squabble every now and then."

A wave of guilt nearly knocks me off my feet. "Digger ..."

He smiles and tilts my face up to his. "What is it, darlin'?"

"There's something I've been meaning to tell you."

"What's that?"

I feel his breath as he holds me close, and it breaks my heart to let him know I've been lying to him all along—especially after what he just said about being honest with each other. "I have a—" I look down and cough.

He places his hands on my shoulders and holds me back to look at me. When I look up into his eyes, I see amusement.

"What's so funny?" I ask.

"Are you about to tell me you have a job?"

Now I'm totally speechless.

"Puddin', darling, I'm not stupid. I've known for quite some time that you've been working at that little dress shop in town."

"You have?"

He continues to smile as he nods. "And I've been wondering when you were going to get around to telling me."

"Are you ... mad at me?"

"No, Puddin'. When I first found out, I was a little hurt that you didn't bring it up, but then I realized it was important for you to have your own little thing on the side." He chuckles. "I'm just glad it's not another man."

25

Shay

Someone could have knocked me over with a feather when I read that note Sara left on the console table in the foyer. She must have dropped it off when she knew no one would be home. She didn't want to face us!

The whole idea of Sara running off with Justin is so disconcerting, but Sally needs me, so I have to pretend to be strong. She's been walking around like a zombie ever since we got the news. "Sally, sweetie, you need to start making some bows. Those orders keep coming in, and I'm worried you'll get behind."

Her chin quivers, and her shoulders slump as she shakes her head. "I can't do it without Sara."

I plant my fists on my hips and give her the same look my own mama used to give me when I needed what she called an extra dose of some serious talkin' to. "And why not?"

She lifts her arms in helplessness and drops them to her sides, slapping her thighs. "I don't know. We've just always done everything together. We even shared a room until we moved out on our own—and that seemed weird at first."

"Just like this seems weird now. But you'll adjust, like you did before, and eventually you might even like being on your own."

Sally shakes her head. "No way. I don't think I'll be able to function without her." She lets out a dramatic cry. "How can I live without her? Our business needs both of us. I can't do it all by myself."

"Oh, come on, Sally. It's not like you won't see her. She's on her honeymoon, but she'll be back." I give her what I hope is a reassuring smile, even though I'm not sure of anything I'm telling her. This blindsided me as much as it did Sally, but I can't let her see that I'm anything less than confident that Sara will resume her position with their business.

"But what if she doesn't want to make bows anymore? What will I do then?"

That isn't something I considered. "Is Justin well-to-do?"

"Not really, but he does okay. He's a mechanic down at Freddy's Tire and Lube."

"Oh." I went to school with Freddy, and I just happen to know he's doing quite well for himself, even though the biggest thing I remember about him is how dirty his fingernails used to be. His business is successful enough for him to have several commercials on TV every day during the early evening news, but I doubt he pays his hired help enough to live lavishly. "At least she won't have to worry about her car not running."

My feeble attempt at humor doesn't go over very well. Sally's lips tighten, and her chin quivers again.

"Everything will be fine." The instant that comes out of my mouth, I regret it. That's not what Sally wants to hear.

"No, it won't. Everything is terrible, so don't try to tell me otherwise."

"Look, Sally, everyone has rocky times, and this is one of those curveballs life throws at us." I close my eyes. Did I just say that?

"You're kidding, right? This is not just a rocky time. It's the end of life with my sister."

Now I'm getting annoyed with her. I've never liked teenage drama, and she's much too old to be displaying it. "Remember that you're a smart woman, your sister is your business partner, and I live across the lake from you. Your mama and daddy love you, and you have lots of family nearby, so you have a pretty decent support system. You'll never be alone, even if you want to be."

She pouts and folds her arms, reminding me of my brother's daughter Hallie when she doesn't get her way. "But I want everything just like it was."

One thing I've learned in life is that as soon as you like how things are going, they change. But fortunately, it works the other way, too.

"Trust me," I say, hoping to end this conversation. "Things will get better. In the meantime, you have your own life to live." I give her one of the looks Mama used to give me. "So pull on your big-girl panties and start livin'."

I try to think of something different to talk about, but Sally's phone rings, so she walks away to answer it. It's Saturday, and we have church tomorrow. I wonder if Sara and her new husband will show up. I can't remember seeing Justin at church, but I go to the early service, and there aren't all that many people in the younger crowd there at that time.

Sally comes walking out of her bedroom, a hint of a smile playing on her lips. "That was Sara. She asked me if I still wanted to be her business partner."

I smile. "And you said yes, right?"

"Of course I did." Sally sighs. "Another thing she told me was that she can't live in Justin's apartment because he has a couple of roommates who are slobs, so she wants to bring him here to live."

"Here? In this condo?" A mix of dizziness and nausea wash over me. The different dynamic of having a man in the house will throw everything off. For one thing, I won't be able to come out to the kitchen for my morning coffee without a bathrobe. At least that's temporary since I'll be moving out soon, but I can't see Sally being any happier about it than I am.

Sally nods. "I told her when you'll be closing on your condo, so I think they'll probably wait until then."

"That's probably a good idea. This is a good-sized condo, but having that extra person might be pushing it a tad."

"I am so relieved I'm not losing my sister." She blows out a breath of relief. "Everything will be just like it used to be."

She can't possibly believe that. Or can she? Surely Sally realizes that her married sister won't have as much time for her as she once had. Or maybe she needs to hold on to this fantasy to keep from emotionally falling apart.

My phone rings and it's Mama, so I go into my room to take the call. She starts talking about Sara's elopement without bothering to ask how I'm doing. "Do you have any idea how long Sara's been dating that boy?

I don't remember anyone saying anything about him. How could she do something so impetuous?"

I know more than I'll tell her in this conversation, so I try to think of a vague way to answer. "Well, she has known him most of her life. They went to school together, and according to Sally, she's liked him for a long time."

"But have they been dating long enough to get married?" The judgmental tone of Mama's voice reminds me of my own when I first found out.

"That's a very subjective thing, Mama. One of my classmates married her high school sweetheart after dating him for almost four years. They got divorced a year later."

"You didn't answer my question."

"I'm not sure, but it hasn't been long."

Mama makes another one of her sounds of disapproval. I hate having conversations like this about things that are none of my business, so I decide to change the subject to something that is my business.

"I'm moving next week."

"But I thought ..." She sighs. "I don't know what I thought. So what happened, and exactly when are you moving?"

"The owner doesn't have to have surgery, so they'll get their things out the day before closing. I'll have the cleaning crew go in right away, and I can move right in after I sign the papers."

"That's a good thing, right?"

"It is. I'm looking forward to having my own space again."

"After you move out, what will Sally do?"

She obviously won't let up. I shouldn't be surprised. But still, I'm holding onto the fact that Sally and Sara's living arrangements are no one's business but their own. "I'm not sure." It looks like, no matter what I say, we'll keep going back to what Mama called about. "She misses Sara quite a bit, even when I'm here."

"I can imagine. Those twins have always been attached at the hip. I can't imagine either of them without the other."

She continues on and on about how they've always been together, so much so that even the family can't tell them apart. I half listen and half try to think of something to end this conversation.

"It'll take time, but everything will work out."

Mama sighs. "Yeah, and maybe this will be a good thing for Sally. She might get out more and find her own guy."

"It's way more important that she find herself first." I hear the annoyance in my own voice, but I can't help it.

"Oh, sweetie, I know. And I'm sure you'll find someone, too … eventually."

26
Missy

All it takes for a prideful man to fly into a fit of rage is his wife asking him to go get his hearing checked. I'm fully aware of what I'm getting myself into when I do it, so I brace myself. The timing has to be perfect, so I wait until evening when all the kids are in their rooms.

"Foster, when was the last time you had a physical?" He doesn't respond, so I ask again in a louder voice.

He makes a face. "You don't have to yell."

"You didn't answer me the first time I asked."

"You only asked once." His chin juts out enough to remind me that I'm dealing with more than hearing issues. "Why do you want to know?"

I shrug, trying to act nonchalant, but I've never been good at hiding my feelings. "It's just that we're not getting any younger, so we should probably get checkups more often."

"When did you have your last one?"

I think for a few seconds. "I think it's been a couple years. Why don't we go together?"

He flaps his hand from the wrist. "Nah, you can go without me. I'm healthy as a horse."

A deaf horse. "Maybe so, but wouldn't you feel better if you knew for sure?"

"Look, Missy, I know how I feel, and I feel just fine. Why would I want to go to a doctor who pokes until something hurts and then gives me a pill for it? Nope. I'll pass, but if you want to go, then have at it."

"I thought it would be nice if we—"

"Nope. I'm not doing it." He lowers the footrest on his recliner, stands, and stretches. "I'm going to bed now. I'm plum tuckered out from all this nagging." He leaves me sitting in my chair, staring after him.

I want to pick up something and throw it at him, then toss back a shot of the strongest thing I have hidden in the back of the pantry, but that's the old me. The new me has been through counseling, so I know there are other ways to cope. I pick up the phone and call my cousin Shay.

"What are you doing for lunch tomorrow?" I ask.

"I was planning to pick out paint for my new living room, but if you have a better idea, I might change my mind."

I smile. Shay has always been one of those family members I'm proud to be kin to. She has her act together, and nothing rattles her. And she never turns her back on a family member, which is precisely why I called her. "Want to meet for salads at the Lettuce Leaf?"

"Sure, that'll be good."

After we hang up, I plop back down in my chair. Just knowing that I'll soon be able to talk to an adult who actually listens makes me feel better. The only problem with Shay is that she's never been married, so she's not able to relate to dumb husband antics. She has even been known to tell me I shouldn't complain since I chose to marry Foster.

Now that I think about it, I wonder if I should have called someone else. Someone who gets the predicament I'm in. Someone like Puddin'. But the big problem with Puddin' is that she's married to my cousin, and she is too sweet to gripe about him to me, and I'm pretty sure she's a whole lot happier than I am. So it'll be all me, sounding like a terrible, disloyal wife.

And maybe that's exactly what I am—a disloyal wife who doesn't appreciate the good things about my husband. I rummage around the junk drawer and pull out a pad of paper and a pencil that looks like a beaver got hold of it from all the gnaw marks on the wood. I sit down at the kitchen table and jot numbers one through ten so I can list Foster's good points.

First, he makes a decent living, so I've never had to worry about not having a roof over my head. That's a big deal. The money I make at my job goes to paying off bills and enabling us to take vacations, even though we haven't taken one in a while.

Second, he's been a good daddy to our daughter Wendy. In fact, when

Wendy's school prom came up, she didn't have a boyfriend, so he offered to go with her. A wild-eyed look came over her, and she didn't waste any time finding another boy to crush on. Of course, it doesn't take much searching when you look like my daughter. To top it off, she has mastered the smoky eye with makeup, so when she gives the guys one of her smoldering looks, there's no hope of escaping.

Third, I know what it feels like to be madly in love with Foster. In fact, I want it back, which is why I've hung in there so long.

Coming up with ten things might be tough. Everything past number three seems lame, so I put down the pencil, get up, and start pacing until I feel my eyelids grow heavy and I know it's time to go to bed.

When the alarm clock goes off the next morning, I glance over and see Foster still sleeping with a dreamy smile on his face. He obviously doesn't hear the alarm.

I reach over and give him a gentle nudge. The instant I make contact with his shoulder, he scowls.

"What'd you go and do that for?" He props up on one elbow for a second, then flops back on the bed after I get up.

"It's time to get up." I pick up the clock from his nightstand and point to the face. "It's six thirty."

"Give me ten more minutes."

We don't have the kind of clock with a snooze button. Foster insists that our old, windup clock is perfectly fine. And it is, if you can hear it. He obviously can't.

I pull on my bathrobe and go to the kitchen to start the coffee. When he doesn't join me ten minutes later, I go back into our bedroom and nudge him again. He groans and gets up without even looking at me.

Foster has his routine down pat once he gets up in the morning, so I know that he'll shower and shave before coming for his coffee. While he pours it and fixes it the way he likes it—one spoon of sugar and two spoons of the powdered, vanilla-flavored coffee creamer he insists I buy—I'll get his Cheerios ready. He'll sit at the table and ask me if I have any bananas, and within a couple of seconds, I'll hand one to him. I've tried breaking the routine by having his banana on the table or fixing his coffee for him, but it totally throws off his day. In fact, he has even blamed me for ruining his morning by changing things up.

After Foster leaves for work, I get ready for my lunch with Shay. I remember the fact that she's always very punctual, so I do everything in my power to be there on time. However, my phone rings off the hook, and I smear my mascara when I put it on my bottom eyelashes, so I'm five minutes late.

"Sorry I'm late, but—"

She holds up both hands. "Don't worry about it. Life happens. So how's everything going?"

"There's so much, I don't know where to start."

Shay tilts her head and smiles. "Why don't you start at the beginning? That's always a good place."

I begin with my chili cook-off win. "I was so excited to take home the big prize ... until I looked around and saw that I didn't have anyone there to support me."

Her lips twist. "Welcome to my world."

"I'm sorry, Shay. I didn't mean—"

"I know. So tell me what happened next." She leans forward and gives me an encouraging look.

I can't even begin to express my appreciation for Shay. She is such a good listener, and I never feel like she's judging me. "We really should get together more often," I say.

She nods. "I'd like that. So what happened after you won the chili competition?"

I tell her about the way Foster didn't seem to care and how he seemed so wrapped up in his fishing trip. "I was really getting miffed at him for being so thoughtless, until I realized something I should have seen a long time ago." I pause to take a breath.

"And what should you have seen?"

"He can't hear."

"Can't hear or won't listen?"

I hold my hands out to my sides. "He can't hear half of what I say. My husband is almost deaf."

"I've heard a lot of wives say that about their husbands, but it's usually selective hearing."

"No, it's not like that with Foster. He really and truly can't hear. I've been trying to figure out what's wrong with him for quite a while, and then we went to Stephen's."

Shay's eyebrows shoot up. "Y'all went to Stephen's? Wow!"

"I know, right? Anyway, after it seemed like he was ignoring people there, I finally realized he simply can't hear."

"As in, you really do think he's deaf?"

I nod. "I've been bubblin' and fumin' inside for years, thinking he's been ignoring me and thinking about what he's about to say next, but all this time—"

"Most people do that, you know." Shay rubs her finger along the edge of the fork as she ponders the situation. "But if he's really hard of hearing, he needs to see someone. Hearing aids keep getting better all the time."

"That's the problem. He doesn't want to see someone. He says he feels just fine."

"I'm sure he does." Shay shakes her head. "But how do you feel?"

"That's just it. I'm angry all the time because I'm the only one who's listening."

"Being married isn't easy, is it?" She grimaces and gives me an apologetic look. "Sorry. I know those are words a single woman should never say to one who's married."

"But it's true." I watch Shay's expression become more pensive and worry that I'm scaring her away from ever getting married. "Marriage isn't all bad, though."

She makes a funny face. "Nothing is *all* bad."

Okay, time to change the subject before I have her committing herself to forever-after singledom. "So are you going to the reunion?"

"Yeah, I'm going." She leans back and sighs. "I can't figure out why we keep having so many. Seems like one a year would be plenty."

"I reckon the older folks are starting to think about their mortality, and they're worried they won't live until next year."

Shay laughs. "But they always do."

27
Shay

When I hear about other folks' marital problems, it should make me happy I'm single. But it doesn't. In fact, it generally does the opposite. I'm just as miserable as they are, and I have no one but myself to blame.

I've had coffee with Elliot a couple of times, and each time, he brings up his ex more than I'm comfortable with. I understand that she's still fresh in his mind, but he is adamant about the fact that he's completely over her.

Maybe I'm being too cautious, but I don't want to date him until I'm sure he's ready to focus on our relationship without constantly being reminded of anything, good or bad, from his marriage. Deep down, I think that time will come.

Something I really like about him is the fact that he's not so money focused that it rules his life. He gave up a six-figure income to come back to Pinewood to teach high school business and help coach the football team. That says a lot about his character.

While it breaks my heart that he has to spend so much of his paycheck paying off the bills from his marriage and divorce, it shows his commitment to doing the right thing. But it also reminds me that his ex will be on his mind for a while, as he plows through the mountain of bills.

Life isn't bad, but it's not exactly how I would have ordered it. The twins have come to some realizations that mirror mine, and I'm amazed by how quickly they've learned about all the kinks in the road of life. Sometimes we all feel sorry for ourselves, even when we know we should be counting our many blessings.

Actually, I'm not always miserable, and I suspect the twins aren't either. But I do have a lot of days when I'm down. Fortunately, I'll be busy for the next couple of months getting my new condo just like I want it, so I won't have time to think about the fact that Elliot isn't ready to be in a relationship yet. If I'd been younger when he returned, I might have given in to the temptation to get involved with him anyway. But years of experience and watching other people have made me more cautious. Maybe too cautious.

I look around at the bare walls of my condo and try to get a feel for what I should do. Fortunately, everything is in decent shape—even the carpet and linoleum that I plan to eventually rip out. I like hardwood floors in the living room and tile in the kitchen and bathrooms. I've seen enough HGTV home-makeover shows with the twins to know what I want, and it's not cheap.

The kitchen is rather tired looking, but unlike the twins, I don't mind the bisque appliances as long as they work. I'll save my money and replace them in a year or so, after I decide whether to go for the super-deluxe fridge with the French-door top, bottom freezer, and pullout snack drawer or the more traditional side-by-side model, which is really all I need.

I despise the fluorescent lighting that's still in the bathrooms, and there aren't enough lights in the kitchen, so I make a note to call my electrician to come out and add more canned fixtures and pendant lights in both rooms. While he's there, I'll have more outlets put on the back porch, since I'll be doing quite a bit of entertaining out there. I'm not that great at grilling, but since my place comes with a built-in grill, I'll get better.

I've been staring at walls, measuring, and planning for almost an hour when my phone rings. It's Mama.

"What have you decided to bring to the reunion besides the eggs?"

"Nothing yet."

"Well …" Mama's voice drops to a whisper. "I've heard that there'll be at least three lasagnas and a couple of creamy chicken casseroles with peas."

"Sounds good."

"Are you being sarcastic?"

"No," I reply. "I'm serious. I like lasagna and chicken casseroles."

"I'm sure we'll have a lot of elaborately decorated cakes, too. You'd think some of the people in our family have nothing better to do with their time than spend hours making sure their fondant rosettes are perfect."

"Okay." A smile tweaks my lips, but I try not to let her know I'm amused. "What are you bringing?"

"One of the lasagnas. You know I make the best."

"What else?" I ask. Mama does make the best lasagna, but she also likes to be the one who brings the most dishes to the reunions. "Any dessert?"

"Maybe some 'nana puddin'."

"Sounds good. What else?" I know that once Mama's pump gets primed, there's no stopping her.

"At least one salad, probably with broccoli and nuts. And maybe a vegetable dish or two."

"Then I don't have to bring anything since you'll have it all covered."

"Shay! You're a grown woman. You have to bring something."

"I was just pulling your leg, Mama. In addition to the deviled eggs, I'll bring a three-bean salad, and maybe some of those spoon rolls like I used to make when I lived at home." I pause. "If I have time, I might even make some meatballs."

"I don't know, Shay. All of that is pretty basic, and you know how the women in our family can be."

Yes, I do know, but it doesn't matter whether they think my contributions are basic or elaborate. One of the main reasons I'm bringing so much stuff to the reunion is to keep Mama from being ashamed of her daughter's manners.

"Hey, Shay!"

I turn around and see Sally grinning at me. And right behind her is Sara with a sullen, very thin, somewhat shaggy guy. "Mama, I gotta run. My decorators are here."

"Tell Sally and Sara I said hi."

I press the Off button on my phone and drop it into my pocket. "Well, what do y'all think?"

Sally spins around with her arms open wide. "I think this is wonderful, but you sure do have a lot of work to do."

"That's not very nice," Sara says as she steps forward. She crinkles her nose. "You're not keeping those hideous appliances, are you?"

I go over my plans with them, even though it's really none of their business and probably nothing they're interested in hearing. "I need to get the Jacuzzi professionally cleaned, and then I'll have y'all over to hang out on my patio."

"We'll bring the steaks."

I glance at the boy who just spoke as he remains standing in the girls' shadows. "You must be Justin."

"Yes, ma'am." His Adam's apple bobs as he swallows hard.

"Well, congratulations and welcome to the family."

His deer-in-headlights look endears him to me. I want to give him a hug and let him know everything will be all right, but I'm not totally sure that's accurate. With the family reunion coming up soon, there's no telling what he's in for. I've seen the way the older women in my family grill newlyweds, and it's not pretty. And I'm sure he'll get an extra dose of it since they eloped. If there's one thing the women in my family like more than reunions, it's weddings, with funerals being not too far behind.

Sara frowns as she nudges her new husband. "Say something, Justin."

He gives her a confused look, glances at me, and shifts his feet. "What do you want me to say?"

She rolls her eyes and lets out a soft groan. "Never mind." I smile at her, but she doesn't meet my gaze.

It's not a good sign when newlyweds act this way. I decide to try to fix things between them. "There really isn't much he can say. I'm sure it's still pretty overwhelming."

Sally's jaw tightens. It's obvious that she's still unhappy about her sister's impetuous move, but she knows there's absolutely nothing she can do about it now.

Normally, I welcome silence, but this is awkward. I rack my brain to think of something else to say.

Justin finally speaks up. "I'm pretty handy, so if you ever need work done, I'll be happy to do it." Now he looks directly at me, letting me know there is one thing he's confident about.

"Why, thank you, Justin."

"No problem."

Sara grimaces, while a slight smirk forms on Sally's lips. Both of the girls know that I hate it when people say, "No problem," instead of, "You're welcome." There will come a time in the future when I'll tell him, but this isn't it. I decide to make more small talk.

"I understand you're a mechanic at Freddy's."

He nods and shifts his feet again. "Yes, ma'am."

"How long have you been working on cars?"

"About ten years."

My eyebrows shoot up. This boy can't be much older than the twins, so that would put him in his early twenties.

Before I have a chance to comment on how young he must have been when he started, Sara speaks up. "He used to help his daddy work on old cars in their backyard when he was a kid."

That makes sense. I grin at him, hoping he'll crack and smile back. "It's nice to have a mechanic in the family."

"Yes, ma'am."

He might not say much, but he has the "ma'am" down pat.

28

Sally

It really bugs me that Shay is trying so hard to be nice to Justin when he's the person who ruined my life. I mean, I don't expect her to be mean to him, but why can't she at least let him know how she really feels? Granted, she has never said anything negative about the situation, but surely she must think Sara did the stupidest thing ever by running off and getting married.

I'm glad Sara isn't moving out, but I can already tell that there will be problems having Justin in the house. He hasn't moved in yet and doesn't plan to until Shay is in her own place.

But then again, maybe he'll be handy to have around, like when the toilet runs and runs in the middle of the night like it did right after we moved in. Shay knows what to do, but Sara and I haven't got a clue.

Ever since my sister eloped, I've been on an emotional roller coaster. One minute I'm hoppin' mad, and the next minute I think it might be a good thing. Then he comes around, and I see an intruder who took off with my sister without bothering to ask how I feel.

I know it's not all about me. Sara has reminded me of this over and over. But still, in my mind, it is partly about me. I mean, I have feelings, too, and she is my sister. People seem to think I'm the smart, strong one, but I know that Sara's just as smart and strong, only she's quieter about it. Besides, part of my strength comes from knowing she's always there.

We're back at our condo now. I'm in my room while Sally and Justin take over the living room. I hear footsteps then a knock on my door.

"What?" I haven't been able to keep the shrillness out of my voice since he's been here.

"The guys are having a party tonight," Justin says. "Wanna go?"

"Where?"

"The apartment." He pauses. "My old place."

"Will Sara be there?" I ask.

"She said she will, but only if you go."

I smile. At least I still carry a little clout with my sis. "I'll think about it."

"Don't think too long. Chevy needs to know how much beer to buy."

Without wasting a second, I hop off my bed, storm across my room, and fling open the door. "Tell Chevy that I don't drink beer, and neither does Sara."

"How do you know she doesn't?" Justin tilts his head.

I see Sara come up from behind her husband, a scowl making lines across her forehead. "She knows me better than anyone else. I'm not sure I want to go to this party."

"But—" He frowns and glances back and forth between Sara and me, as though he's not sure what he's gotten himself into.

"I hate being around a bunch of drunk people," Sara continues. "They act so stupid, and it embarrasses me."

I decide to tag-team, something she and I do so well. "Not to mention the fact that if someone drives home drunk, you'll be liable."

"I will?" Justin now looks completely bewildered.

"Yes, and wouldn't it be a shame to go straight to jail right after your honeymoon?"

Justin frowns as he drops his gaze. It appears that he still hasn't mastered adulthood.

I glance over in Sara's direction and see that she's slightly amused. I'm not sure she believes what I just told her husband.

"Yeah," I continue. "Y'all can be in some serious trouble if you throw a party and let people drive home with alcohol in their blood."

Justin's gaze shoots up as he has clearly has an *aha!* moment. "Then everyone can just crash at our apartment for the night." He brushes his hands together. "Problem solved."

Sara takes hold of Justin's arm and leads him away from me. I go back into my room and close the door as my sister's whispers grow louder and sound more desperate. I can't help but feel smug about her being upset. Serves her right since she didn't talk to me before eloping.

When my cell phone rings, I glance at it and see that it's Mama. Although I'm tempted not to answer, I take a deep breath and press the Talk button. Before I have the word "hello" out of my mouth, she starts on one of her rants.

"I can't even tell you how many times I've tried to call Sara, but it keeps going to voicemail. What is going on with that girl? Has she lost her mind? Can't you keep track of her? You're her sister *and* her roommate. Didn't you stop her and ask where she was going when she left to elope?"

"Are you saying it's my fault she did something stupid?"

"I didn't say it was your fault, but you could have stopped her."

Whoa. "Mama, let's start with first things first. I had no idea she was going to elope, or I would have tried to stop her. And it's never been my job to keep track of her every time she walks out the door. She's a grown woman."

Mama sighs. "I know. I'm sorry, but I'm so worried about her. She always was the one who flew by the seat of her pants, while you've always been so predictable."

Predictable, huh? Maybe I need to work on that. But I don't think this is the time to discuss me when Mama is clearly on a Sara kick today.

"Maybe she has her phone ringer turned off," I say.

"What's the point of having a cell phone if you turn off your ringer? She won't know when people want to talk to her."

That's the point, but I don't say it to Mama, with her fussing and fuming. "She's here now. Do you want me to go get her?"

"No, I don't want to bother her since she clearly doesn't want to be bothered." Her voice has taken on a whole new tone, and it's gone from being accusatory to pitiful. "And she obviously doesn't want to talk to me for some reason, even though I'll always be her mama."

Okay, so now she's moved on to the guilt phase. "I'm sure she'll want to talk to you. Let me go get her." I make a point of clunking the phone as I put it on the dresser.

"Sara," I say as I open the door. "Mama's on the phone. She wants to talk to you."

"What phone?" she hollers.

I walk around the corner and see Sara and Justin snuggling on the sofa. They have obviously made up. "My phone."

"Why did she call your phone to talk to me?"

I widen my eyes, then narrow them, our signal that we can't discuss something. Then I mouth that she needs to go in my room and talk to our mama. "My phone's on the dresser."

She gives me an incredulous look. "Why didn't you bring it to me?"

I give her the biggest fake smile I can manage. "I thought it might be nice for you to have a private conversation *with our mother*."

"Oh." She stands, leans over, and drops a light kiss on Justin's lips. "Hold that thought. I'll be right back." And then she leaves Justin and me alone, in awkward silence.

After the most excruciatingly quiet ten seconds of my life, I decide to say something. "Shay's place is nice, isn't it?"

He bobs his head but settles his gaze on the floor. "Yeah, it looks pretty good."

Okay, this is going nowhere. "Are you excited about moving here?"

He shrugs. "Not really."

29

Shay

The past several weeks seem to have crawled, but I'm finally in my new condo. Granted, not everything I wanted finished before moving in got done, but I'm fine with that. Having my own space is a huge deal to me, which makes me think I might be past the point of ever finding someone to settle down with.

Even though not all the work is done, I can do the rest at my own pace. One thing that life experience and maturity have taught me is that if the kitchen and bedroom are set up and there's a clear path to the bathroom, that's all you really need. Boxes are still stacked to the twelve-foot ceilings in the living and dining rooms, but that's okay. I have a corner on the sofa with a good view of my big TV that Justin mounted on the wall the day I moved in. He's a lot smarter and more capable than he acts or looks.

Now I have to start thinking about the reunion, like what to wear and whether or not I should ask Elliot. Although he still needs a little bit of time to get past his anger toward his ex, I think he's come a long way. I want to ask him, and I know having him there will keep my aunts and uncles from making jabs about my not settling down.

Truth be told, I'm probably just as settled as the married folks. I'm sure they think I'm living the life of a wild and crazy bachelorette, while the wildest thing I do is watch *The Bachelorette* and shake my head about the bad decisions those new celebrities make in front of a national audience. I've even been known to throw a piece of popcorn or two at the TV when they do stupid stuff.

I call Mama to ask her opinion about different foods I should bring in addition to what I've already told her. After our last chat, I know I need to bring more than one thing, or I'll be known not only as an old maid, but a stingy old maid.

"Bring whatever you want, dear." I can tell Mama's in a hurry to get off the phone, which makes me smile.

"Maybe I'll just stop at the store on the way and pick something up from the—"

"No, don't do that. You need to cook something and leave the packaged items to the younger people."

"You originally told me to bring potato chips." I can't help but be suspicious of Mama when she changes like this.

"After I thought it over, I realized you were right. You've had to figure out how to cook since you live alone." She pauses. "So just make sure that whatever you bring is delicious."

"Like what?"

"Whatever you cook best."

"I'm pretty good at making chili."

"No." Mama coughs. "Missy likes to bring chili. Remember last year when she brought three different kinds?"

"Yes, I do remember. A group of men hovered around the slow cookers and argued about which one was the best."

"Bring whatever you want, but not chili." I can hear the anxiety in her voice, which probably means that she's running late for something.

There is one thing I know that might slow her down. "I'm thinking about bringing a date."

"You're *what*?"

Oh yeah, that totally worked. I can't help but smile at the surprise in her voice. It's rare that I manage to pull off something she doesn't expect.

"Say that again, Shay, only speak slowly. I don't think I understood you."

"I said I might bring a date."

Mama sighed. "Please don't tell me it's Elliot. He's not—"

"We went out to dinner and had coffee a couple of times. He's a very kind man." Why do I feel like I'm back in high school, begging for approval?

"Come on, Shay. You can do better. He's a divorced man."

"As are most single men my age. I've known him most of my life, and he's really nice."

"You didn't really *know* him when you were growing up. He was just an acquaintance you pined for when you were a silly teenage girl. How many heart-to-heart conversations have you had with him?"

I want to ask how many heart-to-heart conversations she had with Daddy before they got married, but I don't dare. "Please trust me, Mama."

"I do." Mama lets out one of the sighs I've come to know so well. "Shay, sweetie, I understand why you feel like you need to do this. Teenage crushes tend to stay with people for a long time, and it takes true love with someone else to get over them."

"Maybe so." I stop to take a breath and make my voice sound more adult. "But we hit it off so well we decided to go out again."

"But do you have to bring him to the reunion?" She pauses. "I love you so much, and the very thought of someone hurting you goes all through me. Are you sure you want to ask him?"

"I would like to, but he might not want to go. I haven't asked him yet."

"Maybe he has other plans." I can hear the hopefulness in her voice.

"Or maybe not. Regardless, I'll come up with more yummy things to bring."

"How about a Jell-O mold?"

I cringe. There's at least one Jell-O mold at every reunion, and I don't think I've ever seen anyone eat it. "Maybe."

"Gotta run, sweetie. Please think long and hard before inviting Elliot." She coughs. "Love you."

After we hang up, I look outside and see that it's raining. Normally I welcome these afternoon showers that cool things off and make the Mississippi summer evenings more bearable, but I don't see a break in the overcast sky. I was hoping to set up my patio table and umbrella so I could get outside and enjoy the Jacuzzi that I just spent a fortune having cleaned, only to find out it needed fixing. So I paid someone else to come do that. This is the day I planned to grill some salmon and corn after taking a long soak in the hot tub with the jets aimed at my shoulders to work out some of the kinks from sitting at my desk all week. Oh well. Maybe I can do it tomorrow after church.

My phone rings, so I quickly grab it off the table and glance at the screen. Once again, disappointment swells inside me. It's my brother.

"Hey, Digger."

"What's wrong, Shay? You sound like you just lost your best friend."

"Nothing's wrong. I'm just trying to figure out what to do next in this condo."

"Moving's rough. I don't envy you. I wasn't kidding when I offered to help out."

"I know, but we had more people than we needed, with the twins and Sara's husband, Justin."

"So you're all buddy-buddy with the new guy in the family, huh? Just don't let everyone else know." He lets out one of those comic-book evil laughs that used to get me in trouble when I slugged him afterward. "The reason I'm calling is to let you know that the secret is out."

"Secret?" I think back to anything either of us might have said to the other that is supposed to be a secret. "What are you talking about?"

"I know about Puddin's job."

"Oh." I'm not sure if he's aware of how much I know, and I don't dare speak up. Besides, he might just be fishing for more information than Puddin' was willing to give.

"She said you knew."

"Uh-huh." Why did Puddin' go and tell him that? I sure hope he doesn't get upset that I didn't tell him.

Digger laughs. "I've known for a while, too, and I've just been waiting for her to come out and tell me. What blows my mind is the fact that you managed to keep it such a secret. You didn't give me any clue whatsoever."

"I wouldn't have kept it a secret if it weren't so important to Puddin'. I hope you're not upset with her."

"I'm not. The only thing that upsets me is that she would think I wouldn't want her to be happy."

"It's not that she doesn't think you want her to be happy. It's just that you have been so emphatic about not wanting your wife to work. You took such pride in her staying home with the kids."

"Did I?" He pauses. "What I meant to say was that I didn't want her to *have* to work. There's a difference."

This conversation has stalled with semantics. "So what do you think about her job?"

"Honestly, I don't have many thoughts about it. She still manages to do everything she ever did, and Jeremy seems happy. And now that the cat's outta the bag, she seems happy and relieved. I can't complain."

I suppose that's as much as I can expect from my brother, but I wish he sounded more supportive. It would have been nice to hear him say that he was over the moon about his wife taking the reins and doing something she wants to do while still being a super mom and wife. I'm not sure how she manages, and I suspect she has many of the normal frustrations of career moms, even though it's a part-time job. But Puddin' will never complain.

"Maybe she can offer to work in the front, now that you know about her job."

"What do you mean?"

"Amanda kept her hidden in the back office so people wouldn't see her."

"Because of me?" I can hear the hurt in my brother's voice.

"Yes, because of you. Someone in town was bound to let it slip that they saw your wife working at La Chic."

Digger lets out a sigh of what sounds like frustration. "I had no idea she was that worried about letting me know. I'd never want to make her afraid of me."

"I don't think she's afraid of you. It's just that . . ." How can I talk about his ego without bruising it?

"It makes me wonder what else she's keeping from me."

"I'm not one hundred percent positive, but I don't think she's keeping anything else from you."

"I hope not. All I've ever wanted to do was be a good husband, father, and provider."

My brother is so sweet but clueless. "Why don't you just ask her and let her know that you'll support her in whatever she wants?"

"But what if she wants—" He cuts himself off. "Okay, I'll do that."

"If it makes you feel any better, all she wants to be is a good wife, mother, and caretaker." As I say that, I realize that my brother and Puddin' are perfectly suited for each other, and as much as I appreciate their relationship, but wouldn't want it for myself, I'm still a tad jealous. It sounds contradictory, but who can account for feelings?

30
Puddin'

I wish I hadn't told Digger that Shay has known about my job for a while. When he said he planned to call her and ask why she didn't tell him, I realized that I was betraying the person who had to risk her brother's trust to protect me.

My mama used to tell me that lying is never good because not only do you have to remember who you told what to, you wind up with the lies pilin' up on each other and eventually falling like dominoes. I'm pretty sure that's what's happening now.

Sometimes the guilt I feel overwhelms me and practically renders me useless. After seeing Shay in church yesterday, I'm worried she might never speak to me again. Normally, she makes her way over to me for a quick chat before she goes to the Bible study, but not yesterday. When I glanced up to look for her, she'd disappeared.

If it weren't for having to take care of Jeremy's needs, I might have called in sick today. I look at my child's face that's smeared with grape jelly. He should be able to find his mouth at his age, but he gets more food on it than in it.

Now the guilt kicks me even harder. Have I somehow neglected our youngest child just to fulfill something inside me that should have waited another couple of years?

"Mo'." He thrusts his sippy cup toward me.

I smile down at his sweet little face as I take the sticky cup from his pudgy little hands. "Sure, sweetheart."

I pour half apple juice and half water into his cup before snapping the lid back on and handing it to him. He grins up at me. "Kankoo."

At least he knows he's supposed to say "thank you" when I do something for him. "You're welcome, sweetheart."

He chugs some of his juice before putting the cup on the table. "Skoo?"

"Yes, you have school today, but we have to get you cleaned up first. Are you finished?"

With a nod, he extends his hands toward me. My heart melts as I pick him up and carry him to the bathroom to wash his face and brush his teeth. Out of all of our children, Jeremy has been the easiest baby and toddler. I'm sure I was a nervous mom with Trey. Hallie and Brett couldn't have been more different, and they fought constantly. I think I spent more time breaking up their fights than lovin' on them like I do Jeremy.

Maybe I'm not such a bad mom to Jeremy, after all. He seems well adjusted, and he enjoys his friends at our church preschool, where he's learning praise songs and short Scripture verses. He doesn't speak well, but he can make noise and sort of carry a tune. As much as I tried to teach the older kids when they were younger, they squirmed until I let them go play with their toys. Jeremy might be developing some of his skills later than the others, but he's getting a more solid Christian foundation. I'm pretty sure that's the most important thing we can do as parents.

Now that I think about it, maybe I neglected the other kids more, even though I stayed home with them full-time. I doubt Trey ever attends church now that he has a choice, and the other two ... well, they find every excuse in the book to stay home on Sunday mornings.

After I finish getting Jeremy ready, he throws his arms around me and gives me a huge, sloppy, wet kiss on my cheek. Then he pulls back and cups my cheeks in his sweet little hands. The smile on his face warms me from the inside out, and I'm tempted to call in sick so I can stay home and cuddle with him.

"Skoo?"

I fight back the love tears as I nod. "Yes, sweetheart, let's go to school."

He squirms to get down, so I lower him to the floor. Then he takes my hand and leads me to the door.

I walk him into the education wing of the church, where the teacher and her assistant greet him. As soon as he sees one of his friends, he runs into the classroom squealing with delight, and both of them fall into the middle of a pile of foam blocks, scattering them everywhere. Their giggles grow louder.

His teacher smiles at me. "Jeremy is such a happy child. Everyone around him adores him."

I lift my chin but force myself not to let on how proud I am. "Thank you."

"No," she says as she glances over her shoulder, then back at me. "Thank *you* for doing such a wonderful job with him."

How does she know I need the validation? It must be written on my face, but that's fine. Now I can go to my job feeling like I own the world. I love my work, my husband accepts it, and my child is well adjusted, even though he's a little behind on his speech. That'll come later, so I'm going to try hard not to worry about it. Not today. This is a day for celebration.

Amanda glances up as I walk in, then she does a double take. "You're floating a couple inches off the floor. What's got you in such a good mood?"

I head back to the office where I drop my purse, then I go back up to the front. "I just feel good today. Not having to keep this a secret sure does make it more fun to come here."

"I hope you continue feeling that way." Amanda closes the cash drawer and leans against the counter. "Now that Digger knows you work here, can you help out a little more with the customers?"

I blink. Today keeps getting better. "I think I can manage that."

"I am so relieved. I didn't want to hire anyone else, and it's getting to the point where we need more help." She tilts her head but breaks eye contact. "I have some personal things I have to do today."

Then I remember that I can only work when Jeremy is in preschool. "Don't forget that I have to pick up my little boy by two."

"No problem." She smiles. "Do you think you can do the books in between customers? I'll pay you a little extra."

"I don't see why not." Most weekday mornings aren't terribly busy, even though there are some regulars who prefer to come in when it's not crowded.

"I should be back by lunch."

It takes every ounce of self-restraint not to push her out the door. "Then go. I'll be fine."

Amanda reaches beneath the counter and gets her handbag. "Are you sure?"

"Positive. Now get on out of here before I throw you out."

She laughs on her way out.

And that's when my wonderful day ends. Amanda has barely been gone ten minutes when I get a call from Jeremy's preschool.

"He's been hurt, Mrs. Henke. We had to call an ambulance."

My heart nearly stops. "Where is he now?"

"On the way to Pinewood General."

31

Shay

"Slow down, Puddin'. I can't understand a thing you're saying." Between her hiccupping sobs and disjointed sentences, the only words I can make out over the phone are "my baby" and "hospital."

She clears her throat and sniffles. "Can you come to the shop and keep an eye on things until Amanda gets back?"

"I'm sorry, Puddin', but I'm at the office—"

"He's hurt, and I can't just leave here."

"Who is hurt?"

"Jeremy." A loud sob nearly deafens me, so I hold the phone away from my ear. "They just called me from the preschool."

Now I'm really confused. "Where is Amanda?"

"She left me in charge of the shop. I've tried calling her, but she's not picking up."

"I'm sure she'll understand if you have to leave."

"Please, Shay, this is the first time she's ever trusted me with the shop, and I don't want to mess up." She stops to blow her nose.

I glance at my desk with papers scattered all over it. Most of my work this morning involves reading agreements and signing them, with an occasional phone call for clarification—nothing urgent. "Okay, Puddin'. I'll get there as fast as I can."

"You are an angel." She sniffles again. "Hurry up."

After stuffing the papers into my work tote, I go up to the reception counter. "There's been a family emergency, so I have to leave for a little while. If anyone needs me, I'll have my cell phone on."

A concerned expression washes over the receptionist's face as she nods. "Let me know if there's anything I can do."

Puddin' is standing at the front window when I pull up in front of the shop. By the time I get out of my car, she's out the door, waving. "I'll call you as soon as I know what's going on."

Without another word, she disappears around the corner, leaving me to figure out what I'm supposed to do. I've never worked in a clothing shop, but how hard can it be? Fortunately, I have a little bit of cashiering experience from a job I had during college. But unfortunately, cash registers have changed, and I have no idea how to operate the one in the shop.

I don't have time to pray that no one needs a new dress. A carload of women from the Junior League pulls up behind my car, and they pile out. I hold my breath, hoping they walk right past the shop, but I should know better.

One of them narrows her eyes. "Shay Henke, what on earth are you doing here? I thought you—" She stops herself, raises her eyebrows, and lifts her hand to her mouth. "I'm sorry. It's none of my business."

I force a smile at the women who never gave me the time of day when we were younger. "Don't worry about it. My brother's wife works here, and she had an emergency, so she called me to come help out since she couldn't find Amanda." I quickly clamp my mouth shut as I realize I'm rambling.

"I hope it's nothing serious." I can't remember her name, but I do know we had tenth-grade biology together. She and I have always traveled in different circles.

"Me, too." I glance around. "What can I help you ladies with?"

They all look at each other before turning to me with skeptical looks on their faces. "We all need dresses for our Junior League Fall Ball."

One of the women laughs. "Well, Rita needs a dress today. The rest of us are going to crash diet for a week before we start looking in a couple of weeks."

Rita! That's her name. I offer up a silent thank-you and gesture toward our ball gowns. "I'm not sure what all Amanda has, so please feel free to look around."

Rita casts a frown toward me before turning to her friends. "I don't even know where to begin. Amanda has always started a room for me and brought the dresses to me."

I open my mouth to apologize, but one of her friends takes charge. "Why don't you find one you like, and while you're trying it on, the rest of us can bring you things we think you'll like?" She turns to me and gives me a discreet wink before tilting her head toward Rita.

"Okay." Rita walks up to the rack and stares at it like she's never gone clothes shopping before. I vaguely remember that she was voted "Best Dressed" back in high school, so I wonder if she's always had things brought to her.

She finally selects a blue sequined gown that even I, with my untrained, unfashionable eye, know will overpower her. But I don't say a word as she lifts it off the rack and carries it into the fitting room.

While two of her friends start perusing the ball-gown section, the friend who spoke up walks up to me and whispers, "We tried to talk her into waiting since the Ball isn't until fall, but she's afraid everything will be picked over. She's spoiled rotten, but we love her anyway."

I stifle a laugh. I'm relieved I'm not the only one who's been thinking that thought as I go back behind the counter and pull out one of the vendor agreements that I need to read.

"I think this is the one." The sound of Rita's voice catches my attention.

When I glance up, I'm shocked by the gaudiness of the gold-glitter dress she's looking at in the mirror. "Are you sure?"

She spins around to face me, a humongous grin plastered on her face. "I think I look like a princess."

Her friends stand behind her, all trying hard to stifle their laughter. At this moment, I realize they're getting their kicks at her expense.

"Did you choose this dress?" I ask as I walk out from behind the desk to get a closer look.

She shakes her head and points to her friends. "No, they brought it to me."

"You know ..." I fold my arms, lift my hand to my face, and tap my chin. "I think you'll look good in anything you try on, and I think there might be something even better for you."

"You do?"

The expectant look on her face touches my heart—something that surprises me. I nod. "Yes, in fact"—I walk over to the rack and quickly skim the selection in her size before pulling out a lighter blue one that matches her eyes—"this one is really lovely."

She turns to her friends. "Do y'all think that's too plain for the ball?"

Before they have a chance to respond, I speak up. "It might look plain on the rack, Rita, but once you put it on, it'll come alive. You don't need all that glitter to look fabulous." I have no idea how to speak the language of fashion, but I do remember some things from my college Marketing 101 class. "It'll bring out the color of your eyes, and with the right accessories, you'll be the prettiest princess there."

I cast a narrow-eyed look at her friends and silently dare them to disagree. They actually look a little intimidated as they just stand there and awkwardly wait for Rita to make her decision.

After a tense few seconds, she nods and reaches for the dress. "I doubt anything will come even close to the one I'm wearing, but I don't have anything to lose by trying it on."

She disappears into the dressing room. Her friends have clearly gotten the message, so they avoid eye contact with me once she's out of sight. Good. I go back behind the counter, read the last paragraph that I'd started, and sign my name to the agreement. I laugh at myself because it's the boldest signature I've done in a long time.

Yes, there's definitely something empowering about putting haughty folks in their place. I reach into the jewelry counter and pull out a necklace that I think will look perfect with the dress. I go back to the fitting room and hand it to her. She gives me an apprehensive look but takes it.

When Rita walks out of the fitting room, it's almost as though someone turned the lights on brighter. She looks prettier than I've ever seen her, and that's saying a lot since she's always been one of those girls people couldn't stop staring at.

I give her friends a don't-mess-with-me look before I give Rita my full attention. Her mouth hangs open as she looks at herself in the mirror.

"Shay, this is the most beautiful dress in the entire world. If I didn't care about messing up my makeup, I'd give you the biggest hug ever."

I smile and try to contain my joy. "It looks lovely on you." Now I know what it feels like to work in a dress shop, and I like it. In fact, I like it so much I'm downright giddy.

Rita turns to her friends who are now clustered together like little minions eager to serve their queen. "What do y'all think?"

"Maybe you should—" The friend who seems to be the ringleader glances at me, stops herself mid-sentence, and smiles at Rita. "I think it looks beautiful. You should get it." The other two women give enthusiastic nods.

"Then it's settled. Now all I have to worry about is the shoes." She turns to me. "What color shoes should I wear?"

I look down at the hem of the dress and slowly shake my head. "Something simple that won't compete with the dress."

"I have some glass slippers."

Of course she does. I smile and give her a thumbs-up. "Perfect."

"I'll go take it off now so you can wrap it up for me." She turns and floats back to the fitting room.

Panic sets in. Not only do I not know how to run this cash register, I'm not even sure what she means by wrapping it up. The cashiers where I shop drop my things into a bag that might or might not have tissue paper, but that's the mall for you.

I'm about to ask if she can come back for the dress later, after Amanda gets back, when I see a blur of motion on the other side of the large display window. Puddin' comes walking in, sending a flood of relief through me.

"How's Jeremy?" I ask, trying not to show anything but concern.

Puddin' rolls her eyes. "He fell on the playground and skinned his elbow real good." She flips her hand from the wrist. "There was absolutely no reason for them to take him to the hospital. He was bloody and all, but it was just a skin abrasion."

"I'm sure they wanted to make sure nothing was broken," I say.

She shrugs. "More like wanting to cover their..." She looks around and apparently notices the customers for the first time. All four of the Junior League ladies are standing there, listening to everything. She narrows her eyes and gives me a questioning look. "How is everything here?"

"Just fine." I gesture toward Rita, who hasn't yet taken off the dress. "Doesn't that dress look lovely on her?"

"Oh my." Puddin' walks over to Rita, gently places her hand on her shoulder, and turns her around. She stands back to take a better look. "You look absolutely stunning."

Rita grins. "Shay picked it out."

Puddin' gives me a look of incredulity. "You did?"

"Yep. Looks like I'm a natural with fashion."

Now she looks me up and down and lets out a deep chuckle. "Maybe with other people's fashion."

I realize she thinks I'm strong enough to take comments like that, but deep down, I wither. Of course I know I'm not a fashion plate, but I've always thought of myself as somewhat stylish.

"Thanks for dropping everything and coming," Puddin' says. "I can take it from here."

"You're welcome." I pick up my work tote and head for the door, slowing down momentarily as I pass the bank of mirrors.

Puddin's right. I need to start thinking about my own fashion—or lack of it.

32
Missy

"I don't need to get my hearing tested." Foster looks me in the eyes with an expression of utter defiance.

I have to stand my ground. "Maybe not, and if that's the case, you can say, 'I told you so.'"

Foster's forehead creases. "I don't want to wear one of those ugly hearing aids."

"Some of them aren't ugly."

He gives me one of those you've-got-to-be-kidding looks. "They are all ugly."

"Some of them you can't even see." I pause for a moment. "Did you know that my brother wears a hearing aid?"

"You've said that, but he never wears it when we're around him."

I fold my arms and grin. "George always wears it when he's awake. It's one of those that fits inside the ear, and you can't see it unless you're looking for it, and even then it's hard to see."

"But what if I need the other kind?"

I close my eyes and count to ten before focusing my attention on my very stubborn, very proud husband. "We'll deal with that if it happens. The most important thing is to find out if you have a hearing problem, and if so, how bad it is." I place my hand on his. "Foster, I know this is difficult for you, but your lack of hearing is causing a lot of problems." I swallow hard and try to give him a loving look, even though I'm extremely frustrated. "I don't think you hear well at all, and the only way we'll know is to get it tested."

I'm pretty sure his hearing is about as bad as it gets, just this side of being deaf. Right now I have to face him and shout for him to hear me. When I turn away, he doesn't respond. I can't believe I'm just now figuring it out. All these years, I've thought he was ignoring me because he didn't think anything I said was important. It started so long ago that it'll take a long time for my resentment to subside.

He purses his lips and slowly shakes his head. My heart tightens as I see that he's on the brink of tears. "Will you still love me, even if I have hearing aids?"

Now my heart melts. "Of course I will."

Finally, he lifts his hands and lets them fall to his sides, making a slapping sound. "Okay, I'll get checked if you'll make the appointment for me."

Some women I know might think it's ridiculous to be asked to make their husbands' doctor appointments, but I don't. Foster never went to the doctor until we got married, and the only reason he goes now is to make me happy—or, more likely, to keep me from nagging. And I've made every single doctor and dentist appointment he's ever had.

"What's for supper?" He opens the oven door and looks inside. "There's nothing in there."

"That's because I'm making salads tonight."

"Salad?" A look of disappointment covers his face. "What kind of supper is that?"

"A healthy one."

"Can't you fry some chicken or something to go with it?"

I fold my arms and lift my chin before looking him in the eyes. He's a good foot taller than me, but I have to take a strong stance on this issue. His blood work came back showing that his cholesterol is slightly elevated.

"What?" He leans against the kitchen counter and tries to stare me down, but he quickly realizes he's no match for me when I'm this determined.

"Frying chicken *or something* would defeat the purpose of having salad."

"But—"

"Don't worry, Foster. I'm putting meat in the salad. And eggs."

"I thought eggs were bad for you."

"Nope." I brush my hands together. "That's old medical news. Eggs are actually good for you."

"Says who?"

I think for a minute before shrugging. "Whoever decides those things."

He lets out a sardonic chuckle. "If they keep doing like this, we'll eventually find out that salads are bad for you and fried food is good." He rolls his eyes. "Or candy will keep you strong and make you live longer."

"Actually—" I stop myself before telling him that some fried food actually is good for you, if you fry it in the right kind of oil. And dark chocolate has something in it that is good for your heart. There's no point in confusing the issue right now, especially since I'm still trying to make a point that we need to improve our diets. When Wendy was younger, he told her that candy corn was a vegetable. I know he was teasing, but I worried she'd actually believe him.

"Is Wendy gonna be home for supper?" He opens the fridge and takes a long look at the contents before pulling out a block of cheese.

"No, she's working, and after she gets off, she's going out with some friends."

I walk over to him and take the cheese from him. But as I open the refrigerator, he grabs it out of my hand and gives me a look that lets me know he's not stopping until he wins this battle, so I back away.

"What did you say? Speak up."

I repeat myself, only louder.

"She needs to spend more time at home." Foster puts the cheese on the counter and goes over to the pantry, where he grabs a box of crackers. "Tell her she can't go out so much."

"You tell her. She's your daughter, too."

"But she listens to you. I'm her fun person." He fakes a grin before picking up the cheese slicer.

I feel the same way he does about Wendy, but how do you tell your daughter, who is an adult—although barely—and about to go off to college, that she can't do something that's harmless? We've never had a lick of trouble out of Wendy. She was a wonderful baby who napped twice a day from birth and slept through the night when she was a couple months old. She was cute and funny as a toddler and only rarely threw a temper tantrum, unlike my brother's twins, who ganged up on him and his wife when they didn't get what they wanted. I used to watch in horror as Sally and Sara got the best of him and his wife.

Wendy has always been a straight-A student, and she just graduated from high school with honors. I look at Foster, who has neatly stacked a little square of cheese on each cracker. He gives me another closed-mouth grin before shoving a whole cracker into his mouth, one of his ways of letting me know he doesn't have anything else to say.

"I'll talk to her, but I don't know that she'll want to hang out here with her boring mama and daddy."

He sits down at the kitchen table, swallows his cheese and cracker, and shakes his head. "She's never complained about us being boring."

"She's never complained about anything," I remind him as I walk over to the table and sit down across from him. "When you were eighteen, did you enjoy staying home with your family?"

"I moved out when I was eighteen." He lifts another cracker, repositions the cheese, and inspects it. "But she's a girl. It's different for her."

I laugh. "At least you admit to a double standard. I'll talk to her and let her know we'd like her to spend more time with us. Any idea what we might do with her?"

He shrugs. "Same thing we always do. Watch TV."

"Oh, I'm sure that'll make her want to stick around more. Come on, Foster, let's do something fun as a family."

"We're going to your family reunion, remember?"

"I said something *fun*."

He snorts. "I hear ya. Let me think about it."

The sound of a car pulling into the driveway quiets us. A few seconds later, Wendy comes storming into the house, nostrils flaring, eyes red-rimmed, and chin quivering.

"What happened?" I jump to my feet and put my arm around her.

She yanks loose and runs out of the kitchen. I turn to Foster and see he's just as confused as I am.

After a few seconds, Foster gestures toward the door leading to the rest of the house. "Go check on her."

All sorts of things run through my mind as I head to Wendy's room. I knock. She doesn't answer, but I hear a muffled sob.

I knock again and try to open her door, but it's locked. "Wendy, honey, can we talk?"

"No."

"Please? I really want to help with whatever is upsetting you." Could I sound any lamer?

"There's nothing you can do about it." Her harsh tone shocks me. She's never spoken to me like this before.

"Wendy, open this door right now."

I half expect her to tell me to buzz off, but instead, I hear her footsteps padding toward me. She opens the door a couple of inches, runs toward her bed, and flings herself across it face down.

A lump forms in my throat at the very thought of something upsetting my near-perfect child this much. I walk over to the edge of her bed, sit down, and start rubbing her back. Her muscles tighten.

"Stop."

I pull my hand back. "Just tell me what's going on, Wendy. I might be able to help you."

Her sobs stop, and she slowly turns her face toward me. "There's nothing you can do about it."

"How do you know?"

"Because I'm such a loser no one can help me."

This is the first time I've ever heard such negative words come out of my daughter's mouth. "Please, tell me what happened."

"Jake thinks I'm a dork, and my friends all hate me."

"Oh, honey, I'm sure your friends don't hate you. If there's been a misunderstanding ... My voice trails off as I realize she mentioned a name I haven't heard before. "Who's Jake?"

She slowly sits up, picks up the corner of her sheet, and wipes her eyes before finally looking directly at me. "Jake is the guy I've been in love with for the past year. Melanie posted a picture of him and Tabitha on Facebook."

"Maybe they're just friends." I have no idea what I'm doing, since this is totally unfamiliar territory for me.

"They were making out."

"Well, maybe …" My heart feels like it's about to rip in two. For the first time ever, I have no answer for my brokenhearted daughter.

33

Shay

I pick up my phone during lunch on Friday, search for Elliot's number, and start to press it. But then the old doubts resurface. Our coffee chats have been fun, but in spite of the butterflies I feel every time I'm with him, he's been treating me like a friend rather than someone he's interested in dating.

The old self-doubts creep back into my head. I think back to all the times when I wanted nothing more than to be with him, but I let my own feelings of inadequacy in the social department hold me back. Then I remember what he said about his feelings toward me. Is it possible that everyone is filled with insecurities in high school?

Nah. Not everyone. Just people like me. Elliot said that because he was trying to be nice. Or maybe not.

Okay, this is ridiculous. I have never been indecisive in my whole entire life, and I don't plan to start now. I'm calling, and if he takes issue with that, it's not my problem.

Oh man, I wish I could believe that. But regardless, I'm going to ask if he wants to go to my family reunion, and the ball will be in his court. He can say yes, and everything will be just fine. Or he can say no, and then I'll wait for him to make the next move.

Before I have another chance to chicken out, I press the number, knowing that if I end the call, he'll know I tried to get in touch with him because my name will show up on caller ID. I hold my breath as his phone rings once … twice …

"Hey Shay, I was hoping you'd call. Do you think enough time has passed for us to get together again, only this time as more than friends? I've been doing a lot of thinking."

I slowly let out the breath I've been holding. "I think so."

"Would you like to go out tonight?"

Be still my heart. "I would love to." Then I remember why I called. "Speaking of going out, I was wondering . . ." I cough. Maybe a family reunion isn't the best place to take him.

"What were you wondering?"

Okay, it's now or never. "Would you like to come to a little family gathering with me in a couple of weeks?"

"If you're talking about one of the famous Bucklin reunions I've been hearing about practically all my life, yes, I absolutely would love to go."

I let out a nervous but relieved laugh. "I don't know about famous."

"Oh, trust me, they are, at least in South Mississippi. I've been hearing stories about those events ever since I can remember." He chuckles. "Is it true that your cousin Pete tried to ride one of the buffaloes at your grandparents' farm?"

"Well, yeah, but it didn't last long."

"I know. I heard. How about your cousin going into labor and her baby being delivered by a couple of your aunts?"

"That was actually my brother Digger's wife, Puddin', who went into labor. We thought she'd give birth to Jeremy right there, but they managed to get her to the hospital on time before he made his entrance."

"Or exit." Elliot laughs. "I do know one thing for certain. I don't want to go anywhere near Digger's two older boys when they have bows and arrows."

"I don't think Julius does either. It took the doctors in the emergency room almost an hour to get that arrow out of his rear end."

"As I said when you first asked, yeah, I would love to go. It sounds like a blast."

"Good." I chew on my bottom lip, hoping he'll bring up tonight again.

"How about something casual tonight then?"

Whew. I'm relieved he mentioned it because I know I wouldn't have. "Casual is fine."

"I'll pick you up around seven, if that's okay."

I normally eat earlier, but I'll grab a snack so I'm not so hungry I eat like a pig when I'm with Elliot. "I'll be ready."

The afternoon gets crazy with all kinds of problems, from late deliveries to a life-and-death need for a dozen cases of Spam in one of the country grocery stores to be delivered before the end of the day. Top that off with the regular end-of-the-week reports, and I'm busy right up to quitting time.

I can't remember a time when I've been so happy to greet the weekend. Not only has this been one of the craziest workweeks I've had since I started at Southern Foods, I have a date with my lifelong crush. Talk about a roller-coaster ride.

Once I arrive home, I grab some cheese from the fridge and crackers from the pantry and munch on them while standing in front of my closet trying to decide which top to wear with my favorite pair of jeans— the ones with the bling on the back pockets and waistband that doesn't give me muffin top. I'm not heavy, but some of my jeans cut me off at the worst part of my waistline, making me self-conscious.

I opt for the peasant top that has a wide neckline and shows off my collarbone rather than my cleavage. Even though I want to hold Elliot's attention, I want it the right way, and that doesn't involve having him stare at my chest all evening.

My hair isn't terrible, but it's been a while since I had it trimmed. Puddin's words about my tight hairdo play in my mind, so I put it up in a loose French twist and pull a few tendrils down to soften the effect even more.

I'm glad the twins spent a little time with me, teaching me the tips and tricks of contouring, bronzing, and highlighting my cheeks. Until they got hold of me, I never gave my high cheekbones a second thought. Now I know how to play them up with makeup.

In the back of my mind, I hear Sally's directive to focus on the eyes or lips but not both. I take a step away from the mirror to get a better overall look and decide to add more eye shadow, liner, and mascara, which means I'll need to go with a nude lip.

I pull out my cross-body handbag and transfer a few essentials from my everyday purse. A quick glance at the clock lets me know I only have a few minutes before Elliot is due to arrive, so I slip into some wedges that add a couple inches of height without being too obvious. I'm average height, but being taller always seems more elegant.

Once I'm satisfied with my overall look, I go into the living room to wait. And wait. When he's ten minutes late, I get up off the sofa and start pacing. Another ten minutes later, I go to the kitchen to get a drink of water. The knock finally comes at the door at seven thirty. Maybe I misunderstood the time.

I put my hand on the doorknob, close my eyes, take a deep breath, and open the door. His eyes widen as he looks me over.

"Come on in." I take a step back.

He walks inside, never taking his gaze off me. "You look amazing, Shay."

I nearly choke. No one has ever said anything like that about my looks before except Mama, who has always said I'm pretty to her.

"Um ... thank you." Heat flames in my cheeks. I have to look away to keep from being so flustered I can't talk. "Would you like a drink?"

"I don't drink."

"Sweet tea." I manage a smile. "That's the strongest drink I have."

"In that case, I think I'll start drinking. Sweet tea sounds good."

As I pour his tea, my stomach growls, reminding me that it's way past my dinnertime. I should have had another cracker. I turn around to hand him the glass, and he grins.

"You're really hungry, aren't you?"

I nod. "Starving."

"Me, too." He downs the tea in just a few seconds flat before putting the empty glass in the sink. "Let's go."

On the way to his car, I think about the fact that this is my second real date with the man of my dreams, and I wonder if I can get away with saying that we're dating. It's probably a stretch at this point, so I decide to wait until we go out a third time.

Elliot gives me a choice of several places, and I pick Catfish Jack's because it normally has the fastest service. He nods. "That's what I was hoping you'd say."

When we pull into the parking lot, I remember that Friday night is all-you-can-eat catfish and hush puppies. The parking lot is practically full, and there's a line of people waiting to be seated.

He turns to me. "Would you rather go somewhere else?"

"We could, but they're usually pretty good at handling crowds here."

He grins. "Smart girl."

At that moment, one of the cars parked close to where we're waiting starts to back out. "Your timing is good."

He pulls into the spot, turns to me, and squeezes my hand. "*Our* timing is good."

If my heart beats any faster, it will bounce right out of my chest. I force myself to appear as normal as possible and smile back. I don't dare say anything because, if I do, I'm sure my voice will squeak.

As we walk toward the entrance to Catfish Jack's, Elliot takes my hand as though it's the most natural thing in the world. I see a few familiar faces turning to look at us. I lift my head a couple inches.

We're barely inside the restaurant when Gavin, one of the guys Elliot used to hang out with in high school, approaches and slaps Elliot on the back. "Hey, bro. Heard you were back in town." He looks me over and grins. "Who's your date?"

I give him a curious look, and Elliot laughs. "Don't tell me you don't remember Shay Henke."

Gavin's eyebrows shoot up. "Shay Henke? Whoa. What have you done with the nerdy girl?"

34

Sally

Getting up before the crack of dawn is something I haven't had to do in years. I trudge out to the driveway before sunrise, shove the car key in the ignition, and turn it. Nothing happens.

Oh man, this couldn't have happened at a worse time. I have to be at the apparel show in Jackson in two hours, and it'll take me at least that long to drive there and find a parking spot.

After a couple more tries, I get out, slam the car door shut, and storm back inside the condo. Justin blinks. "What's got you all worked up?"

"Car won't start." I head to the kitchen, grab a glass, and fill it with water. After I drink it, I go back out to the living room and see that Justin is gone.

I dig my cell phone out of my purse and start to look up the automobile club when the door opens, and Justin comes inside brushing his hands together. There's a smudge of oil on his arm.

He grins. "All fixed."

"All fixed?" I lift an eyebrow.

He nods. "Yeah, it was just a loose wire. Your car should be fine now."

"Are you sure I don't need a new battery?"

"Positive."

Feeling doubtful, I head out to my car and turn the key. It starts right up. I glance toward the door and see Justin standing there, watching. I smile and wave. He lifts his hand, wiggles his fingers, and disappears inside.

Maybe having Justin for a brother-in-law isn't so bad after all. This isn't the first time he's done something nice. A few days ago, I came home from working out to a full chicken dinner that Justin had prepared. And before that, he changed my tire before I even realized it had a nail in it. When I thanked him, he just shrugged and said, "It was startin' to look a little squishy on the bottom."

Those are the good things, but I'm still struggling with the ways he annoys me. For instance, I have to put on a bathrobe before leaving my bedroom every morning, and I can't sit in front of the TV in the living room to paint my toenails because Sara said that kind of thing grosses him out.

On my way to Jackson, I try to focus on the positives of having Justin living with us, but the negatives keep popping into my head. Sara seems fine with everything as it is, and during the times I've tried to talk to her about it, she gets surly. Sometimes I feel like the crazy person in the house, and maybe I am. But I sure do miss how things used to be.

I glance at the empty seat next to me. Sara used to go with me to these things, but now she's more focused on being a wife than a business partner. When I asked her if she could go with me today, she just shook her head, looked away from me, and said she had plans. I can tell that something is up, but I haven't had the time to figure out what it is.

After a half hour of thoughts that make my frustration even worse, I turn on the radio and listen to the news on Sirius. I'm not sure why, but these days, I'm more interested in talk radio than music. It could be that, since Justin has been in the house, he has his music playing nonstop. When I asked Sara why he doesn't use earbuds, she said they irritate his ears. She obviously doesn't care that the noise coming out of his phone irritates my nerves.

When I get to the apparel show, various people greet me by name—some of them calling me Sara, others getting it right. A couple even ask where my sister is.

I make the rounds and chat with various people who have placed orders with us for their stores or wholesale companies. When I first came up with the idea to have a wholesale business, Sara didn't think people would be willing to pay the same price that we get on Etsy. After the first show, she was sold. I'm a little bit sad about being here alone, but I'm finding that it's actually a little easier to get around.

"Hey, Sally."

I turn around and find myself face to face with one of the men Sara and I met at the show in Mobile. "Hi, Tom."

He leans over and looks behind me before straightening up. "Are you here alone?"

I nod. "Sara has something else to do today."

"Good." He makes an apologetic face. "Sorry, but I've been wanting to ask you out since we first met, but I didn't want to leave anyone out."

That's when it dawns on me that he actually called me by the correct name. "How do you know I'm Sally?"

He grins and shrugs. "I don't know. Maybe it's the way you walk or the way you make eye contact when we're talking. I can just tell."

Now he has my attention. Very few people actually pay that close of attention to see the differences between my sister and me.

"So how about it? What are you doing for lunch?"

"Depends." I fold my arms and rock back on my heels. "What do you have in mind?"

"There's a nice little café down the street, if you don't mind walking."

"As a matter of fact, I prefer walking."

He smiles. "It's a date. I need to get back to my company's booth. Where would you like to meet?"

"I'll stop by your booth. What time can you get away?"

He glances at his watch. "How's eleven thirty?"

"See you then."

I walk away feeling as though I'm floating a few inches above the concrete floor. Tom Flaherty is one of the best-looking, nicest men in the children's fashion industry. In fact, last time Sara and I saw him, I told her that. She just shook her head and said she thought he was sweet but not all that good looking. Seeing the differences between Tom and Justin, it's obvious that she and I go for different types.

Now I'm happy that I'm here alone. I go from booth to booth and take orders without having to discuss anything with my sister. I know what we're capable of producing, but she has always wanted to be in on the decision making, so we've stepped aside to discuss each and every order.

It's finally time for lunch, so I round the corner and head toward Tom's booth. His back faces me, so he doesn't realize I'm there.

"Remember that woman I told you I thought was beautiful and smart, but she's always with her sister?" I hear him say. "She's finally here alone, so I'm taking her to lunch."

A combination of joy and embarrassment washes over me as I stop and make eye contact with the woman he's talking to. I make a gesture for her not to say anything, and she glances away. After a brief moment of hesitation, I move forward.

"Here she comes," the woman says. "Enjoy your lunch."

As we make our way down the aisles, he tells me about his company and the fact that his mother and sisters managed to talk him into quitting his industrial sales job to work with them. "I never saw myself selling children's fashion."

"Do you regret it?" I ask.

"Never. In fact, if someone from my former industry offered double my salary, I'd have to turn them down. There's something special about working with family and knowing that your coworkers have integrity. I was never sure before."

"I totally understand. I used to be in banking, and wild horses couldn't drag me back to that."

He motions toward a small café and opens the door for me. "It's a hole in the wall, but the food is delicious."

After we order, the server brings our drinks and a basket of dinner rolls. Tom folds his hands in his lap, lowers his head, and appears to say a blessing, so I do the same. When I open my eyes, he grins.

"I think my dream has just come true," he says.

"What dream?"

He sighs and shakes his head. "I probably shouldn't say this, at least not yet . . ."

"Say what?"

"I don't want to scare you away."

I lift an eyebrow. "Should I be scared?"

"I hope not." He gives me a serious look. "I've been chatting with you for the past year or so, and every single time, I want to get to know you better. But there's one thing that's of the utmost importance to me." He takes a deep breath and blows it out. "My faith is the number one priority in my life, even before family."

My heart hammers hard in my chest. "Faith is important to me, too."

"You are talking about Christian faith, right?"

I tilt my head to the side. "What other kind of faith is there?"

35

Shay

I can't be more excited about the fact that Elliot has agreed to go to the reunion with me, but I know some of my uncouth family members will probably bring up the fact that he's divorced and probably make a big deal of it. It'll be embarrassing as all get-out, but a lot of my kinfolk are very outspoken.

"What's wrong, Shay?" he asks over lunch on Sunday after church. "You've been mighty quiet all day."

I shove the lettuce around on my plate. "Nothing's really wrong. It's just that..." How do I tell him that he'll most likely be grilled by at least one person, while an audience of aunts, uncles, and cousins watches? Why did I think it would be a good idea to ask him to my family reunion?

The lines of concern on his face deepen. "Did I say something to upset you?"

Without hesitation, I meet his gaze and shake my head. "No, Elliot. You've been a perfect gentleman." I close my eyes momentarily and ask God to give me the right words. "Ya know, when I asked you to go to the reunion with me, there was something I didn't consider."

"So you don't want me to go now?"

"I do want you to go, but... well, some of my family might be... sort of..."

"They don't like me?"

"Oh, I'm sure the ones who know you like you just fine."

He frowns. "Is this about the fact that I've been married before?"

I nod and make a face. "Yeah."

Elliot puts down his fork, buries his face in his hands for a few seconds, then looks me in the eyes. "Shay, I like you a whole lot, and I'm willing to walk across hot coals if you want me to."

"That is so sweet." Facing Mama and some of my aunts might feel like he's walking across hot coals.

"But I don't want to make you feel bad. If you've changed your mind, I certainly understand."

I shake my head vehemently. "No, I haven't changed my mind. I just want to make sure you know what you'll be getting yourself into."

"You're worth whatever I have to go through." He grins and gives me one of those looks that make my toes curl. "We're in this together."

He has some things to do this afternoon, so he takes me home. As soon as I walk into my condo and see the still-unpacked boxes stacked in the corner of the living room, I realize I've neglected my own place. I change into some shorts and a T-shirt and go back out to the living room to tackle the monster that I've been ignoring.

A couple hours later, my stomach starts to rumble, so I head to the kitchen. When a knock sounds at the door, I do an about-face and answer it. Sally stands there grinning at me.

"Come on in." I step to the side and let her in. "I was just about to cook supper. Want some?"

"Sure." She follows me to the kitchen and plops down at the table.

"Where's Sara?"

Sally shrugs. "Somewhere with Justin, but that's not why I'm here."

I pull out some ground beef and shove it into the microwave to thaw. "What's going on?"

"I think I'm in love."

"Really?" I can't help but smile. "Who's the fortunate guy? Do I know him?"

"No. He's someone I know from the fashion shows."

"What's his name?"

"Tom Flaherty." She grins back at me. "He works for his family's children's fashion business."

I think back over our conversations and try to recall his name but can't. "Have you ever mentioned him before?"

She shakes her head. "There was nothing to say until now."

"What makes you think you're in love?"

Her dreamy expression intensifies. "Everything about him is perfect, from the way he looks to his faith."

"His faith?" I pause as she nods. "Did y'all discuss Jesus?"

"After telling me how much he loves his family, he said that his faith is the only thing that is more important."

"That's a good start." I try to think of a way to let her know that love takes longer than a single conversation. "Just be careful, okay? Not that I've ever been in love, but ..." I give her one of those helpless looks.

"Oh, I know." A pragmatic look replaces her dreamy expression. "When I said I was in love, what I should have said was that he said all the right things to make me think there might be something there."

Ah, now that's the sensible Sally I know. It's one of the biggest things that make her different from her more impetuous twin. "It's nice to get off to a good start in a relationship. Do y'all have plans to get together again?"

Her eyes light up. "He's coming through Pinewood on his way to the coast next week, and I asked him to stop by for dinner."

Between the two sisters, Sally is the better cook, but she still needs some work in that area. "Would you like me to help you?"

She nods. "Can you? I mean, will you?"

"Yes, of course." After all, these girls let me stay with them, rent free, while I waited to close on my condo.

"You are the best cousin ever!" I brace myself for a hug, but she maintains her distance. "I was thinking it might be fun to make a casserole."

A casserole isn't the most romantic dish I can think of, but it's probably safe. "Why don't I come over and help you prepare one, and you can stick it in the oven an hour before you plan to eat. Add a salad, and you've got a meal."

Now she grabs me for a bear hug. "I'm pretty sure he's the man of my dreams. If he likes my casserole, I'll have to become a better cook. Can you teach me before he figures out that I have no idea what I'm doing?"

I laugh. "You're better than you think you are, but sure, I'll show you how to make a few basic meals and teach you some things that'll help in the future."

"The future." She says that with a sigh, so I know it's loaded with thoughts of this man. Her phone chirps, and she pulls it out of her back pocket, looks at the screen, and squeals. "It's him."

I chuckle. "Don't keep him waiting. Answer it."

36
Puddin'

For the first time in my adult life, I feel free and unrestrained. My marriage has always been pretty good, but with strong-willed young'uns and housework and holding down a job no one knows I have, I've felt tense as a fiddle string.

Jeremy is still recovering, but he's doing just fine. In fact, he's proud of the scab that remains on his elbow, and he shows it off to anyone who is willing to look. His preschool teachers have apologized for overreacting and thinking he might have broken his arm. I'm just relieved everything has turned out as well as it has.

I have the job of my dreams, and to top it off, Digger not only knows about it, he encourages me by saying he's proud of what I've managed to do. If I had to make a bet on his reaction a few months ago, I would have put money on him pitching a fit and making me quit.

One of the things I look forward to when he gets home from work now is telling him about my day at the shop. He laughs at some of the things the customers do, and at times he even offers suggestions on how to deal with some of the more difficult situations.

For the past couple of days, Amanda has had me working out on the sales floor as much as back in the office doing bookkeeping. Seems I have some decent fashion skills, too. Who knew? I'm certainly surprised.

I've never been known as a fashion plate, but I have an eye for what looks good on other people. In fact, one of the women who has been shopping at La Chic ever since it opened will now only work with me. I think that's why Amanda sticks me out on the floor as much as possible.

Most days now, I go in early and start out in the office, making sure all the bills have been paid and the deposits have gone into the account. After I finish the bookkeeping, I check the sales floor to see if I'm needed. More times than not, I am.

The store has only been open a few minutes on Tuesday when Amanda comes to my office door. "Would you mind keeping an eye on the sales floor? I need to make a couple of personal phone calls."

"Sure, I'd be happy to." I walk out on the floor and see that there aren't any customers, so I take advantage of the down time to do some organizing.

I sort through the clothes on the racks and pull out anything that's been on the floor since the last season to put it on the clearance rack. The volume of apparel we sell amazes me, and I still can't get over how much people are willing to pay for it. Even some of the clearance items are priced higher than my budget will allow.

The bell on the door jingles. "Hey Puddin'."

I spin around and see a regular customer who buys a new dress every single month. "Hi, Ms. Bailey."

"Got anything new?" She takes a quick look around before making a beeline for a round rack of dresses. "Looks like you do."

"I'm making room for even more stock we're getting in tomorrow." I put down the tops I'm holding and walk over to where she's already thumbing through the dresses. "Did you see that yellow one?"

She pulls out the dress and holds it up. "This one?" Before I have a chance to respond, she grins. "It's gorgeous. Here, be a dear and start me a room."

"I'll be happy to."

"If you see anything in a size large—"

I interrupt her. "You mean a size *lovely*?" I grin. "I prefer to call them sizes sweet, marvelous, lovely, and extra lovely."

She smiles back. "Why, yes, dahlin'. I like how you think."

An hour later, Ms. Bailey walks out with the yellow dress, a green one, and accessories to go with both of them. Amanda comes out of the back room and shakes her head.

"Ever since you started selling, my profit has gone up by about twenty percent."

I smile at her. "That's because I understand the value of accessorizing."

"Well, you're good at it, which is why I'm thinking about hiring another bookkeeper so you can always be out here."

My heart sinks. Even though I enjoy the change of pace that helping customers gives me, I still love making the numbers balance. "I really don't want you to do that."

She frowns. "But"—she shakes her head—"so you like bookkeeping?"

I smile and nod. "I don't just like it, I love it. In fact, it's like a game to me, making all the columns balance."

Amanda purses her lips and looks out over her store before turning her attention back to me. "I suppose I can let you do both, depending on where you're needed."

"That would suit me just fine." I sigh. "Sometimes I feel like this is my store, but I don't have to worry about paying the rent or staffing."

She laughs. "Actually, you *are* the one paying the rent, and since we only have one other person working here now, staffing isn't an issue."

"I'm just writing the check," I say.

Now that I think about it, Amanda is right. She owns the place, but with me here, all she has to do is show up and sign stuff that I don't have the authority to sign.

"What day did you say your family reunion is on?"

"This coming Saturday. Why?"

"Saturdays can be pretty busy. I'll try to get Helen to work that day."

"Haven't you already asked her?"

She shakes her head. "I've had a lot on my mind, and I forgot."

I can tell she's been preoccupied lately. "Is everything okay?" Most of the time, Amanda maintains a professional distance, in spite of the fact that we used to be friends, but every once in a while she forgets she's my boss, and she vents. I try my best to be a good listener.

"There've been rumors that Ted might be transferred, and he just heard from the higher-ups that it's happening by the end of the year."

"Can't he ask to stay here?"

"He did that last year, and his boss told him that if he wants to move up with the company, he'll eventually have to take a transfer." She grimaces. "And apparently, eventually is now."

This is a problem, since Amanda will want to move with her husband. "What are you going to do about this place?"

"I'm not sure. I'll probably have to sell the shop."

My heart sinks. Right when everything is just like I like it, this has to happen. "When will you know for sure?"

"Next week."

I stare at her in disbelief as she turns and walks back to the office, leaving me standing on the sales floor wondering about my own future. I've managed to save money from the job, but the job has saved me from worry and boredom. Now I have to decide what to do if she does sell. Maybe the new owner will want to keep me on, but there's no guarantee that'd work out.

Why can't things stay as they are? I don't like change, but it keeps happening. I should have known that my life was too good to be true.

37

Shay

I get ready for the reunion with a mixture of excitement and trepidation. I have my outfit picked out, the dishes I'm taking planned and shopped for, and my date with Elliot all set. He acts excited about going, but deep down in my insecure self, I'm not sure. In fact, I'm not sure about anything anymore.

Until recently, I've been content in my old condo, the job I've had forever, and being single and on my own. Now that has all changed in what seems like the blink of an eye, but in reality, I think my dissatisfaction has been brewing for a while.

I wish I could be more like Sara and Sally, who both take life as it comes—sometimes with a smile, other times fighting back. I plan first, and when something I don't expect happens, I just take it and wonder how on earth I might have missed something.

For the past week, Mama has called me several times a day. She wants to know if I'm sure it's a good idea to bring Elliot, how I'm doing with the dishes I'm bringing, and what I'm wearing.

And this morning, she wanted to know if I've thought about what to do for my grandparents. That's the only thing I don't have covered, but I know it's important to do something special. After all, as Mama says, they're not getting any younger.

I sit down with a pen and paper, jotting down ideas and crossing them out. Granny Marge and Grandpa Jay already have plenty of family portraits with the grandkids and great-grandkids lined up in awkward poses, wishing the person would hurry and snap the camera so we could let go of our fake, plastered smiles. They have more knickknacks than Granny Marge will be able to dust in her remaining lifetime if she starts now.

After racking my brain to the point of pain, I open my laptop and Google meaningful gift ideas for old people. Lap robe? No way. Personalized journals? I scrunch my nose as I try to imagine either of my grandparents sitting still long enough to write down what they do. A book on how to age gracefully? Eek! No way. Knitted scarves? I laugh at the image that brings to mind. Granny Marge and Grandpa Jay are both into jeans and wash-and-wear tops. They both have their favorite sweatshirts with goofy sayings, so that's an option. It still doesn't seem like the best gift for these two people who act half their age.

I call Sally. "Have you thought about what to get Granny Marge and Grandpa Jay?"

"What to get them? What's the occasion? It's not their birthday, is it?"

"No, but Mama reminded me that they're not getting any younger."

"No one is." Sally pauses. "But I guess it's not a bad idea to do something special for them. How about dance lessons?"

I laugh as I realize that suits them better than anything I've come up with. "They might like that."

"I know they will. They've been talking about taking ballroom lessons at that new dance studio in Hattiesburg, so why don't we all chip in and give them a series of lessons?"

"Know what? You're pretty smart."

She laughs. "I know. Sara got the looks, but I got the brains."

Now it's my turn to laugh. Not only are they identical twins, but their mama, my cousin Sheila, has made it clear that the twins not only look alike, they have the same IQ. They just choose to use it differently.

"Why don't I send an email to everyone?" Sally says. "I'll use the family loop and take Granny Marge and Grandpa Jay's names off."

"Good idea." I reach over and close the lid on my laptop.

"The only problem I see is that everything in Granny Marge's closet is casual or church clothes. She'll need a pretty dress that moves with her."

"I'll call Puddin' and see if there's anything at La Chic we can get her." I'm glad I at least have one decent idea.

"Grandpa Jay has plenty of suits from back in the day." Sally chuckles. "I remember thinking how goofy some of those suits looked, but now they're back in style."

"It happens."

I call Puddin' and talk about getting Granny Marge a dress, and she thinks it's a great idea. "She'll need one with a full skirt for twirlin' on the dance floor," she adds.

"Perfect."

"What size do you think she wears?"

"A ten, maybe?"

"That sounds about right. I'll pick out a pretty dress for her, and if it doesn't fit, I'll bring her into the store and help her get something else."

After I hang up, I sit and stare at the table. Now that I've finished the busywork, all I have left to do is prepare myself for showing up at the reunion with Elliot. The second thoughts about inviting him are nibbling at my head and my heart. There's no telling what some of my family members will say or do, and I would never want to embarrass Elliot or be embarrassed on his behalf.

I have two more days of work before I can devote all my time to getting ready for the reunion. I remember the days when all I had to do was show up. Of course, I spent an hour or so picking out something that I thought was cute, in case one of my cousins brought a friend. And someone always did, but it was always too awkward to see if there were any sparks.

After I get home from work on Thursday, my phone rings. It's Elliot. "Hey, Shay, I almost forgot to ask what you want me to bring."

"Just yourself."

"Aw, come on. I know how these things work. Everyone brings something to share. I'm actually a decent cook."

"Do you *want* to bring something?"

"I do. Besides, it'll be less awkward if I have something in my hands when I arrive. I know it'll be uncomfortable for you at first, so if I bring something with printed copies of the recipe, I'll have something to talk about besides my divorce."

I smile and realize I have nothing to worry about. He has this whole thing more figured out than I do. "Sure, if you think it would make things easier, by all means, bring something."

"Which do you think would be better—peach cobbler or stuffed redfish?"

"You know how to make both of those?"

"I do. I had no choice but learn to cook, since my ex thought a home-cooked meal meant ordering something to be delivered."

I laugh. "It doesn't matter which you bring. My family will be duly impressed with either one."

After a few seconds of silence, Elliot speaks up. "Shay, are you sure you want me to go to this thing with you? I'll understand if you've changed your mind."

"Of course I'm sure." I clear my throat to try to get rid of the tinny sound of my uncertain voice. "I wouldn't have asked you if I didn't want you to come."

"Just making sure."

38
Missy

What can you say to your daughter when she tells you she's changed her mind about going to college because it's a waste of time and money? She has enough scholarships to cover her tuition for two years at the community college, but she says it'll be wasted on her.

"I'm such a loser." Wendy's words from a few days ago keep ringing through my head.

This has been going on for several days now, and nothing I say seems to work. Finally, I decide to just let her deal with whatever's bothering her and try again after the reunion.

It's Friday, the day before we're all gathering at Grandpa Jay and Granny Marge's house. I only worked a couple of hours this morning, so now I'm getting the salad ready for the reunion. I cooked several varieties of chili and froze them over the past week, so all I have to do in the morning is take them out to thaw. Foster went up to the attic to pull down my extra Crock-Pots to heat them up in.

I've just started tossing the salad when I hear footsteps behind me. "Mama?"

I turn around and see Wendy, her face pale, her eyes wide but without her usual raccoon makeup. "Hi, honey. Want to give me a hand with the salad?"

"Sure. What do you need?"

"I have some olives in the pantry. Can you open them for me?"

We work together in silence for about a minute before she starts talking. "Mama, do you think I could handle being a nurse?"

"Yes, I've always thought you'd be a good nurse." I try to keep my voice on an even keel and not ask her all the questions that have been racing through my head. "Why?"

She hands me the open can of olives, plucks one out, and leans against the counter. "Do you know Carla Fitzsimmons?"

"Yes, her mother is a doctor at the Pinewood General Hospital, right?"

She nods. "She told me that I don't have what it takes to be a nurse."

I drop the tongs I've been tossing the salad with and spin around to face my superintelligent, supercaring daughter. "Why would she say such a thing?" Before Wendy can answer, I continue. "It ticks me off to think someone like Carla Fitzsimmons would say something so mean to you. Is she jealous or something?"

Wendy nods. "I didn't realize it until last night. I thought she knew what she was talking about because her mother is a doctor and all."

"What happened last night?"

"She didn't get accepted to the community college, so when she found out I did, she tried to drag me down." She pops the olive into her mouth, chews a couple of times, and swallows. She doesn't appear as devastated as she did last time we talked.

But still, my heart sinks at the thought of anyone being mean to my baby. "Don't let her do that to you, honey."

Wendy gives me a comforting grin. "I won't."

"So you're back on for college?"

She grabs another olive from the can and bobs her head. "Maybe." And then she leaves.

It's difficult that it has to happen this way, but I realize my daughter has just learned a valuable lesson about human nature. While some people sincerely care about their friends, others are fine as long as you don't have more than they do. Once you get something they want, they'll scratch and claw until they drag you down into the pit with them.

Foster calls. "I'm not sure I'll be able to make it to the reunion. It's tomorrow, isn't it?"

"You know it is, Foster. What happened?"

"Some of the guys at work are going on a one-night hunting trip."

"Foster . . ." Oh, what's the use? I just clamp my mouth shut and fume.

"You know how I love to hunt."

"If you don't go to this reunion with me, you'll have to go hunting for a place to stay."

"Aw, come on, Missy. It's not like anyone will know I'm not there."

"I'll know."

"You also know I hate those things."

I have to bite my lip to keep from telling him all the things I do that I hate. The pressure in my chest builds, but I manage to keep my mouth shut.

"Missy? Are you still there?"

"I'm here."

"So you're telling me I can't go hunting?"

"No, Foster, I'm not telling you anything of the sort. You're a grown man, and you can do whatever you feel you need to do."

"Okay, thanks, Missy. I'll tell the guys."

After I hang up, I want to scream. The anger inside me has reached its tipping point, but there's absolutely nothing I can do about it.

I take a few slow, deep breaths, just like I saw that yoga woman on YouTube do when I went looking for a way to relieve stress and anger. It helps, but it doesn't make it go away.

After I finish throwing the rest of the ingredients into the salad, I cover it and stick it in the fridge. I'll make the dressing in the morning and toss it into the vegetables when I get there.

I spend the remainder of the day frantically straightening the house, folding the laundry that's been sitting in the dryer since early this morning, and plumping the sofa cushions. Since tomorrow's the big day, I haven't got anything special planned for supper tonight. I figure I can fix canned soup and sandwiches, or we can order a pizza.

Foster is due to come home soon, and I don't want to be in the kitchen waiting for him, so I go to our closet and try to find the perfect outfit for the reunion. I shove all of my pants to one side and look at each one with a critical eye. Uncle Bubba made a comment at the last one about how my backside needed a "wide load" sign. That's why I now have a slew of tunic tops that cover my seat.

Every now and then I glance at the clock to see how much longer before I have to face my husband. He's always had a mind of his own and done whatever he wanted to do, regardless of how I felt about it. But

I would think that a family reunion with a wife who has stuck by him through thick and thin would be more important to him than a bunch of smelly guys on a hunting trip.

At a little after three o'clock, I hear the door from the garage slam shut. Foster is home early. I hear the rattling of bottles as he rummages around inside the refrigerator looking for something to drink.

I take a deep breath, shut my eyes, and ask God for forgiveness for my thoughts. I know it's wrong to be mad all the time. *Lord, help me deal with Foster and not always be so angry.* Then I head to the kitchen.

Before I have a chance to open my mouth, he looks over at me, grins, and opens his arms wide. I just stand there and stare at him.

He gives me a look of confusion. "Are you mad at me?"

I shrug. "I don't know."

"Well, you shouldn't be. I told my buddies that I'm going to the reunion with my family."

I blink. "You did?"

39
Shay

I'm glad I decided to make a variety of things for the reunion. After all, Elliot will be with me, and I want to show him a side of me he's never seen.

I make another run to the grocery store, where I run into Aunt Willa Dean. She looks me up and down before settling her gaze on mine. "Hey, Shay. Looks like you've lost some weight since last time I saw you. Have you been dieting?"

"No, ma'am. I've just been working hard and trying not to eat too much dessert."

"Well, don't work too hard. It's difficult enough to find a good man as it is, and I'm sure you won't find one if you're stuck in an office all day." She grins and shakes her head. "I know girls like to be skinny, but I do think that real men like a little meat on their girls' bones."

It takes every ounce of self-restraint not to tell her what I'm thinking. I smile back. "I'll keep that in mind."

"I hate that we had to miss the last reunion, but Irby won that cruise, and we couldn't very well pass up the opportunity to go to the Caribbean. Say, Shay, have you ever gone on a Caribbean cruise?"

I shake my head. "No, can't say that I have."

"If you ever find yourself a man, you might want to think about it. They're so romantic, and the food ..." Her eyes roll back. "They put out so much heavenly food, you could eat yourself silly." She laughs. "That's pretty much what Irby did, but not me. No, sirree. I spent most of my time playing bingo, jogging around the deck, playing charades, and taking art classes."

I have no idea what's so romantic about that, but of course I keep that thought to myself. "Sounds like fun."

"Oh, trust me, it is." She glances at her watch. "I better run. See you tomorrow, hon."

As soon as Aunt Willa Dean turns the corner, I give my buggy a powerful shove toward the condiments to fill in what I don't have from the prospective vendor's samples. I love my family, and I would do anything for them, but they sure do get me riled up. It's like they know what my weaknesses are, and that's what they zoom in on.

"Whoa there, Shay. What's got you all up in a dither?"

"Sally? What are you doing here?"

She shrugs. "I'm trying to figure out what I can bring that's not stupid."

"Stupid?" I try hard not to laugh. "I don't think anything you bring will be stupid." I pause. "I thought you were bringing pies."

"That's what Sara and Justin are bringing."

"Bring whatever you want, then. I don't think anyone will expect a lot."

"I know. I just don't want to be one of those people who brings bags of chips or rolls from the bakery."

"So what are you thinking?"

Sally lowers her head and sighs. "I burned what I was planning to bring, so now I have to figure out something else."

"You can always do a Jell-O mold or ambrosia." I can't help but giggle.

"Right." She rolls her eyes in typical Sally style. "I don't want to bring home something that no one else has touched."

I think for a moment and decide to let her have one of my dishes. "I have an idea. How about meatballs?"

"Meatballs? Who makes those?"

"I do. Come on. I'll help you with them."

"Are they hard to make?"

"Not if you know what you're doing."

Sally lets me lead her to the meat counter, then over to the canned tomato products. "What will we put the meatballs on?"

"You can do pasta, or you can buy a bunch of toothpicks and let people think they're hors d'oeuvres."

Her eyes light up. "People like to eat stuff with toothpicks. I'll do that."

"And how about stuffing some celery?" I gesture toward the produce section. "You can do a tray with celery stuffed with pimento cheese, hummus, and peanut butter. If you make it all pretty on a bed of lettuce and put a few cherry tomatoes on the platter for color, people will think you're the best cook in Mississippi."

Sally follows happily along and picks up everything I tell her to. "Shay, you're a genius."

"I'll be over to help you with that after I finish shopping."

She wiggles her fingers in a wave and leaves me standing there wondering what to do. I've just helped her shop for one of the main things I was planning to bring to the reunion.

Since I know there'll be plenty of dense, rich casseroles, I head for the produce department. I load up on peppers, zucchini, tomatoes, and green beans. Although I'm still not sure what to cook, I know I can chop and freeze whatever is left. Then I wheel my buggy toward the eggs, grab several dozen, then go toward the checkout.

"Shay!" I glance up and spot Aunt Faye letting go of her buggy and coming toward me with open arms. "I see I'm not the only one who does last-minute shopping."

"It's good to see you." I glance at her buggy and slink back when I realize I'm still not up to the family standard of overflowing bounty. Healthy produce will never stand up to one of Aunt Faye's chicken-fried steaks smothered in gravy and onions.

She leans over and looks at the contents of my buggy. "Looks like you're just getting started, so I won't keep you."

At that moment, I know I'll be up until the wee hours of the night, fussing over the stove, worried that whatever I bring won't be enough. "See you tomorrow."

She smiles and walks back to her buggy before turning around. "Oh, by the way, I hear you might be bringing a guest. Will I be hearing wedding bells soon?"

I have no idea what to say, so I smile back and shrug. "You never know."

"Ooh, this sounds promising. I guess I better run. I have a lot to do tonight to get ready for the big day."

After she goes to the checkout, I stand there staring into my buggy. I have to come up with something else. Even though I know I'll never be able to compete with some of the older women in the family, I need to at least hold my own.

As soon as Aunt Faye is out of sight, I pull out my cell phone and click on my favorite recipe site. My eyes aren't what they used to be, so I pull out the readers I picked up from the drugstore, put them on, and shop for more ingredients. I even pick up a couple more overpriced casserole pans because I don't have time to make a stop at Walmart.

An hour and a couple hundred dollars later, I'm on the way to my car. I turn on the radio, but the music irritates me, so I shut it off. The stress from this reunion is overwhelming, and I regret inviting Elliot. Not only am I worried about the family's reaction to him, but I don't want him to see me like this.

I promised to help Sally get ready for the reunion, so I put everything away as quickly as possible, fill the dishwasher, grab the detergent from beneath the sink, and squirt it into the little fill cup. Then I turn it on so the dishes will be clean and ready to use when I get back home.

40

Sally

If I'd known how easy it was to cook, I would have done it a long time ago. All you have to do is follow directions, and voilà! You have a meal.

"See?" Shay takes a step back so we can both admire our finished dishes.

"Can I try one of the meatballs?" I reach for one, but she swats my hand.

"No, you've tried enough already. If you keep going, there won't be any to bring to the reunion."

I glance at the stuffed celery that I ordinarily would have walked past. But it actually looks good, nestled into a bed of curly lettuce and embellished with cherry tomatoes. Food presentation is sort of like little girls' hair bows. You can take something that's just okay and jazz it up with a little bling to make people want it.

"Fine, then I'll take one of these instead." I grab a hummus-stuffed celery stick before she has a chance to react. "It looks like a boat."

Shay folds her arms and grins back at me. "Let's see what you think about it. Go ahead and taste it."

I bring it to my mouth and stick out my tongue to check out the hummus. I wanted to get the kind with garlic and hot peppers, but Shay said it's best to get the plain one in case folks have allergies.

After I chew and swallow the first bite, I shake my head. "It's kind of blah."

"So why don't you put a little Tabasco on it? You can put some on the table tomorrow in case other people like it spicy."

"I'll do that."

Shay is wiping her hands on the dish towel, so I have a feeling she's about to leave. "Why don't you stick around for a little while? Sara should be home soon, and I'm sure she'd want to see you."

"I have to go home and fix what I'm bringing." She gives me a hug before reaching for her purse and walking toward the door. "Besides, I'll see her tomorrow." She puts her hand on the knob then pauses. "How are things with Justin?"

I shrug. "Okay, I guess. It's just that he's … I don't know … always there. She and I don't have much time together, just the two of us."

"She'll always be your sister, no matter what. I don't think anything can possibly come between the two of you."

"Someone needs to tell Justin that."

"I'm sure he knows." Shay opens the door. "Don't forget to stick those meatballs in the oven to heat them up before you leave."

"Shay?"

She stops and turns to face me. "Did you need something else?"

"I just have a question." I take a deep breath to stop the tears that bite the backs of my eyes. "Do you ever think of the questions you'll ask God when you get to heaven? Like about why He lets certain things happen?"

She gives me a half-smile, sort of like the one Mama used to give Sara and me when she felt bad for us. "When I get to heaven, I think my mind will be on more awesome things than questions that came up during my earthly life."

"Oh." What else can I say?

"I think everything will be clear once we're in heaven. This is all petty stuff that we worry about way too much."

I hang my head. "Yeah, you're right."

As soon as she leaves, I wait a couple of minutes before I go back into the kitchen, grab a couple of meatballs, and pop them into my mouth. They are absolutely delicious.

I cover them back up and stick the pan in the refrigerator. Now I need to think of something to do before I go crazy and eat the whole pan of meatballs. I glance over at the platter filled with little celery boats. Too bad they don't taste as good as they look.

The sound of a key in the door lets me know Sara and Justin are home. I pretend not to notice when they appear at the door of the kitchen.

"Hey, Sally, we got an extra pie for us," Justin says.

I glance up and see that they are each holding two pies. "That's nice. What kind did you get?"

Justin looks at Sara then smiles at me. "We got apple for the reunion but pecan for here. Sara says that's your favorite."

"I like it with ice cream."

"That's why we stopped at the grocery store on the way home." Justin sets the pies on the table and lifts the bag from the crook of his elbow. "Why don't we have some now?"

Without another word, I fetch some plates from the cabinet. I'm touched that they'd think of me and bring home a pecan pie, since I know Sara barely even likes it.

"So, Justin, what's your favorite kind of pie?" I ask as he scoops a dollop of ice cream onto each slice.

He shrugs. "I like just about anything."

I've seen that. He'll eat whatever is in the fridge without making any negative comments, regardless of what it is.

After we finish our pie and ice cream, I start to get up, but Justin points to the chair. "Stay and talk to Sara. I'll clean up."

I blink and raise my eyebrows before turning to Sara. She grins and winks. "He's sweet, isn't he?"

I'm starting to see what Sara likes about this boy, but I'm not about to say he's sweet. Not yet, anyway. "That's nice of you, Justin."

"So how's everything going with Shay?" Sara asks. "Did y'all get some stuff made for the reunion?"

"A whole bunch of stuff." I tell her about the meatballs and stuffed celery.

She crinkles her nose. "Stuffed celery? I don't know if anyone will eat that, but maybe someone will."

"It's actually pretty good. You might want to try some."

Justin glances over his shoulder. "I love stuffed celery. What did you stuff it with?"

"Pimento cheese, hummus, and peanut butter."

He grins. "Did you make any extra? I'd love some now."

I hop up, open the fridge, and pull out the platter. "I'll slip a couple of each out for you now." I tilt my head toward Sara. "Want some?"

She narrows her eyes as she scrutinizes it. "It does look good."

I reach for one with peanut butter and hand it to her. "I think you'll like this one." Then I get the bottle of Tabasco out of the cabinet and put it on the table. "This is good with the hummus."

After Justin finishes the dishes, he wipes his hands and unrolls his sleeves on his way to the table. "I'll take some hot sauce."

As he munches on the stuffed celery, I watch his look of appreciation, and I have to admit it feels good to know someone likes my cooking. "How is it?"

"The best I've ever had."

"Wow, Sally, I'm impressed. You're becoming Ms. Homemaker." Sara turns to Justin. "Isn't she?"

"Absolutely." He beams at me. "You'll have to teach Sara how to make this."

If Justin hadn't cooked more meals than Sara since they've been married, I might have made an issue of his comment. But I can't do that, especially after the kind thing they did for me.

"I'll be happy to teach her whatever I know, if she's ever home long enough."

Justin gives me an odd look, and guilt washes over me. I need to control my sarcasm until he figures out that's my way of dealing with things I don't understand.

41

Shay

As I walk home, I think about the relationship between Sally and Sara. They were long overdue for some changes, but this one has obviously blindsided Sally.

I can't help but wonder how Sara would have held up if Sally had eloped. Probably not very well. Although Sally is struggling with Sara's decision, she's clearly the stronger of the two. I doubt anyone else in the family—besides their parents, of course—sees the differences. In fact, when people talk about them, they usually just say, "the twins." Unfortunately, I'm guilty of having done that before I really knew them.

I turn onto my street and think about the work I have ahead of me. I'll need to put the clean dishes away then cook for a couple of hours. After that, I need to figure out what to wear. I planned to get a new outfit, since Elliot is going with me, but time just got away from me.

"Hi there!"

I turn around and see one of my new neighbors getting out of his car. I wave back. "Hey."

"Welcome to the neighborhood." He takes a step toward me and extends his hand. "I'm Joe Stanford."

"I'm Shay Henke." I accept the handshake but quickly pull away the instant I feel the chemistry. He has something that transcends good looks, and I feel a bolt of attraction that catches me off guard.

"Are you new to Pinewood?"

I shake my head. "No, I've lived here all my life. In fact, I just moved from the other side of the community."

"Oh." He shoves his hands into his jeans pockets. "I was hoping you were brand new so I could show you around."

"How about you? How long have you been in Pinewood?"

"About a year and a half." He glances over his shoulder. "Would you like to come over for a few minutes? I just finished making a cobbler, and I'm afraid if no one helps me, I'll be tempted to eat the whole thing myself."

I laugh. "I don't know."

He gives me an exaggerated puppy-dog look. "Please?"

There is no way I can turn him down now. "Okay, but just for a few minutes. I have a ton of stuff to do."

"You've got the whole weekend," he says as he gestures toward his condo.

Once we get inside, I smell the wonderfully sweet aroma of peach cobbler. I take a long look around. It's not heavily decorated, but I can tell he has varied interests. There's a bow and arrow mounted on the wall over the TV. On a side table, he has a variety of sports trophies lined up. An open Bible holds court in the center of a rough-hewn coffee table.

"I see you're an athlete."

He lifts his hands and chuckles. "Guilty as charged."

I glance back over at the Bible. "And a Christian?"

"Yes, absolutely. How about you?"

I nod as my pulse picks up even more. "I am."

"Then you probably won't run away when I tell you I'm the youth pastor at Cornerstone Community Church."

"I go to Pinewood Community Church."

"Good church." He points to the kitchen. "Ready for some cobbler?"

"Absolutely." I ate a half dozen meatballs at Sally's place and nibbled on some celery, so I might as well have cobbler and call it dessert.

He prepares a couple bowls filled with cobbler and ice cream and places them on the kitchen table. As we eat, we take turns asking each other questions about our pasts. I'm having the time of my life when I look up at the clock on the wall and realize how late it's getting.

I carry my bowl to the sink. "I had a wonderful time, Joe, and your cobbler is delicious, but I really need to run."

"It's early."

"I know, but I have to get some stuff ready for my family reunion tomorrow."

He narrows his eyes. "You wouldn't happen to be going to the Bucklin family reunion, would you?"

"How did you know?"

"Then I'll see you there. In fact, that's why I made the cobbler. This one is a mini. The big one's in the fridge."

"Why are you—I mean, you're not a long-lost cousin I don't know about, are you?"

He belts out a hearty laugh. "No, I'm friends with Faye and Dennis Wright. I think they felt sorry for me because I don't have any family here."

"Faye and Dennis are my aunt and uncle."

"Pinewood is a small town, so I shouldn't be surprised." He pauses and gives me a lingering look. "But I am. Pleasantly surprised."

"You didn't have to make a cobbler. There's always a big spread. In case Aunt Faye and Uncle Dennis didn't tell you, all my aunts and cousins like to see who can one-up everyone else."

"I hate to go to something like this empty-handed." He walks me to the door and stops. "I'm delighted to know you'll be there. At least I'll have someone a little closer to my age to talk to."

I leave his place with strange feelings surging through me. I'm not sure whether I should be happy or sad that he'll be at the reunion, since I'd like to get to know him better. For the first time ever, I have two interesting guys in my life, and I find it confusing.

Then I kick myself back to reality. I just met Joe. Besides, Elliot is my date, so I need to stop thinking like this. I let out a sigh. I need to focus on all the work I have ahead of me tonight and stop thinking about all the what-ifs.

As soon as I open the door to my condo, I see water trailing out of the kitchen and onto the brand-new wood floors. I drop my purse and rush into the kitchen, where I wade across the lake covering the floor and open the dishwasher. What on earth? The whole thing is filled with suds.

I grab the closest dish towel and drop it onto the floor. A lot of good it does, so I tiptoe out of the kitchen and to the linen closet, where I pull out all the towels to sop up the mess. It takes me almost an hour to get all the water off the floor. When I open the cupboard beneath the sink, I realize what happened. In my haste, I reached for the regular dishwashing detergent rather than the kind for dishwashers. The bottles are similar, and I've been so absentminded lately, I haven't paid close enough attention to what I'm doing.

The whole time I clean up the mess, I fuss at myself. This is one of the reasons I shouldn't have let myself get mixed up with men. They mess with your mind. It's a man who stepped into Sally and Sara's life and disrupted it. It's a man who has Sally wanting to suddenly get all domestic, even though he'll be sorely disappointed when he finds out she doesn't have a homemaking bone in her body. And it's a man who has me doing crazy stuff. Well, actually, it's now two men. Who'd have thought?

Two hours later, I have the mess cleaned up, a couple of respectable casseroles ready to be heated, and some cookies baked. I'll make the deviled eggs in the morning because I want them to be fresh. I don't think all this work will impress anyone in my family, but at least I won't be going empty-handed, or worse, be the person who brings bagged potato chips and napkins.

42
Puddin'

"Mommy, I want some dat." Jeremy points to the batter I'm mixing for his birthday cake I'm bringing to the reunion.

It's late. I've already served Jeremy his supper, but Digger called and said he won't be home for a while. It's much later than Jeremy should be up, but he napped longer than usual this afternoon. Besides, I'm enjoying his company.

I smile down at Jeremy, and it dawns on me. He just said a complete sentence. Excitement courses through my body as I bend over and look him in the eyes. "Jeremy! What did you just say?"

He points. "Dat."

"No, say the whole thing, Jeremy."

His little face scrunches with confusion. "Dat!"

"You said, 'Mommy, I want some dat.'" I push my face closer to his. "Can you say it again?"

His little chin quivers before I realize I'm holding onto his arm and squeezing so tight it's bound to leave a bruise. I quickly let go.

"Okay, sweetie, you can lick the bowl when I'm all done."

His near-tears face now beams. "Kankoo, Mommy."

I try not to show my joy over the fact that he's at least given me more than one-word commands. Twice now. That's twice more than ... well, ever.

After I pour the batter into the cake pans and swirl them around to level it out, I set the bowl on the table in front of his booster seat. He climbs up like a little monkey, gets into position, and grins before turning his attention to the bowl. Before I have a chance to give him the spoon, he sticks his hand into the bowl, scrapes a bunch of batter off the sides, and shoves it into his mouth.

I know I'm not supposed to give my young'un cake batter with raw eggs, but I've done it for all four of them, and nothing bad has ever happened. In fact, I've never known anyone who's gotten sick from it. If I ever tried to wash the bowl before offering it to whoever's in the kitchen, I'd have more squawking than you hear in a hen house.

After he's all done, I lift him off the booster seat and carry him to the sink. He sticks his hands under the running water, rubs them together, and holds them up.

"See, Mommy? All keen."

"Jeremy!" Now I want to fist-pump all over the place, but I don't want to scare my little guy. So I just smile at him and place him on the floor. "Yes, sweetie, all clean."

"Go pay now?"

"Sure, go ahead and play while I clean up the rest of the kitchen."

As soon as Jeremy leaves the kitchen and goes to his toy box in the corner of the dining room, I grab my cell phone and call Digger. It rings twice before he answers.

"Whatcha need, Puddin'? I'm in the middle of a delivery."

"I just wanted to tell you that Jeremy has been making sentences."

"I know. He's been doing that for several days. Look, hon, I'd love to chat, but I really need to go. The lady is waiting for me at the door."

Now that my bubble is burst, I fold my arms and rock back on my heels. Why am I just now hearing about Jeremy making sentences?

After I allow myself to wallow in self-pity and a little bit of guilt for a few minutes, I get to work on the casserole I'm taking to the reunion tomorrow. Digger has been getting on my nerves more than usual lately. I'm doing all this work for his family reunion, making sure the house is clean, doing all the laundry, and cooking all the meals. I have supper on the table within five minutes of when he walks in the door every evening, giving him just enough time to change clothes.

Yeah, I've always done all of that, even after I started working. But he knows I have a paying job now. You'd think he might want to contribute to some of the household chores. But no, all he does is eat his supper, ask what's for dessert, then go into the living room to watch TV, leaving the dirty dishes for me to do. By myself. Alone. While he relaxes. I've heard other wives with bigger things to complain about, so my guilt level rises again. This is something I'll eventually need to discuss with him, but not now. I'm too busy.

I've just stuck the casserole in the oven when Jeremy comes running back into the kitchen. "Ook, Mommy. Airplane."

"Yes, sweetie, I see your airplane."

He zooms his little wooden airplane around me before running back to the dining room. I stare at the door as I think about how my baby is growing up and I'm the last to see it happening.

Amanda calls. "Do you know where the order form for the winter collection is?"

"Yes, I put it in the top drawer, in the pending order file."

She laughs. "That's logical. I'm afraid my brains aren't working very well lately, with all the stuff I have to do to get ready for the move."

"Did you hear back from the Realtor about that lady who is interested in buying the store?"

"She likes it, but she doesn't want to give me what I think it's worth."

"You don't have to sell, you know. I can run it for you, and we can hire another part-timer."

Amanda clears her throat. "I know. I might have to do that, but I'd really like to sell it so I won't have to think about it anymore."

"I thought you liked having the store."

"It was always my dream, but ..." Her voice trails off.

"So you're saying it wasn't what you thought it would be like?"

"Pretty much. I envisioned being surrounded by fashion and pretty things all day. I thought people just like me would come in and buy everything I show them. But it's nothing like that. It's more ... well, more businesslike than I ever thought."

"And that's the part I like."

"I know you do. Too bad you can't buy it."

My entire body goes numb. The thought of purchasing La Chic has never even crossed my mind. Until now.

"Who says I can't buy it?"

She lets out a soft laugh. "You know Digger would never go along with that."

"Maybe. Maybe not."

Amanda sighs. "I have someone else looking at it tomorrow afternoon. It's a man who owns a chain of different retail stores, and he says this will fit with his brand."

"You don't sound terribly excited about him."

"I'm not. He plans to come in and completely redo everything, including staff."

"Are you saying—?"

Before I can finish the rest of the sentence, she replies, "I'm afraid so. He told my Realtor he has his way of doing things, and it's nothing like how we're currently doing them."

"Please don't sell to him."

"I'm so sorry, Puddin', but if he offers my asking price, I'll have to."

Now I know I have to buy her store. It's a matter of self-preservation. All I have to do is think of a way to bring it up to Digger without having him go ballistic.

43

Shay

I wake up the next morning feeling like someone hit me over the head with a two-by-four—not that I know what it feels like to be hit over the head with a piece of wood. Or with anything else, for that matter. It is just something Daddy used to say after a rough day, and now I get it.

Before I sit up, I squeeze my eyes shut again and pray that the day will be smooth and nothing terrible will happen. I know better than to pray for everything to be rosy because this is my family reunion, and that would be totally unrealistic. I'm fully aware of the drama some of the people in my family drag around with them everywhere they go. And being honest with myself, I realize that I'm more worried about taking Elliot to the event than I realized. It might be fine, but it can also turn out to be a total disaster. What was I thinking?

My thoughts drift to my new neighbor. Joe seems very comfortable about going to my family reunion, even though he doesn't know most of my relatives. I have a feeling his confidence is more like mine—new but developed. And then I remember that sometimes my self-assuredness is a facade. Deep down, I know who I am and where I come from, and there's no reason to be too full of myself based on that.

I wonder if Joe has a big family and whether or not he plans to stay in Pinewood very long. Some youth pastors go from church to church until they eventually move up to the lead position at the church, or burn out and go into another field altogether.

After a few more minutes of procrastination, I finally get up and head to the kitchen for coffee. One thing I've counted on since adulthood is the first sip of the first cup of coffee. There's just something about it that lets me know I'm still alive. And it helps to have a shot of a special flavoring in my morning dose of caffeine.

I sit down and take a few sips while staring at the news page on the screen of my tablet. It reminds me that what I worry about is mostly first world problems, and that folks in other countries would give anything to have them. Even in my world, there are hungry people—folks who are down on their luck and haven't had the advantages I've had in life.

Mama used to organize a group at church to help feed the homeless in Hattiesburg. We'd all convene at the church once a month and go through the donation boxes from people bringing in canned goods on Sundays. From that, we'd decide how many people we had food for and divide it as equally as possible. Then someone would pull the church van up to the multipurpose room's door, and we'd load up. After that, I was never sure where it went, since Mama didn't want me going wherever it was. She said she wanted to protect me, and now I wonder what she wanted to protect me from, since I never heard about any homeless person in Hattiesburg hurting someone.

After I finish my coffee, I take a shower and slip into some shorts and a T-shirt. I don't want to mess up what I plan to wear to the reunion.

Most of the food I've cooked goes into the oven to be heated up, then I set about the task of cleaning the condo so it isn't a mess when Elliot arrives. I've barely finished when my phone rings. When I see that it's Elliot, I half hope he's calling to say he can't make it. Maybe this is the Lord's way of reminding me that He's in control.

"Hi, Shay. I just wondered if we might need extra ice."

"Oh." I think for a minute. "No, I'm pretty sure that's covered."

"I thought I'd ask since I'm at the store now." He pauses. "I'll see you in an hour and a half." He lowers his voice. "I sure hope your family is okay with my being there."

After we hang up, I head back to the kitchen to check on the food in the oven, boil the eggs, and put the finishing touches on the platters in the fridge. I got a little carried away last night and put together a few last-minute concoctions. With my family, more is always better.

As I work, I ponder my conversation with Elliot, and I'm ashamed of myself for half hoping he'd called to say he couldn't make it. He did sound nervous, so at least he's prepared. And then it makes me smile to think that this Pinewood golden boy might be insecure about anything. I've always thought of him as the most confident guy in our high school, but we've been out of high school for a long time now. I need to remember that things change. I've gained confidence, so why shouldn't someone who seemed to have boatloads of it back then slide in the other direction? I'm sure that must be more common than I ever realized.

Before I finish getting ready, I turn off the oven and assemble the deviled eggs. As soon as Elliot arrives, I can get everything ready for transporting.

I start to put on the outfit I'd originally planned to wear but change my mind because it now seems too boring. Instead, I slip into some casual taupe linen slacks, a turquoise tank top, and a peach-and-cream striped overshirt. Then I put on a necklace that pulls all the summery colors together before sliding into my favorite jute sandals. I pull my hair up into a messy bun like the younger girls wear these days. It took watching several YouTube videos and lots of practice before I managed to master the technique, but I think I look pretty good.

I'm thankful that my skin is clear today because I don't want to wear too much makeup on such a hot day. A swipe of coral lipstick gives me the finish I want. Then I stand back and take a good, long look at myself in the full-length mirror. Before I have a chance to get too caught up in self-admiration, my doorbell rings.

The instant I open the door, Elliot's eyes widen. "Whoa. You look—" He lowers his head. "I've already told you this."

"Told me what?"

"The fact that you look amazing."

Yes, he has told me that. The first time I was embarrassed but flattered, but now it seems like overkill, and I'm a tad annoyed. I wonder if this is something he always says when he picks up a girl for a date.

My mind flashes back to Joe. I can't help but think he'd have something more appropriate to say. Something more meaningful. Something less canned.

"Whatcha thinkin'?" Elliot asks.

"That I need to get the food out of the oven and fridge and put it in boxes so the hot food will stay hot and the cold food will stay cold."

"Do you have the boxes, or do I need to go get them?" The eagerness in his voice touches my heart.

"I have them in the garage." I hold up a finger as I back away. "I'll be right back. Why don't you fix yourself a cup of coffee while you wait? It's still hot."

44

Missy

"What's the worst that'll happen if I don't go?"

"You said you'd go with me. Are you going back on your word?" I'm super annoyed by the fact that Foster keeps changing his mind.

His lips form a straight line as he stares at me. "I didn't say that."

"Come on, Foster. It's just one day out of your life."

He places his fists on his hips and shakes his head. "I wish that's all it was. Your family has more reunions in one year than mine has in a lifetime."

"The most we have is two a year," I remind him. "And you always have a good time when you go."

He snickers. "Is that what you think?"

Tears spring to my eyes before I have a chance to stop them. I've always bent over backward to make sure Foster gets his way, and I'd like for him to at least be nice on these occasions.

He steps closer and cups my chin in his hand. "Missy, darlin', you're a wonderful wife, but you have to admit this is asking an awful lot from someone who hates crowds."

"How about all your fishing and hunting trips? I can't think of anything more crowded than six or eight grown men in a little cabin."

Foster drops his hand and shakes his head. "That's different."

"It's only different because you want to go."

"There you have it. I like fishing and hunting. I don't like family reunions and having to pretend."

"But I do." I step back, lower my head, and pull my lips between my teeth as I think about his last statement. "What do you mean, *pretend*?"

He makes a face. "I have to pretend to be having a good time."

"That's because you don't allow yourself to have fun."

"Then why don't you go and have yourself a good time?"

"What will I tell everyone?"

He shrugs. "Maybe say I didn't want to go, so I'm home watching a game on TV."

I roll my eyes. "Oh, that'll go over like a lead balloon."

"You sound just like my mama."

Finally, I let out the loudest sigh I can manage. "Fine. Stay here and watch your stupid TV like you do every Saturday when you're not hunting or fishing. I'll go do something meaningful with the people who will always be there to support me no matter what." I give him a harsh glare before walking out of the room. So much for my resolve to not be so mad all the time.

I make as much noise as possible getting all the food ready to bring to the reunion. Foster shows up at the kitchen door and gestures toward the pans of food. "Want me to carry that to your car?"

"Nope. I can do it all by myself."

"But it's heavy." He walks over to the table where all the pans are laid out on trivets. "Mmm. Smells good. Mind if I put a little on a plate for later?"

I swat at his hand. "Keep your hands off this food. It's for the reunion."

"But I won't take much."

"You heard me, Foster. If you want some of this, you'll have to come to the reunion to get it."

He lifts both hands and backs away from it. "Okay, fine. Have it your way. I'll just fix myself a peanut-butter-and-jelly sandwich while you're feasting on this delicious food."

"That's your decision." I go out to the garage and get a couple of boxes to make transporting the food easier.

"Sure you don't need some help?"

"Positive." I stack the pans in a crisscross manner to keep them from sinking down into each other. Then I carry them to my car, doing my best to ignore the man who alternates between the sensitive and loving man I married and some guy who is too clueless to understand why his macho actions bug me.

"Aw, Missy, don't be like that." He takes a step closer but backs off when I snarl at him. "I thought you'd understand."

"Then you weren't thinking with your brain."

He lifts one eyebrow, gives me a strange, head-tilted look, then goes inside, leaving me to finish loading the car. I force myself to plow ahead and not get too caught up in my hurt feelings. I don't want anyone in the family to ever know there are problems in the Montague house.

I go back inside and pick up a couple more pans to load in the car. I've barely arranged them when I turn around and see Foster standing by the door, buttoning his good work shirt like he's going somewhere. I have one more load to bring to the car, so I edge past him without making physical contact.

As soon as I turn my back on him, I feel his hand on my shoulder. "Missy, let me help you."

"I'm fine. I can do it."

"No, you can't. I'm your husband, and it's up to me to do things for you." He gives my shoulder a gentle squeeze. "It'll only take me a couple shakes of a donkey's tail, and I'll have everything ready to go." He turns me around to face him. "Then we can get on over to the reunion and help the folks set up."

I raise my gaze to meet his. "What did you say?"

"I'm going with you." A hint of a smile plays on his lips. "I'm really sorry for being so dense. I know this reunion is important to you. Why you want me to go, I have no idea, but after thinking about it, I'm actually kinda flattered that you do."

"Really?" I narrow my eyes and give him a long, hard look. I can't help but wonder what he's up to or what he wants from me. And then a wave of guilt washes over me. I want to be appreciative. I know how much he hates being around my family. Besides, I'm partly to blame for the way he acts because I've given in so much and become an enabler. "Are you sure?"

Foster smiles and drops a kiss on my nose. "Positive. I feel bad that I didn't take your feelings into consideration." He chuckles. "Besides, I heard Bucky just got back from a trip to South America, and I want to know how the fishing was down there."

I should have known. "Okay, that's fine. You can talk to Bucky all day if it makes you happy."

He tilts his head. "Are you being sarcastic?"

"Me?" I laugh. "Never."

"You're really good at it, ya know."

I give him a curious look. "Good at what?"

"Sarcasm. You're funny, too, but I don't like to always be the subject of your sharp tongue."

"Sorry. I'll try to do better."

He gives me one of those grins that melt my insides. "C'mon, let's move this stuff over to my truck."

"Why can't we just take my car? It's already packed."

"Are you kidding me? You drive a lady car. We're taking my truck."

The finality in his tone lets me know there is no room for arguing, so I nod. Giving in on this is the least I can do since he's definitely going with me now. It takes us less than five minutes to move everything to the backseat of his oversized cab. Then he makes a nest with some blankets and towels to cradle the Crock-Pots. After we have all of those loaded, he covers them with a tarp.

45

Shay

I keep thinking about Elliot saying I look amazing. It sure would be nice if he truly believes it.

"Are you sure we were supposed to turn back there?" He glances at the GPS on his dashboard. "It doesn't look like there's anything out here."

I laugh. "I'm positive. I thought you knew where we were going."

"I thought I did, too." He turns to me and flashes what would have been a knee-weakening grin until recently. "But even if it isn't the right turn, I can't think of anyone I'd rather be lost with."

He's saying so many sweet things, I've almost forgotten that I had a momentary regret about asking him. As silence falls upon us, I decide to get the conversation going again to keep from getting buried in my own doubts.

"How did you learn to cook so many different things?"

Elliot smiles again, only this time not as wide. "I don't want to discuss my ex, since I'm supposed to be past that, but I will say that she was never into anything domestic—cooking, cleaning, or any of those things. I had no choice but to learn."

"Oh." I know he's making a conscious effort not to discuss her, but there are a few things I'd like to know before I let my heart completely melt for him. "Does she work?"

He lifts a shoulder in a half shrug. "She does some volunteer work, and she shops, but she's never had a regular job."

"Did you want her to work?"

"It really didn't matter to me whether or not she worked. I made enough money so she could stay home if she wanted. But if she had a burning desire to have a career, that would have been fine, too."

So their divorce has nothing to do with his ex being too wrapped up in a career. I want to ask more questions, but I don't want to upset Elliot. And I did make a big deal over his wallowing in the past.

"Look, Shay, I understand why you want to know what happened in my marriage, and I'll tell you all about it." He gives me a very sweet, apologetic look. "But let's not do that now. I'd like to enjoy today with you and your family."

I nod. "That's fine. Sorry if I overstepped."

"You didn't." He narrows his eyes and points to the right. "Is that where we're going?"

"Yes." My palms grow clammy. I'm excited and happy to have Elliot with me, but I'm nervous, too. Most of my family members are very outspoken, and there is no telling what they'll say to him.

"I see a house and a double-wide mobile home. Who lives in them?"

"Grandpa Jay and Granny Marge used to live in the house, but when they got enough money, they bought the house of Granny's dreams."

A smile tweaks the corners of Elliot's lips. "The mobile home?"

"Yeah." I let out a laugh. "She remembers being a little girl and visiting a friend who lived in a double-wide. She thought it was the nicest house she'd ever seen, and that's what she always wanted."

"At least she knows what she likes."

"Oh, yeah. Granny Marge has always known what she likes, and she won't hesitate to let you know what it is."

"Who lives in the old house now?"

"No one. They call it their guest cottage."

He chuckles. "Why not? It's theirs to do with what they want."

I have to admit that he doesn't seem to have a snobby bone in his body, unlike the last guy I dated. When he met a couple of my cousins, he called them rednecks. I laughed and said I had a little of that in me, too, but he didn't mean it in a fun way. In his eyes, it was an insult. That was the last time we went out.

I decide to address that with Elliot. "Some folks might balk at attending a redneck reunion, but you don't seem to mind."

He bursts into laughter. "Are you kidding? Those are the best kind. In case you don't already know this, our families are similar."

That's what I'm talkin' about.

He pulls up beside my Uncle Bubba's tricked-out truck with the flame decal on the sides, custom fluorescent hubcaps, and contrasting running board with flashing lights. "Nice wheels," Elliot says. "I bet whoever owns that piece of work gets attention on the road."

"That would be my Uncle Bubba, and yes, he does."

Elliot chuckles. "I'm not surprised. If I remember correctly, Bubba has always enjoyed being the center of attention, but I can't say I blame him. My daddy says Bubba was the Pinewood football hero back in the day."

I grin. "And you were the football hero of our day."

He turns to me and places his arm on the back of the seat, letting his hand brush my shoulder. I tingle at his touch.

"Let me tell you a little secret, Shay. As the wide receiver, I made the touchdowns, but if it weren't for the quarterback and the fullbacks, I wouldn't have been able to do a thing. We had an awesome team."

I love the fact that he's giving credit to the other guys on the team. "But you still caught the ball and managed to get to the goal without being tackled."

"Good coaching, a smart quarterback, and the biggest guards in the division helped me do that." He turns away and opens his door. "We need to get out and put this stuff on those tables while there's still room."

It blows me away that Elliot has brought more dishes than me. He has casseroles, pans of meat, and desserts.

"Were you up all night cooking?"

He nods. "Yeah, pretty much. I want to impress your family."

I can't believe he's actually admitting this ... unless he's just saying it for a reason I don't yet know. It's hard for me to believe that someone like Elliot would be so eager to impress my family after all these years.

Elliot pulls out a couple of the smaller casseroles and hands them to me. "We'll have to make several trips."

"That's fine."

Once our arms are loaded up with pans, we make the trek to the tables that I know have been labeled by Mama and some of the other OCD family members. Heaven forbid we put a dessert on the salad table or vice versa. That would rank up there with breaking the Ten

Commandments, which is saying a lot since my family takes God's Word very seriously.

We've barely put everything down when Uncle Bubba approaches, slaps Elliot on the back, and reaches for a handshake. "Hey, guy. I heard you were comin'. So whatcha been up to all these years?"

Elliot shakes my uncle's hand. "Not much. Just working hard."

"Yeah, I hear that's how most people make a livin', but not me. I'd rather let the land do all the work for me. Did you hear about how we struck oil?"

Elliot glances at me, gives me a subtle wink, then turns his attention to Uncle Bubba. "Seems I heard something about that. Congratulations."

Uncle Bubba belts out one of his hearty chuckles that vibrate a room when he's indoors but just sound loud out here. "Somethin' pretty special about an old redneck like me makin' good."

Uncle Irby steps up from behind. "You got that right. Take a redneck and put a million dollars in his hand, and what do you have?" He momentarily pauses, but before anyone has a chance to answer, he delivers the punch line. "A rich redneck with enough money to stock a chewin' backy warehouse for life."

My uncles have a good laugh, while Elliot only smiles. I can tell he's trying hard to be friendly, but he still looks uncomfortable. And I don't think they're funny at all.

I gesture toward Elliot's truck. "Come on. Let's get the rest of the stuff."

"Y'all need any help?"

"Thanks, Uncle Bubba, but I think we've got this."

"No problem. I didn't want to help anyway."

As soon as we're out of hearing distance, I turn to Elliot. "Sorry about that. He can be rather crude."

"Trust me, I understand much better than you realize. Your family doesn't have anything on mine, though I don't think any of my uncles have struck oil on their plot of the family farm." We get to his truck, but before he opens the door, he gestures around the land. "Is any of this yours?"

"What do you mean?"

"This is family land, right?'

"Yes, but most of it still belongs to my grandparents. Some of my relatives have asked for their inheritance early, and they gave it to them."

"Oh." He is silent for a few seconds. "Will some of this be yours eventually?"

Something inside me triggers an alarm. I wonder if he's being so charming because he thinks I might strike it rich from the family land someday.

46
Sally

Sara knocks on my bedroom door, but before I have a chance to tell her to come in, she opens the door. "Are you sure that guy's gonna show up?"

"He said he would." I'm getting mighty nervous. Tom told me he'd be here at ten o'clock, and it's already fifteen after.

"Justin and I will wait a few more minutes to make sure everything's okay."

"No, y'all go on without me. I don't need anyone else making sure everything's okay."

"Why are you acting this way, Sally?" Sara crosses the room and sits down on the edge of my bed.

I glare at her before turning back to the mirror and pretending to fix my makeup. She doesn't need to know how insecure I'm feeling right now. "I'm not acting any way. I just don't like you hovering over me."

Sara laughs. "Not too long ago, you were the one doing the hovering. I couldn't make a move without you right there next to me, telling me what to do and how to do it."

"Nuh-uh."

"You sure did." Sara sighs and smiles at me in the mirror. "But if you want to know the truth, I really didn't mind. In fact, I liked it. At least, most of the time I did." She smiles and sighs. "I knew you did it because you cared for me."

I don't feel like having this conversation now. "Where's Justin?"

"He's out at the truck, trying to get the bugs off the windshield while we wait for your guy." She makes a face. "Those bugs are gross, so I told him I'd wait in here."

Now it's my turn to laugh. "Are the pies ready to go?"

"Yeah, and we picked up some chips and dip. That stuff you made looks amazing. Justin and I both took another look at them."

I stop what I'm doing as a sense of dread washes over me. "I hope you didn't eat any of it."

"Just a bit last night, after you went to bed. Those meatballs were good."

I spin around and glare at her. "You knew I didn't want you to eat those meatballs."

"I'm just kidding, Sally. We took another peek, but I told Justin you'd have a hissy fit if we so much as took one."

I roll my eyes. "Why do you keep doing stuff like that to me?"

"Because you're funny when you get mad." She stands and straightens her top over her jeans. "I hope he gets—"

The doorbell interrupts her. "That's probably him."

"You wait right here. I'll answer the door. He's late, and you don't want him thinking you're waiting by the door."

"I'm not a teenager, silly." I start for the door, but she pushes me back into my room.

"I said I'd answer the door." Sara gives me one of the looks Mama used to give us when she meant business.

The sound of male voices in the living room lets me know Justin has already invited Tom inside. "Now you don't have to."

"Then let's get this show on the road."

Both Justin and Tom look up and smile as we enter the room. And even though Tom is as white-collar as Justin is blue-collar, they seem to be hitting it off quite well.

Justin gestures toward his new friend. "You didn't tell me he's into cars."

Tom shuffles his feet and grins. "My uncle has a dealership, and he used to let me hang out with the mechanics."

"That's how I learned, only not at a fancy dealership. My daddy has a tree in the backyard that gives just the right amount of shade to keep from burnin' up."

Sara grins as she glances at me. "Now that our guys have met each other, let's get going."

"Why don't we all go in my car?" Tom asks. "It's plenty big enough, and it'll be fun."

"Sounds good to me." Justin lifts a questioning eyebrow at Sara. "Okay with you?"

Sara turns to me with the same inquisitive expression. I nod. "Sure."

After we load up the car with what Shay and I prepared and put Sara and Justin's pies and chips in the trunk, we all pile into Tom's very fancy car with the plush seats. "Nice wheels," Justin says. "I bet this vehicle set you back a pretty penny."

Tom glances at me with a half smile. "It wasn't cheap, but I plan to get my money's worth. I'm not into trading cars every other year. I had the last one until it fell apart."

The guys do most of the talking while Sara and I listen and send visual signals via the mirror on my visor. I can tell she's amused. I am, too, but it would be nice to have a conversation we can all enjoy.

After we turn off the main road, I have to give detailed directions, since some of the country roads aren't on his GPS. "You weren't kidding when you said this was out in the boonies," Tom says.

I scrunch my face and look at him. "I didn't say that."

Justin howls with laughter. "I did."

I don't find any humor in that, but I don't say anything else about it. There's no point in voicing my thoughts about my sister's husband's opinion or choice of words.

Tom has brought some things, so the four of us load our arms with the massive amount of food. As we get closer to the crowd that has already formed, Sara slows way down.

Justin stops and turns his head. "C'mon, poky."

"I'm coming." She and I look at each other, and in that instant, I realize she's scared silly to face the rest of the family with her new husband.

I lean over and whisper, "Don't worry. I'll be right here if you need me."

A slight smile forms on her lips, and she nods. "I know."

The instant Aunt Lady spots us, she puts down the towel she's holding and practically runs toward us. "There you girls are. I've been wonderin' if y'all would be here." She makes one of her many faces—this one feigning a blend of joy and exasperation—and looks directly at me. "It's getting mighty late."

Tom starts to apologize, but I stop him with a smile and headshake. There's no point in anyone putting the blame on someone they haven't even met yet.

"We wouldn't miss this for anything." I pause and nod toward my sister. "Would we, Sara?"

Aunt Lady walks over to Sara, places her hand on her shoulder, and glances down at her belly. "Do we have a little one on the way?"

Sara glances down at her shirt. "No, I don't think so. Why?"

Aunt Lady rolls her eyes and shakes her head. "Then why would you run off and get married like you did? Do you realize you've taken away the opportunity for your whole family to see you say, 'I do'?"

"I—"

"But that's okay. Some of us have decided to throw you a combination shower-reception. Then you can throw the bouquet. You can at least do that much for us, can't you?"

"I guess." Sara gives me a helpless look. "But you really don't have to go to all that trouble."

"It's no trouble at all. We're havin' it at my house on account of it being the only place big enough for all the people we plan to invite."

My heart goes out to Sara. I'm not happy about her elopement, but she and I both abhor being the guest of honor at this type of thing. The last time Aunt Lady planned something for us was our surprise "coming out" party after we'd already told Daddy we didn't want to have a formal debut. We'd barely graduated from high school and were still trying to figure out what to do with our lives. Throughout the party, people asked us what we were doing, if we were going to college, whether or not we planned to stay in Pinewood, and if either of us had marriage prospects. It traumatized both of us so much we never even mentioned it after that night.

Aunt Lady continues to jabber on and on about flowers for the occasion and whether or not it should be a formal sit-down dinner or more casual buffet. Justin's eyes keep getting bigger by the moment. I have to stifle a giggle. I've never seen him this scared. Most of the time he wears a blank expression, and this other side of him endears him to me more than I'm happy to admit.

"What kind of flowers do you want in your bouquet?" Aunt Lady asks.

Sara tilts her head. "Do I really need a bouquet?"

"Of course you do. What else would you toss?" Aunt Lady takes hold of Sara's hand in both of hers. "You don't think you'll get away without the bouquet toss, do you? Why, you simply can't leave that out. It's the best part."

"I don't—"

"Yes, you do. We can't disappoint all the young single women in the family, now can we?" She turns to me and winks. "I'm sure Sally will be right up there with all the other girls who are eager to catch the bouquet so they can hook their own prince."

If I didn't know my aunt, I'd never believe anyone would say such a thing. But Aunt Lady has been embarrassing Sara and me—and I'm sure everyone else in the family—since I can remember. I sure hope Tom doesn't hold her against me.

47

Shay

Elliot is more attentive than I ever imagined he'd be. On the one hand, I love having him with me, but on the other hand, I'm starting to question his motives. I'm concerned about a couple of things now. First of all, I don't want him to think that I'm a ticket to wealth, but he'll eventually figure that out on his own. I'm also feeling kind of squirmy about the rather off-putting stares we're getting from some of my cousins, aunts, and uncles.

We pass one of my great-uncles with a crowd of little boys around him. "Looky here, young'uns. I'm gonna put these goobers in this Co-cola, and watch what happens." The instant he drops the peanuts into the liquid, it starts foaming. All the boys make appreciative sounds. My great-uncle leans back in his chair, a self-satisfied look on his face. "Now what do y'all think of that? Pretty nifty, huh?"

Elliot chuckles as he leans down and whispers, "My daddy used to do that."

I look over at him and see that he's still smiling, and now I know what my grandfather meant when he used to say something made his heart smile, because that's exactly what I'm feeling right now.

A strange expression comes over Elliot as he stares off to my right. "Don't look now."

Of course I look. How can I not?

Uh-oh. Aunt Lady has just left Sally and Sara, and is now heading toward us. "Shay, darlin', it's so good to see you here." She turns toward Elliot and flashes her biggest smile. "And you finally brought a man. Isn't he good lookin'?"

"Aunt Lady, you know Elliot Stevens, don't you?"

She makes an exaggerated surprised face, letting me know it's all an act. She knows exactly who he is. "Why, Elliot Stevens, I do declare. I thought you moved away and got married."

He rubs his chin and gives her an awkward look. "I did, but it didn't work out, so I'm back in Pinewood."

"Oh, honey, I'm so sorry. Look at me, stickin' my foot in my mouth and not mindin' my own business." She grins at me. "I'm glad you have Shay here to help you get over your failed marriage." She lowers her voice. "She's gettin' up there in age, and some folks seem to think she might wind up bein' an old maid." She nudges him. "But maybe she's just waitin' for the right man who has his own problems."

She couldn't have said anything worse if she'd planned it. And she probably did. I start to say something, but Elliot squeezes my hand.

"I'm just happy to be here with Shay. I never thought I'd have a chance with her because she's always been one of the prettiest girls in Pinewood, and she's smart, too." He lets go of my hand, places his arm around my shoulders, and grins down at me. "That's a bonus."

For the first time I can remember, Aunt Lady is momentarily speechless, but she recovers quickly. "Well . . . that's nice, Elliot. Why don't you two chat with some of the young people? Did y'all see the twins?"

As soon as she floats off to spread her Lady-like cheer, Elliot chuckles, but he doesn't let go of me. I have to stifle the urge to snuggle closer to him.

I wait until she's far enough away not to hear. I chew on my lip for a couple of seconds. "I guess I am an old maid."

"Don't talk like that. Family members have no idea what they're doing when they give us labels." He gives me another of his appreciative looks. "You are not an old maid."

"Has your family put a label on you?"

He grimaces and nods at the same time. "They used to call me Beast."

"Beast?"

"Apparently I didn't have the best manners when I was little, and I would chase and knock down all my cousins."

I laugh. "I guess you can say you were destined to become a football player."

He laughs, too. "I reckon so. Besides, I get a kick out of people like her. She reminds me of one of my great-aunts."

"She does?"

"Yeah. In fact, all the way down to the fact that she's also a redneck who made it big."

Then it dawns on me. "Are you talking about your great-aunt who invented the pillow that hugs you back?"

"That's the one. Not a single person in the family took her seriously until she bought a cheap, middle-of-the-night TV ad, and that thing started selling like hotcakes. When she started wearing those two-hundred-dollar dresses, all the ladies in the family took notice, but it wasn't until she bought the Ford truck that the men realized she was on to something big."

Now it's my turn to laugh. "Funny how a truck can do that to a man."

"She got my attention, that's for sure." He waves to someone off in the distance. "Your brother and his wife are heading this way."

I glance up and see Puddin' walking toward me like she's on a mission. As soon as she stops, she plants her hands on her hips, gives me a head-bob, and grins. "Hey girl. I hope you don't think you can get away with not giving me a hug." There's something different about her that I can't put my finger on. She extends her arms.

I lean over to give her a hug, and she whispers, "You and I need to talk, but don't say anything to anyone."

When we pull away, she lifts her chin. "So who do you have here? Don't tell me it's Elliot Stevens."

"Okay, I won't." I giggle, something I don't think I've ever done before.

Elliot steps closer to her and extends his hand. "So good to see you, Mrs. Henke."

She lets go of his hand. "Call me Puddin'. Everyone else does."

"Then Puddin' it is." The warmth in his voice soothes me from the inside out, but I'm still not sure about him. "This is some get-together, isn't it?"

Puddin' laughs. "That's a good way of putting it. If you want to know the truth, most of us would rather be somewhere else, but we come here so we don't wind up being the topic of conversation."

I hate to admit this, but she's right. At least, most of the time. I'm not sure how I feel at the moment.

"What did y'all bring?" Puddin' asks. "I want to make sure I try whatever it is. You've always been a good cook, Shay, and your food is much healthier than most." She runs her hands down her sides. "I'm going to have to lose a little of this so my customers will take me more seriously."

Oh, so that's what it is. She's gone from being a bookkeeper to working face-to-face with customers and it obviously agrees with her. I glance over at my brother, who appears rather surly.

"What's going on with you, Digger?" I ask.

He shrugs. "Not much."

Elliot clears his throat. "Are you still with UPS?"

Digger squares his shoulders and nods. "Sure am. Been there for a while now."

"I hear it's a good company," Elliot says.

"The best for delivery service. Our slogan used to be, 'What can brown do for you?' and we still mean it. His puffs his chest so it appears at least half again its normal size.

I pull my lips between my teeth to keep from laughing. My brother has always been proud of his job, and as tempting as it is to crack a sarcastic comment, I would never want to take that away from him.

"Hey, Shay!"

I spin around in time to see Sally strutting toward me with a very attractive man following close behind her. And behind them are Sara and Justin.

"I want you to meet Tom." Sally steps aside as the man I assume is Tom comes forward. "He's in the fashion business."

Before anyone else has a chance to say a word, Puddin' jumps into the conversation. "I'm on the retail side of the business. What are some of the latest trends you're seeing this season?"

Tom grins. "Mostly the latest cartoon characters. I'm in children's apparel."

"Oh." Puddin' slinks back, clearly disappointed. Then she takes me by the arm. "Shay, can I talk to you now? I'm about to pop with some news, and I want to get some advice from you." Her pleading look touches my heart. "Now if the rest of y'all will excuse us." She pauses momentarily. "Oh, Digger, don't forget my photos of the house when you go back to get Jeremy's party hats."

"I thought you had 'em in your phone."

"I do, but it's easier to see them all blown up on paper."

His scowl deepens. At least now I understand his surly expression.

48

Puddin'

"Okay, so here's the deal." I glance over my shoulder to make sure no one else is within listening distance. "Amanda is moving, and I have to buy the store."

"What?" Shay's face scrunches up. "I missed something here. Why do you have to buy the store just because Amanda's moving?"

"Because she doesn't want to run it long distance, she's already put it up for sale, and someone has made an offer." I know I'm talking too fast, but I'm also aware that this family won't give us much time alone. As soon as someone discovers we're away, just the two of us, they'll send a search party.

Shay gives me one of her expressions that let me know she thinks I'm crazy. "Then why can't you work for the new owner?"

"Because the guy is known for cleaning house and starting over with his own people."

"Oh." Shay contorts her mouth. "And you don't want to find another job?"

I groan. "You know that La Chic is much more than just a job to me. It's a calling. It's what I'm meant to do."

Shay smiles. "It's also something my brother has gotten used to." She pauses. "I understand. What can I do?"

"You can help me figure out how to buy the shop. You're good with numbers, and you're the best businessperson I know." She's also the only person I know I can trust.

"Have you asked Amanda how much she wants?"

I shake my head. "No, not yet, because it doesn't matter how much she wants. I simply don't have the money."

"And I gather you haven't discussed this with Digger." She makes it sound more like a question than a statement.

"Are you kidding? There's no telling what Digger might say."

She nods as she places a hand on my shoulder. "Exactly. Puddin', you've been surprised by Digger's reactions in the past. He might just do that again."

"I don't know about this, Shay. It's one thing to have a job there, but a whole other thing to own the place."

"True." Shay chews on her bottom lip for a few seconds before smiling again. There's a twinkle in her eye I've never seen before. "Tell you what. I'll think about it and try to come up with a plan. In the meantime, go have a good time with the family. I know everyone will rave about whatever you brought. They always do."

"Okay." Shay always knows the right thing to say, which is why I'm glad she's my sister-in-law. I have a feeling she'll come up with a solution that I wouldn't ever think of on my own. "Oh, how's everything with Elliot?"

"I wish I knew." Shay scrunches her face before offering one of her forced smiles that I've come to realize is how she keeps from falling apart. She once told me it's all an act when she's in over her head in a social or business situation.

"Tell you what. After we get this thing with the shop settled, I'll see what I can do to help you in the romance department."

Her expression softens, and she laughs. "I'm sure I could use a little help."

Out of the corner of my eye, I see some really cute man coming toward us, his gaze focused on Shay. "Do you know that guy? I don't think I've ever seen him before."

Shay turns her head, then looks back at me, her eyes wide. "He's one of my neighbors."

Okay, now this is getting weird. "Did you invite him?"

"No. He's the youth pastor at Aunt Faye and Uncle Dennis's church. They asked him to come."

"Whew. I was worried you were playing two guys at the same time."

Shay leans back and practically howls with laughter. "Me? I wouldn't have a clue how to play that game."

"I know that. So tell me, what do you think about him?"

Shay's face turns bright red, doing a better job of answering my question than words ever could. "He's nice."

Now I get why she's acting so strange. It's my turn to put my hand on her shoulder. "Oh, I know, sweetie. I know."

"Hi there, Shay."

"Hey, Joe. I'd like to introduce you to my sister-in-law."

After she makes the introduction, he rubs his hands together. "You weren't kidding when you said your family puts out a big spread. I don't think anyone will go home hungry after this."

Before I have a chance to say another word, Elliot and Digger approach, both of them holding big red plastic Solo cups in both hands. Digger gives me mine. "I added extra sugar, just like you like it."

"Did you go to the house for the pictures and hats?"

"I called Trey. He's bringing them."

I don't want to admit that I don't trust Trey to follow through, so I just smile. "Thanks, hon." I turn my attention to Shay and Elliot.

"Wasn't sure if you wanted anything to drink, but I thought I'd take a chance." Elliot hands Shay one of the cups filled with tea. "Digger said you like lemon in yours. I hope I fixed it like you like it." He glances over at Joe, then back at Shay. "One of your cousins?"

Before Shay has a chance to make the introduction, I speak up. Her attraction to Joe is so obvious, I'm sure it'll come out the second she opens her mouth, and I don't think she'd want Elliot to notice.

She gives me an appreciative smile, and I grin right back at her. I love the way she and I can say a lot without words. It's sort of like how I used to imagine husbands and wives communicating, but I've found that's not always the case. In fact, most of the time it isn't. At least not for Digger and me.

Digger lifts his hand and waves. "There's Trey."

I glance up and see him coming toward me with one of my totes, holding it like it might bite him. "Daddy said you wanted this stuff."

As soon as I take the tote, I look inside and see that he brought exactly what I wanted, and I'm surprised. "Thanks, Trey. You did good."

He makes a grunting sound before turning around and walking toward a group of cousins closer to his age. Digger, Elliot, and Joe are talking, and every now and then, Shay speaks up.

I keep an ear open for awkwardness in the conversation, just in case I have to step in and rescue her. It's the least I can do for all the times she's pulled me out of pickles.

Elliot doesn't seem concerned, so I don't think he's aware of the sizzling tension between Shay and Joe. But Shay is still trying to cover up her nerves, so I speak up.

"I have a little album of some photos of our new house." I pull the hot-pink album out of my tote and lift it for all to see. "It's my dream house—the redbrick ranch on a corner lot. It has three whole bedrooms and two full baths."

"I saw it," Marybeth says as she approaches from the side. "It's a quaint little starter home. I'm sure you'll enjoy it until you can afford something nicer."

Deep down, I know that if it weren't for discovering oil on her husband's share of the land, Marybeth wouldn't even be able to afford what she calls a "quaint little starter home," but she still gets my goat. I take a deep breath, count to seven since I can't make it to ten without feeling like I might explode, and turn my attention to Shay's date as I shove the album back into my tote. I can show off later, when that awful, ungrateful woman isn't around.

"Hey, Joe, you mentioned that you brought some cobblers. Which ones are yours?" I point to the dessert table. "Can you show me?"

"Yes, of course." He glances at Shay with a look that melts my kneecaps, so I'm glad I intervened.

On the way to the dessert table, Joe strikes up a conversation. "So how serious is this relationship between Shay and Elliot?"

I don't want to lie and make more of it than I'm aware of, but I also don't want to mess anything up for Shay. So I shrug. "I'm not sure. Maybe you can ask her later."

"I think I will. She's very nice, and of course, it's obvious that she's easy on the eyes." He pauses. "And the most important thing is that her faith seems steadfast."

I like this guy already. Maybe I shouldn't have pulled him away. "I take it you're not in a relationship."

He smiles. "You're a very smart woman." We approach the table, and he points to a peach and a blueberry cobbler. "I made these, and I brought ice cream that's in the freezer over there in the shed."

"I can't wait to try it." I stand there and look around, awkwardness taking over and rendering me incapable of a normal conversation.

"In case you're wondering why I'm not already in a relationship, I might as well let you know that I was engaged until about six months ago. She kept putting off the wedding, until she finally admitted that she couldn't see herself married to a pastor."

"Oh." He obviously recognizes my discomfort, which isn't too difficult, given the fact that I'm not sure what to do with my hands so I'm wringing them. But the fact that he understands the cause blows my mind. Digger never would have been able to do that.

"Most of the time, I don't mind being single," he continues. "But I have to admit there are times when it would be nice to have someone. A person I can call ... well ..." He chuckles. "I'd like some companionship." He laughs. "Man, this is awkward. I'm not sure how to put this."

"Oh, trust me, I understand." I reach out and touch his arm. "You seem like a great guy. I'm sure some woman will realize just how much you have to offer."

"I hope so, but one thing she'll also need to know is that I'll probably never be rich with worldly things."

"The right woman won't care. If she loves you for who you are, it won't even be an issue."

"Thank you so much, Puddin'. Digger is blessed to have you."

Now it's my turn to laugh. "Someone needs to tell him that. I'm not sure he knows."

"He knows, but when the timing is right, I'll say something." He glances over his shoulder toward my sister-in-law. "I think I'll keep my distance today and talk to Shay sometime next week."

"That's a good plan."

After Joe heads off in the direction of Digger's aunt and uncle who invited him, I go back to Shay. She gives me a shy smile and sighs. I know how relieved she must feel.

It's been a mighty long time since I've felt what I think she's feeling at this moment. When Digger and I first got married, our chemistry was sizzling. But now ... well, it's more of a slow simmer. I actually like the way it is now, but I would love a little more heat every once in a while.

"Hey, y'all!" The sound of Aunt Lady's shrill voice and her clapping hands snags my attention. I glance up at the woman with hair that's too red, blush that's too pink, and an outfit that I'm ashamed to say I sold to her. "Bucky and Marybeth have some news they'd like to share, so come on, everyone. Gather 'round."

49

Shay

Elliot leans toward me and whispers, "Any idea what this is all about?"

"No telling." I shake my head. "Aunt Lady has some kind of announcement every year, and it's always something different."

"A lot of your family members look annoyed."

"That's because they are." I give him an apologetic look. "This family has all types."

"Yeah, I've always known that." He gives me a sweet smile that reminds me why I've liked him for as long as I can remember. "But it's strange seeing all of them here in one place."

I hope he doesn't hold some of the people in my family against me. Before I have a chance to tell him that, Aunt Lady starts clapping her hands again. I look up at her, and she has a smile as wide as her face. Her dark-red lipstick is smeared all over her teeth, but I don't think she cares.

"Come on up, Bucky." She reaches for her son's arm, but he yanks it away. His face is bright red, and his wife is glowering at him from a few feet away.

"Just tell us already so we can eat," Uncle Dennis shouts from behind.

Aunt Lady gives up trying to pull Bucky into the circle. "It looks like my son is too shy to tell y'all the good news, so I reckon I must."

"Of course you must," Uncle Dennis says as he approaches her. "Why don't you just tell us and get it over with?"

She cuts a glare in his direction but quickly replaces it with a smile. "I'm sure you all know how delighted Bubba and I were when Gulf States Drilling discovered oil on our property, and then they found even more on the land we gave our kids. Well ..." She turns to Uncle Bubba, and they exchange equally wide smiles before she skims the crowd with her snooty gaze. "Well, Bucky and Marybeth gave them the go-ahead to look some more, and guess what!"

"They found more oil." All heads turn to Uncle Dennis. "Anyone in the family could've told you that would happen. It's no big surprise. There's oil everywhere around these parts."

Aunt Lady appears momentarily frazzled, but she quickly regains her composure. "I bet you they'd find oil on your property if you'd let them drill."

"Of course they would, but I don't care about that," Uncle Dennis replies loud enough for everyone to hear. "I like the land as it is, clean and unblemished. Those rigs are ugly."

Elliot's eyes widen and he gives me an I-can't-believe-this-is-happening look. "This is weird."

"Not really. They do this all the time." I'm surprised that I'm not the least bit worried about Elliot's impression of my family at this moment. If this had happened years ago, I would have wanted to crawl into a hole and never show my face again. But this is my family, and it is what it is.

"Who do you agree with?" he asks.

"I don't know." I shuffle my feet before looking him in the eyes. "I can see both sides. How about you?"

I study his face as he chews his bottom lip. "I reckon I can, too, but it seems wise to think what all you can do with the money if you strike oil."

"But you heard what Uncle Dennis said." I narrow my eyes as I wait to hear what Elliot has to say.

"He could always buy more land with the money from the oil."

"True." His response doesn't hit me well, but I try not to let him know how I feel. "I'm sure everyone has a perfectly good reason for whatever decisions they have to make."

A soft chuckle escapes his lips. "You're so diplomatic, Shay. That's one of many things I like about you."

I try to smile, but I don't feel it in my heart. I'm back to feeling uncomfortable about Elliot now. Some of the things he says are disturbing. Until now, I never saw him as a gold digger, but I'm starting to have my doubts. There is the fact that, in spite of what he keeps saying about not having a chance with me all those years ago, he never really tried that hard. There's a lot to think about, but I'll do that later.

When I glance toward the tables packed with casseroles, salads, pies, cakes, and every other type of food, I see Granny Marge standing at the one holding the meats. She holds up her hands, a sign to get closer so someone can say the blessing before we line up to fill our plates.

Joe steps up from the side. "I've been asked to ask the Lord to bless the food we're about to eat and to give thanks." He opens his arms wide and gestures around. "And it looks like we have a lot to be thankful for because we've been abundantly blessed."

Granny Marge lifts a finger. "Don't forget to pray for my friend Clara. She's still in the hospital."

"Yes, of course." Joe gives her a sympathetic look. "Does she ... I mean, is she terminally ill?"

I brace myself for what I know is coming, and she doesn't let me down. She clucks her tongue and shakes her head. "Joe, honey, we're all terminally ill." She pauses and offers a slight smile. "In fact, not a solitary one of us is getting out of this human condition alive."

"Oh." Joe's face turns bright red. "I didn't mean—"

With a flip of her hand, Granny Marge interrupts. "She's just getting her gallbladder removed, so I think she'll be okay."

"Okay." Joe takes a deep breath and lifts his hands.

A few people chuckle. Elliot whispers, "I know he's clergy, but there's something about him I don't trust."

I blink but don't respond. I'm impressed by how comfortable Joe seems standing in front of my family like this, even though he's never met most of us.

Elliot takes my hand and holds it throughout the blessing. After the "amen," he squeezes my hand and lets go.

"Ready to get some grub?" he asks.

I purse my lips and narrow my eyes. "Better not use that word with some of my aunts. They put a lot of time into preparing this food, and I don't think they'd appreciate having someone call it grub."

"I'm sorry." A look of concern crosses his face. "I have to admit, I'm a little bit nervous. I wasn't sure how people would feel about having me here. Folks in your family don't get divorced, and I know they think something's wrong with me."

He steps forward, picks up two plates, and hands me one.

"Something is wrong with everyone." My tone sounds terse, even to me. I take a breath, slowly blow it out, and try to relax my voice. "We're all sinners, remember?"

"Some more than most, I'm afraid." He points to the array of meats. "I don't know which to choose. Any suggestions?"

"How about a little of all of it? You can come back if you want more."

He gives me an odd look, like he's confused about something, but then he turns around to face the food. "Ladies first."

As we go through the line, I glance up and take quick looks around. When my gaze settles on Joe's, my heart hammers. *Lord, forgive me.*

"Why don't we go sit over there with your brother and his wife?" Elliot says, pointing to a large oak tree with a couple of concrete picnic tables beneath it.

Rather than talk and risk exposing my annoyance with him, I nod, grab a napkin and some plastic flatware, and head straight to the table. Elliot is right behind me.

As soon as we sit down, Puddin' tilts her head, squints her eyes, and slowly shakes her head. "If you boys will excuse us for a couple of minutes, I have something important and very personal to discuss with Shay."

"Again?" I look back at her with curiosity. "I mean, you do?"

She stands. "Yes, I do." The tone of her voice is similar to what she uses with her kids.

"All right, then." I stand up. "I'll follow you."

Puddin' leads the way to another oak tree—one that doesn't have a bunch of people standing beneath it. "Okay, Shay. What gives?"

"What are you talking about?"

"I thought you were thrilled to bring Elliot here, but now that I see you together, you look miserable." She puts her face closer to mine, making it impossible to look away. "Is that the way it is?"

I can't lie to Puddin'. At least not with her looking at me like this. "I'm afraid so."

"What happened?"

"I don't know." I clear my throat, wishing I could say more, but I'm not really sure of anything yet.

"Well, since you don't know, let me take a stab at it."

I blink and meet her gaze again. "Okay."

"There's this crazy chemistry zinging between you and the preacher boy. Is that it?"

I try to stifle my surprise, but she has seen right through me so there's no doubt she'll recognize a lie. "I'm afraid that might be part of it."

She sucks in a deep breath and slowly blows it out. "If it makes you feel any better, he's already asked me about you."

"He has?" I have to hold myself back from showing too much excitement. "What did he say?"

"He asked me if you were in a relationship with Elliot." Puddin' snorts. "This feels so much like high school."

"Hey, Shay!" The sound of a very deep masculine voice behind me snags my attention, so I turn around.

It's Sally and Sara's dad. "Hey, Georgie. Where's Sheila?"

"She's around here somewhere. I got someone here I want you to meet."

I glance at the man walking behind him. He's tall—well over six feet tall—has a little bit of facial hair, is clad in faded jeans, and wears a hat to match his cowboy boots. He almost looks like a caricature of the hero in an old western.

"This here is Dex." George pauses as Puddin' and I get a good look at the man. "And this is my cousin, Shay. I thought the two of you might hit it off."

Dex tips his hat. "How do you do, Shay?"

"Just fine." I have no idea what to do, what to say, or how to act.

He gives me what appears to be a practiced flirty look. "Yes, you certainly are."

"I am what?"

He forces a crooked grin. "Just fine."

Puddin' lets out a groan. I gesture toward her. "And this is my sister-in-law, Puddin'."

"We've met," Puddin says. Without missing a beat, she takes me by the arm and gently nudges me away. "If you'll excuse us, gentlemen, we're discussing something very important. And private."

As we walk away, I overhear Dex talking to Georgie. "She sure don't look like an old maid."

50

Missy

I grab my husband's arm and try to pull him toward the crowd. "Come on, Foster. You can't stand here all by yourself all day."

When he looks at me and yanks his arm out of my grip, I see fear, and my heart melts as I realize it's not stubbornness that almost kept him from coming. "I wish you hadn't made me come, Missy. I'd much rather be home."

"Doing what? Sitting in front of the TV, eating potato chips and that stinky onion dip?" I place my hand on my husband's arm again, only this time I don't try to move him. I feel a tug at my heart as I realize how miserable he is, and the emotion practically makes me speechless. I clear my throat. "Look, Foster, everything's going to be okay. Don't forget that George has worn hearing aids for years."

"I know, but he's part of the family. I'm not."

I let out a grunt. "You know better than that. You became family the second you said, 'I do.'"

"It's still different." His expression turns pouty. "I think I'll just hang out here for a while until everyone else has their food."

"No."

Foster jumps at the sound of my very firm voice. I stand there and wait while he processes the situation, and I can see when it dawns on him that his only choices are cooperating or remaining stubborn . . . and that the second choice comes with consequences. He lowers his head for a few seconds then reaches for my hand. "Okay, but promise you'll stay with me."

In all the years we've been married, I've never seen my husband like this. Even though it's a bit disconcerting, I have to admit that I kind of like having him acting so unsure of himself. It makes me feel important and ... well, motherly.

"Look at all those desserts," he says softly. "Can I have some cobbler?"

I laugh as I see his mischievous grin, but it quickly fades. "You have to eat something nutritious first. Let's start at the salad table."

His frown becomes even more pronounced. "Do I have to?"

"Yes. In fact, you have to take at least two bites of everything before you can go to the dessert table."

He tries to get away with loading up on a so-called fruit salad that's nothing but canned fruit and marshmallows, but I stop him after the first scoop. "Why don't you try some of that tomato-and-cucumber salad?"

We go down the side of the salad table, having the same conversation over and over, until he finally digs his heels in. "This is enough roughage. I'll be spending the rest of the weekend in the bathroom as it is."

"Okay, let's get another plate and get some meat and potatoes," I say. I know he won't balk at that, but I'll have to keep an eye on him to make sure he eats his veggies.

As we load up our second plates, I think about how things have changed between us in such a short time. I never would have insisted on him eating anything a little more than a month ago, but now I feel emboldened. Now that I know he hasn't been intentionally tuning me out, I think there might be hope for rekindling the old loving feeling.

I turn and am starting for the table where Shay and Digger are sitting when Foster clears his throat. I turn around. "What's wrong?"

"Aren't we going to get some of your chili?"

"We have to get bowls, and we don't have enough hands."

He gives me a *duh* look. "Then let's go put this stuff down and come back for it. Tasting some of your chili is one of the main reasons I agreed to come."

I sigh as I realize my husband is sweet-talking me the only way he knows how. And I love him even more for it. I also realize something about myself—that all I need are a few words of affirmation from the man I love.

As we head for the table, Puddin' looks up, waves, and says something to the rest of the people at the concrete picnic table. They all move over to make room for us.

"Hey, y'all," she says. "I've been wonderin' where you were. We saw you for a few minutes, and then you disappeared."

I start to say something about getting lost in the crowd since we're such a big family, when Foster speaks up. "I've been all mopey about these danged hearing aids, but Missy tells me I'm being stupid."

My chin drops. "I never said you were being stupid."

"Not with your mouth, but I could tell you were thinking it." He laughs at himself. "And she's right. Lots of folks wear glasses, and what's the difference? If they help me hear, that's a good thing, right?"

Everyone at the table appears stunned as they nod. Foster has never been this chatty around my family. "Oh, absolutely," Puddin' says. Her voice is quite a bit louder, which I know must bug Foster to no end.

"You don't have to talk so loud now, Puddin'." Foster puts his plates down and points to his ears. "I can hear you loud and clear. I have hearing aids now, remember?"

Her face turns bright red, and her eyes flutter. "Oh, yes, of course. Sorry about that."

"No problem." Foster tips his head toward me and points toward the lineup of slow cookers. "Now let's go get some of the best chili south of the Mason-Dixon."

We're about ten feet from the table when I hear Puddin' call out. "I don't think there's any of your chili left, Missy. Y'all are late gettin' to the Crock-Pot table."

"There'd better be some left," Foster mumbles. "No one makes chili like you."

Puddin' is right. There's not even a smidge of my chili left in any of the Crock-Pots. In fact, it looks like someone licked the inside of a couple of them clean. I glance at all the dials and see that they're still on, so I turn them off and unplug them.

"What are we gonna do?" Foster asks.

"There's more chili in those other pots."

"But I want yours." He pouts again. "I don't want that other cr—"

I stop him. "Don't insult anyone else's chili until you've tried it." I get closer to him and whisper, "You might hurt someone's feelings, so hush now. I'll make you some next weekend if you really want it."

He sighs as he grabs a bowl and scoops half of a ladle of someone else's chili into it. "This doesn't even smell like yours."

Deep down, I'm smiling, but I don't want to let on. "Behave yourself, Foster. We're here to see the family, and the food is just a bonus." As we walk past the dessert table, I see him craning his neck. "Looks good, doesn't it?"

"I think I'll just get mine now." He stops, but I playfully yank his arm.

"Oh, no you don't. You're eating your vegetables first."

"You sound like my mama."

"All mamas sound alike." I nudge him toward our table and follow behind.

Puddin' glances down at Foster's bowl. "I told you there wasn't any left. I heard it was good. You might need to bring more next time."

I nod. "Sounds like a good plan."

"I wanted my wife's chili." Foster starts to pout then looks at me. I shake my head and give him one of those wifely looks.

Puddin' gives him a sympathetic smile. "At least she can make it at home where no one else can get it."

I start to agree with her, but Foster speaks up. "It's not as good at home. I like it better when I get something other people want."

The impact of his comment hits me hard. When I glance over at Puddin', I see it affects her the same way.

As I try to eat, his words ring through my head, and I lose my appetite. Back when Foster and I first met, I was dating someone else. He took a liking to me and pursued me until I stopped seeing that other guy. Now everyone in my family knows my husband has lost interest in me.

I get up before the tears start and take a step toward the old barn that hasn't been used in years. Back when it had chickens and cows, I would go in there and talk to them. They always listened without talking back, and I knew I could count on them keeping secrets.

"Where ya goin', Missy?" Foster gives me a brief glance but quickly turns his attention to his dessert.

"Just over there, to the barn. I heard Grandpa Jay is thinking about knocking it down, so I thought I'd go take another look around for old times' sake."

"Be careful, girl. It's a shambles, and I don't want anything falling on your head. Who'd do my laundry and cook my supper?"

I know he's joking, but it still hurts. And now I understand that it's mostly my fault. I've made life way too easy for him. I have some serious thinking to do, and that's impossible with so many people around. The barn has always been my thinking place.

51

Shay

I almost choke on my pie over Foster's comment. The pain on Missy's face and the slump of her shoulders let me know this hasn't just started. It's deep.

Everyone at the table has grown quiet, even Elliot. I glance at him and see that he's aware of what's going on.

He gives me a brief smile. "Would you like to see if there's any more dessert left?"

I nod. "Sounds good."

We're halfway to the dessert table when Elliot clears his throat and stops. "I'm not sure what just happened back there, but it looks to me like your cousin and her husband have some issues."

"Ya think?" The instant those words leave my mouth, I realize how sarcastic I sound. "Sorry, but I feel bad for Missy."

"So do I." He squeezes his lips together as he shakes his head. "Contrary to what people might think, not all men are pigs."

"Who said they were?"

"No one." He glances over his shoulder toward the table we just left. "I'm not even sure Foster is, but one thing I do know is he could use some lessons on how to treat a lady."

"I agree."

"And another thing." He gives me a sweet smile. "I'm not sure what's going on between us, but I sense a change. I thought you might be interested in seeing how things go between us, but …" He shrugs. "I'm not so sure now."

I sigh. "I'm sorry, Elliot. I've been distracted lately."

Elliot tips his head toward a crowd of my relatives listening to the youth pastor. "Is your distraction named Joe?"

I want to tell him no, that it's more complicated than that. But I can't, in all honesty, make such a statement. So I shrug. "Maybe a little, but there are other things going on in my life."

"I understand." He gestures toward the dessert table. "And believe it or not, I'm fine with that. I've discovered that it's best to wait for things to happen rather than rush them. If you need to get to know him and compare us before you decide who you like better, I'd rather you do it now instead of later."

"Compare you?"

He nods. "I have to put myself in your shoes, and I assume you would want the better of the two guys."

"That makes me sound terrible."

"No, it doesn't," he says. "I'm just being honest and real, which is the best way to start off in a relationship."

Now I'm more confused than ever. I never expected to have this conversation with Elliot, and now that I have, I find his pragmatism odd but appealing.

"Shay, I'm attracted to you, but there is one thing I need to add. Even though I want you to be sure about your feelings, I'm still human."

I'm not sure exactly what point he's trying to make, but I have a pretty good idea. He's not willing to wait around forever. And I get that.

The crowd around Joe starts laughing hysterically. Elliot chuckles. "Sounds like he's charming the socks off your family."

"It does, doesn't it?"

"I wish he wasn't such a nice guy, but I have to admit, I like him, too. I think he and I could be pretty good friends if it weren't for ..."

This whole conversation keeps getting stranger. I'm still attracted to Elliot, but I have to admit I'm confused. One minute, Elliot's the sweetest guy I know. Then someone brings up the oil on the property and I get that strange feeling he's more interested in my family's assets than he is me. Granted, he's never come out and said a single word about any nefarious intentions, but the thought continues to hover in the back of my brain that he might be interested in something other than my wonderful personality and intellect.

"Do you want to go see what's so funny over there?" Elliot turns his head in a teasing manner as he gestures toward the crowd.

I'm dying to see what's going on, but I am with Elliot, and I don't want to be one of *those* dates. "Do you?"

He laughs. "Sure, let's go check it out." He holds out his hand, palm up. "After you, m'lady."

Joe does a double take as we approach, and then he smiles. Directly at me! I sort of smile back, but my lips have started twitching from nervousness. My insides churn as Elliot gently guides me toward the group.

"Come on over, you guys. I was just about to tell another story."

Elliot leans down and whispers, "He said, 'you guys.'"

"What's wrong with that?"

"You're not a guy." He smiles and wiggles his eyebrows. "Your friend Joe may not have noticed, but I certainly have." I can't help but see the look of admiration in his eyes.

I feel a flutter of flattery floating through my body. I know, I know. It's just words and a look. But I've never had someone act this way over me, and I like it.

Elliot gently positions me in front of him so I can get a better view. He's acting rather odd for someone who is worried I'll like another guy more than him, but maybe that's just the southern gentleman coming out. Based on what I know, mamas work so hard to drill it into their male offspring, it runs deep and seeps out of the pores, even to the detriment of the guys.

Joe widens his smile momentarily before beginning his new story about something that happened at his former church. As he delivers one punch line after another, people chuckle. But I don't. There's something about his stories that either don't ring true, or he's telling stories that the subjects might not want people to know about. In fact, some of his comments sound mean. The more he talks, the lower my interest in him dips.

Elliot takes advantage of a brief break while Joe sips some sweet tea. "He's funny, isn't he?"

I frown. "I'm not sure."

He feigns surprise. "You're not sure? Then why are all these folks laughing?"

My frown deepens as I look Elliot in the eyes. "Honestly? I don't know."

"So tell me, Shay. Why don't you think he's funny?" I can see in his eyes that he knows. In fact, that's probably why he wanted me to hear Joe's stories.

"He might not be as nice as I thought he was."

Elliot puts his arms around my shoulders and gives me a squeeze. "That's my girl. You're such a kindhearted person, I can't imagine you ever thinking someone else's troubles are funny."

"You knew this would happen, didn't you?"

He smiles and gives me a clipped nod. "I confess, I had a feeling it might."

"Why didn't you just tell me?"

"Because there are some things a person needs to know firsthand." He lets go of my shoulder and takes me by the hand. "I also have a feeling there are other things on your mind, so why don't we talk about it soon and you can tell me what's going on."

52
Sally

I am so glad I brought Tom to this family thing, but I'm getting annoyed. Justin won't stop talking to him, and he's my date.

My sister and I are sitting on the edge of the tabletop while Justin and Tom talk sports. They've pretty much ignored us for the past half hour.

Sara turns to me with a humongous smile on her face. "Isn't it nice that they get along so well?"

"Just peachy."

"What?" Her joyful expression has turned into a look of disbelief. "I thought you'd be thrilled our guys can be friends."

"I don't know if he's *my* guy." I lift my hands in frustration. "And as long as Justin's around, I'll never know."

"Tell me something, Sally. Why don't you like Justin?"

"Who says I don't like him?"

"Trust me. I know you better than you know yourself. You dislike my husband with a passion."

"I do not." Really, I don't. It's just that, not only has he taken my sister away from me, he's now doing the same thing with the guy I've been wanting to get to know for a long time.

Sara slides off the tabletop and brushes off the seat of her jeans. "Tell you what, sis. I'll see if I can pull Justin away so you can have some time with Tom. Maybe sometime next week we can have a family meeting."

"Family meeting?" I scrunch my nose. "You hated it when Mama and Daddy used to have those."

"I'm an adult now. I understand the value of open communication."

"No," I remind her. "They had those family meetings to tell us it was their way or the highway."

"Whatever. I think it's time for the three of us to discuss our feelings and figure out a way to get along. There's no point in any of us having hard feelings. Justin and I are married, and I plan to do whatever it takes to stay that way."

I know she's referring to my bad attitude when she mentions hard feelings, but I can't help it. She didn't even bother to ask how I felt about her marrying Justin. And sometimes I wonder if she had time to think about her own feelings before taking the plunge.

I get off the table and resist the urge to brush off the seat of my shorts. Now that Sara has decided to move on with her life, I think it's time for us to stop being so much alike. I can't help the fact that we look exactly like each other, but I don't have to do everything she does. I might even cut my hair soon.

"We can have the talk, but I can't promise I'll feel any different about him."

She shrugs. "Suit yourself. I can't control your feelings any more than you can control mine."

Before I can say another word, she walks up to Justin, whispers something in his ear, and walks away with him, hand in hand.

Tom stands there looking at them, then turns to me with confusion. "What just happened?" he asks.

"I think my sister wants to spend some time with her new husband."

"Oh." He slaps his forehead. "I forgot about them being newlyweds."

He clearly forgot about the fact that he's my date as well, but there's no need to remind him now that Sara has taken Justin out of the picture. "Do you want to get more food?"

Tom rubs his belly. "If I thought I could fit anything else in here, I would. It's all so good." He grins. "Your family has a lot of great cooks."

"Everyone brings their best dish here. They like to show off."

"I like your family. Mine is okay, but they're scattered all over the country, and they don't bother organizing anything like this."

"But you still have your immediate family. You get to see them at work every day, don't you?"

He nods in a half-hearted way. "Most days, but my sisters are getting tired of the family business, and sometimes I find myself doing everything without them."

"At least you have job security," I remind him.

"True, but to be honest with you, if I had my choice of jobs, it wouldn't be in the children's apparel field." He steps closer, takes my hand, and holds it between both of his. "One thing I do believe, though, is the Lord has me there for a reason." He widens and then narrows his eyes as if trying to tell me something without saying it.

"Probably."

"I've always wondered what that reason might be." He squeezes my hand and gives me a warm smile.

"One of these days, I'm sure you'll figure it out."

"I think I might have just figured it out. He wanted me to meet you." He opens his arms wide. "And your family."

As much as I've wanted to get to know him, I'm not so sure he's right. But I don't dare say that because I don't want to make him feel bad. Yeah, I like him okay, but he doesn't leave me feeling all giddy inside like I thought he might.

"Why don't we go over there and chat with your other cousins?" He points toward the picnic table where Puddin', Digger, Shay, and the guy she's with are sitting.

"Okay."

I'm not sure what to say to him now that I know he isn't interested in the children's apparel business. Actually, I'm not either, but I'll probably continue making hair bows because it beats working at the bank.

Puddin' grins as soon as we get close to the table. "Hey, y'all. I wondered where you disappeared to."

Digger doesn't even look up, but Shay greets us, too. Her date stands and extends his hand to Tom.

"Where's your sister?" Puddin' asks.

I can tell she's not sure which twin I am, even though I'm clearly not the married one, so I decide to help her out. "Sara and Justin went off somewhere to talk. Mind if we join you?"

Shay makes a gesture toward the other side of the table. "Have a seat. Looks like your meatballs were a hit. They practically flew off the tray."

"I know, right? Thank you so much for helping me with them."

"You didn't have to tell anybody," Shay says.

"It wouldn't be right to take full credit for them." I turn to Tom. "My sister and I never knew how to cook until we bought Shay's condo."

He gives me a curious look. "I'm sure that makes sense on some level."

Shay laughs. "If you hang out with this family long enough, the weirdest stuff will start to make sense."

"I think I'd like that." Tom gives me a look that makes me wonder what I've gotten myself into, and how I can break it to him that I'm just not feelin' it. At least not now.

53

Shay

I can tell Sally isn't as into Tom as he is her, but I see the potential if she'd just relax. Part of the problem might be that she still can't let go of her anger toward Justin for taking Sara away from her. I learned that the bond between twins is exponentially more powerful than most sibling relationships, but I'm not so sure Justin realizes that yet.

Elliot gently rests his arm around my shoulder—something that seems natural for him but odd for me. I've never been one to show affection in public. Or anywhere, for that matter, since I've never been in a long-term relationship. I wonder if having been married gives him a more relaxed manner when it comes to touching.

I turn to him and grin. The corners of his eyes crinkle as they always do right before he smiles, and that feeling I used to have in the pit of my stomach when I watched him from a distance returns. It's sort of a roller-coaster free-fall sensation that radiates throughout my body.

It's weird how I've gone back and forth with my feelings toward Elliot in such a short time. When I saw him in the grocery store after all those years, it was like we'd never left high school. Then I started having doubts, until he gave me one of his looks. My doubts returned, and then we heard Joe talking about the people from his old church. One thing I hate is gossip, even when it's insignificant or if no one in the audience knows the person. It's just wrong in my book. And I'm happy to know that Elliot feels the same way.

The sound of Tom's laughter gets our attention. When I glance over at him, I see that he's laughing, while Sally appears disinterested. Yeah, this thing between them has gone south really fast.

Elliot pulls me closer and whispers, "Sally is clearly not into her date."

"I've noticed. I wonder what happened."

He pulls his arm back and shrugs. "Who knows about matters of the heart? Maybe something bad happened that we don't know about, or maybe nothing happened, and she's just not interested." He pauses and gives me a different look—one I used to see him give whatever cheerleader he was dating back in high school. "Could be that the chemistry between them is off."

"Well, I'm—" I'm interrupted by a loud *ka-boom*!

"What the—" Foster glances over his shoulder in the direction of the sound. "It's the old barn." A few more popping noises echo across the field, and I hear the crackling sound that is clearly fire making its way through the barn. Foster hops to his feet and takes off running. "Missy's in there!" His voice is frantic. "I gotta get my wife! Missy's in there!"

Elliot's eyes widen as he lets go of me and jumps up. "I'm gonna help find her." Without another word, he takes off after Foster. They reach the barn, and without a second's hesitation, Foster flings open the door and they run right in.

My body is numb, but my heart pounds with fear as I squeeze my eyes shut and beg for safety for Missy, Foster, and Elliot. When I open my eyes, I see giant flames licking the side of the barn.

A couple other guys in the family run toward the barn. I look over at the area where Joe was holding court and see him staring off toward them, but he doesn't make a move in that direction. My opinion of this youth pastor has taken a second nosedive, and I know he'll never be able to redeem himself in my eyes.

Someone must have called the fire department because I hear the sound of sirens approaching. One of my uncles and a couple of my cousins are on the Pinewood Volunteer Fire Department, so I figure it must have been one of them since they got here so fast.

An ambulance pulls up behind the single fire truck, and several first responders pile out. "Anyone in the barn?" one of the paramedics asks.

"My cousin Missy went in a little while ago," I say. "And a couple of guys went in after her. I'm not sure if anyone else was in there."

The paramedic, a young woman I've seen around town a couple of times but don't know by name, directs some of the other emergency people before she takes off toward the barn. She looks to be no taller than five feet nothing, but I have no doubt she can handle whatever she encounters. Some people exude competence and authority, and she's definitely one of them.

Elliot and Foster come walking out from behind the barn with Missy between them, her arms slung around their necks, her face bleeding and her outfit ripped in a few places. The expression on Foster's face lets me know he'll need a paramedic's attention as soon as his wife is tended to. I'll never forget the look of shock in his eyes.

Once the men turn Missy over to the paramedics, I can tell Elliot is taking charge by the way he takes Foster by the arm and leads him to another one. He takes off running back toward the barn, where the firefighters are doing their best to control the blaze.

Mama walks up to me, her face filled with concern. "Anyone know what happened?"

The next voice I hear is Grandpa Jay hollering at Julius and Brett. "What in the Sam Hill do you young'uns think you're doing? Someone coulda been killed in that barn."

Julius turns away, but Brett's face is shrouded in fear as his chin trembles. "I didn't think—"

"I know you didn't think, boy, and that's why this happened." Grandpa Jay takes both boys by the arm and drags them toward the double-wide, where Granny Marge is standing at the door. "We've got some talkin' to do."

Julius shakes his head. "But—"

"No buts, young man. You're comin' with me."

A look of fear washes over Julius's face. "Mama?"

"Your mama can't get you out of this one, Julius." Grandpa Jay's face tightens even more. "But I'll give you back to her after I'm done with you."

I shake my head, but before I can get a word out, Marybeth storms past us. "I knew if Julius hung out with Digger's young'uns, something like this would happen."

"Like what?" Mama asks.

Marybeth ignores the question as my cousin Bucky approaches. "You were supposed to have a talk with Julius."

"I did."

"And why was he hanging out with that low-class hoodlum?" Marybeth plants a fist on her hip. "You know those Henke boys are a bad influence."

Out of the corner of my eye, I catch sight of Puddin' storming toward us, her nostrils flared. "Hold it right there, Marybeth. Who are you calling a bad influence?"

"Your children. They're wild and not the kind of kids I want influencing my sweet boy."

"Well, I just happen to know that sweet boy of yours got caught smokin' behind the elementary school three weeks ago."

"Where did you hear that?" Marybeth asks.

"From Patty Anderson."

"Her kids are as bad as yours."

I step between the wives of my brother and cousin and carefully push them away from each other. "Ladies, this isn't the time or place to start laying blame on anyone's kids. We need to make sure everyone is okay."

"Julius is probably in that trailer cryin' his precious little heart out. That boy is so tenderhearted, he can't stand the thought of hurting anyone."

"Oh, give me a break." Puddin' tries to get past me, but I block her again. "If you keep this up, you'll wind up bailin' sweet little Julius out of jail someday."

Marybeth narrows her eyes. "Not before I see you sittin' in court waitin' on a verdict for Brett."

"Trust me, as soon as Grandpa Jay gets done with him, Digger will make him wish he was never born." Puddin' makes a sour face. "And why aren't you with your sweet little Julius, givin' him some mama-love, if he's so precious and tenderhearted?"

54

Puddin'

I've never told anyone before, but I don't have much use for Marybeth. She might be married to one of Digger's favorite cousins, but she thinks she's too good for the family just because they struck oil. I don't hate many people, but I do despise snobs. All they do is try to suck the joy out of anyone they think is beneath them.

To top things off, she thinks that when her young'uns do bad stuff, it's someone else's fault. If she doesn't stop defending them, there's no telling where they'll wind up.

Of course, I'm mad as all get-out with my son for doing such a stupid thing. Why would anyone think it's okay to bring a box of firecrackers into a barn and light the entire thing at one time? I was ready to go pull his eyebrows out as soon as I heard he did it, but Digger insisted on doing it himself.

As soon as Digger's grandfather finishes with the boys, I'm beside my boy in a flash, only I'm not offering support. Instead, I'm hollerin' my head off, making all kinds of threats that involve his ability to have children if he lives to be a man, saying things I'm sure the good Lord doesn't like.

I manage to get one smack on my son's behind before Digger takes me by the shoulders and pulls me away. Tears stream down my face as I continue yelling. Brett might have a good six inches on me, but I've never seen him look so scared as he did when I first went after him.

Digger tells me he doesn't want me anywhere near Brett because I'm too emotional for something like this. He's probably right. I mean, what mama wouldn't be emotional when her son lights a barn on fire and nearly kills someone?

I know my husband, so I'm not worried he'll do anything to seriously hurt our child. He's told us some stories about his shenanigans when he was a kid, and what Brett did pales in comparison to a lot of it. The big difference is that no one ever got hurt on account of Digger's stupidity—unless, of course, you count his backside after his grandpa got ahold of him.

"Is there anything I can do for you?"

I glance up and see Shay standing beside me with a look of compassion on her face. "Nah, I'm fine. I'd like to be alone for a few minutes, though, if you don't mind."

"Of course." She pats me on the shoulder. "I'll be nearby if you need me."

I lower my head, but I can still see her walking away with Elliot. She seems happy with him, but I can tell there's some hesitation in her actions with him.

My sister-in-law is one of the kindest people on earth. Too bad she has never found the right guy to enjoy life with. I like Elliot, but I know her family won't take kindly to her having a relationship with a divorced man. Even Digger has made some comments. I've had to remind him that everyone makes mistakes, so he needs to let his sister live her own life and fall in love with a man who's right for her.

I'm relieved to hear that Missy is going to be just fine. She was on the other side of the barn, near the back door, when the firecracker bomb went off, so she managed to get out before it finished popping. She did get hit by some of the wood that flew through the barn, and apparently she has some mild lacerations on her face and arms. Her clothes are ruined, so I make a mental note to help her pick out something new at La Chic.

About ten minutes later, a sheriff's department cruiser pulls up as close to the barn as it can get, and the deputy gets out. I know he's here to talk to my son and Julius, and I'm all for it. My son needs the fear of the law right now.

I start to walk over to the newer barn to see what's going on with Digger and Brett, but they come out before I get there. "I've got this covered, Puddin'. Let me handle it."

"But I—"

"You heard me." His voice is firm. "Puddin', you're in no shape to deal with this. Besides, I feel responsible for not paying closer attention to my son."

I nod. "Okay, but if you need me, I'll be right here."

"Speaking of sons, where's Jeremy?"

"One of your aunts took him away so he wouldn't have to see all this commotion."

Digger walks Brett over to the deputy, and I watch as they talk. It's obvious Brett feels awful, based on the way he's hanging his head. Digger speaks a little bit, and every once in a while, I see Brett open his mouth. His cheeks are flushed, and his hair looks like he's been through a wind tunnel.

After a few minutes, the officer says something to Digger, who backs away. Elliot joins him, and they say a few words. I sure wish I knew what's going on.

"Oh, for cryin' out loud," Marybeth hollers as she approaches. "What's the cop doing here? You'd think no one ever pulled a prank in this town before." She storms off toward the deputy, her arms flailing every which way, and the shrillness of her voice echoes over the crowd.

Shay magically appears beside me. "Don't say anything, Puddin'. You don't need to get in a fight you can't win."

"I know, but it's hard."

Elliot approaches my other side. "If it makes you feel any better, your son is cooperating with the deputy."

I blink. "What about Julius?"

"Not so much." Elliot glances at Shay, who nods, then looks at me again. "His mama told the deputy that he wouldn't talk without his lawyer."

"What teenage boy has a lawyer?" I shriek.

Elliot nods. "My thoughts exactly. It looks like they're finished with Brett, and from what I gather, he's free to go home. The officer says he suspects the punishment there will be much more severe than anything the sheriff's department is allowed to do."

"So they're getting off?"

"I didn't say that. Both boys still have to go to court, and I wouldn't be surprised if they're sentenced to some sort of community service."

Shay looks back and forth between Elliot and me as silence falls over us. There's no telling what she's thinking, but I sure hope she doesn't think my young'uns are bad eggs. I've spent quite a bit of time trying to drill the importance of being good citizens into their heads. We go to church every Sunday, and I make them do work for others every single chance I get. We've worked at the Interdenominational Christian Food Bank in Hattiesburg, helped build houses for the Habitat program, and served meals at a couple soup kitchens. Brett is the only one of my children who has never complained about any of it.

Granted, Trey and Hallie have given me plenty to worry about in the past. Trey got caught up with a bunch of boys who liked to drag race in Hattiesburg. I talked to him until I was blue in the face, and Digger threatened him to within an inch of his life. So he left home and said he was never coming back. That ended when one of his friends got in a serious accident and became a paraplegic.

Hallie went through a phase of sneaking out with some new friends I never would have approved of. She was a little more difficult to handle because everything she did happened after Digger and I went to bed. However, Digger ended that by sleeping in his rocker-recliner. One night, he caught her tiptoeing through the house. She didn't know he was there because it was dark. When he grabbed her by the arm, her scream was loud enough to wake the neighborhood. And Digger took it to the next step by going outside and embarrassing her in front of her friends. She told us we ruined her life when they quit hanging out with her, but within a week, she was back to doing things with her youth group at church. What still blows my mind is that her grades never dropped, in spite of all her shenanigans.

Jeremy is still too young to do any of this stuff, but I reckon I need to be prepared for anything. Even though he has a sweet disposition now, we know how quickly things can change.

"Are you okay, Puddin'?" Shay asks. "You're being awful quiet."

I swallow hard and nod. "I'm just thinking."

"Don't forget, I'm here if you need me. I don't have much experience with kids, but I sort of remember being one."

Elliot nods. "Same here. Sometimes it takes someone other than a parent to get through to kids."

"Thanks, y'all." I manage a smile. "I hope you were right about the community service. I think hard work is the best way to keep young'uns from getting in trouble."

55

Shay

I can actually imagine Brett doing service for others since Puddin' had him working on a Habitat for Humanity project. But Julius? Not so much. His parents spoil him so much, I don't think he has a clue about helping the unfortunate. I sure hope their lawyer doesn't get him off. Doing something for others will be good for the pampered, rich kid with parents who don't seem to understand true values.

"Has anyone seen Granny Marge or Grandpa Jay?" I shield my eyes and look around.

"They're in their mobile home," Elliot says. "You might want to go see about them."

"Yeah, I think I will."

"Want me to go with you?" He puts his hand on my shoulder as he looks into my eyes.

"I don't think so. There's no telling how they're doing."

"Oh, trust me, your grandparents have seen a lot. I have no doubt they're handling it all just fine." He makes a face. "This sure did turn out different from how I expected."

I feel bad for Elliot. "If you don't want to hang around . . ." I pause and watch for a reaction. "I'll understand if you want to leave. I can get a ride home with someone."

"Don't even say such a thing." He squeezes my shoulder. "Why don't you go see about your grandparents? I'll be right here."

I'm touched by his tenderness, but his comment about the use of the family land keeps popping into my mind. It's hard to get past that.

On the way to the house, I say a brief prayer that I'll have clarity. And before I step inside, I pray that my grandparents aren't a couple of basket cases.

I have to blink a couple of times when I walk inside. Mama is sitting on the sofa, and Grandpa Jay is telling her a story that has her and Granny Marge laughing.

"What's so funny?"

Grandpa Jay turns to me. "I was just tellin' your mama about the time me and some of the boys I used to play with set the outhouse on fire. Daddy gave us a whuppin' I'll never forget."

I'm not sure what to think about this. All my life, I've seen Grandpa Jay as a pillar of perfection—or at least as perfect as humanly possible. He's never raised his voice or acted in any way that goes against his faith when I'm around. He works hard and appreciates all of his blessings, and he never hesitates to thank the Lord for everything. Granny Marge is the traditional female version of him—nurturing, working hard, keeping a clean house, and bringing up all of their children to be God-loving people. Some of their grandkids ... well, that's obviously a different story.

"Missy called from the hospital," Granny Marge says. "She has some cuts, but they're not too deep."

"That's a relief. It could have been so much worse." I turn to Grandpa Jay. "Someone could have been killed."

"Oh, I know that. But no one was, so let's consider it a blessing. The Lord was looking out for everyone."

I'm surprised by how coolheaded my grandfather is over what looks to me like a serious situation. "Anyone know what Missy was doing in the barn?"

"Nope." Grandpa Jay shakes his head. "She knows we've been planning to take that barn down because one of the rafters fell and the rest of them are loose. It was ready to collapse anyway. I'm sure that's probably why she was standin' so close to the back door."

I remember watching her take off with the paramedics. She looked like an emotional mess, so she probably wasn't thinking clearly.

"Those boys will be just fine as long as their mamas and daddies make them suffer sufficiently," Grandpa Jay continues. "When you inflict pain, you need to feel pain in some way, or you don't have a good understanding of how bad it can be, especially at their age." He shakes his head. "It's a wonder anyone lives through the teenage years."

"So you're saying, 'an eye for an eye.'"

He gives me a clipped nod. "Exactly. Shay, you've always been a smart girl, and I don't remember you ever doing anything bad. I bet your mama's proud of you."

Before I can speak up, Mama reaches for me and pulls me closer. "You bet I am. My girl has never given me a lick of trouble, even when she was a teenager. Now Digger ..." Mama shakes her head and clicks her tongue. "That boy is a whole other matter. I'm just glad he's all grown up now, but I hope he gets a grip on his young'uns. That Brett is at such a formative age, and if he keeps hanging out with—"

Grandpa Jay cuts her off with one of the looks he's known for. "Remember there were two of them, Irma. You have to be careful talkin' about kinfolk like that. Especially young'uns."

"I know, but—"

"You don't want Julius's mama talkin' about Brett like he's the bad influence, now do you?"

"No, of course not." Mama's lips tighten.

"Then don't be talkin' about her young'un like there's something wrong with him, other than the fact that he's nothin' but a child in a man's body. I think us grown-ups tend to expect too much from someone who hasn't had enough life experience to understand some of the facts as we know them."

I remember that I have a date out there waiting for me. "I just wanted to check on y'all to make sure you were okay. I'm sure Elliot wonders what's going on."

"You best get back to him then," Grandpa Jay says with a chuckle. "He seems like a good boy."

"He's divorced," Mama says. "I don't know if Shay should be seein' a divorced man."

"Oh, come on, Irma. People make mistakes. How would you feel if Shay was the one who had a bad marriage she had to get out of and someone held it against her?"

"I wouldn't know." Mama lifts her chin in a prideful way. "My kids aren't divorced."

Grandpa Jay tilts his chair back and lets out another hearty laugh. "You got a good point there, but don't forget that you have to get married before you get divorced. Let Shay have some fun seeing whatever man meets her fancy." He stops smiling and tips his head toward me. "As long as he believes in our almighty Savior and commits his life to Him, she can even marry him."

Mama's eyes almost pop out of her head. "You're not talkin' marriage, are you, Shay?"

I glance at Grandpa Jay and see the mischievous twinkle in his eyes. He's clearly pulling Mama's chain. "Not yet."

"Are you ... I mean, do you think—?"

I shake my head. "We've only seen each other a few times, so don't worry."

Granny Marge speaks up. "Your grandpa and I will be ready for the reception if you do, thanks to the dance lessons y'all gave us."

Grandpa Jay groans. "Don't rush things, Marge."

Since I haven't had any long heart-to-heart talks with Elliot yet, I don't want to speak on his behalf about his beliefs or intentions. Instead, I make my way to the door. "If y'all need me, I'll be around for another half hour or so."

Mama turns around and gives me a sad look. "Thanks for checkin' on us. I'll be out there in a little while to see how Digger and Puddin' are holdin' up."

Once I step back outside, I take a look around at the crowd that hasn't diminished as much as it usually would have by this time. My gaze settles momentarily on Joe. He gives me a thumbs-up sign, and I smile. Then I shield my eyes and look around to find Elliot.

"Looking for someone?"

I jump and turn toward the voice behind me. It's Elliot, sitting in a rocking chair on the porch Grandpa Jay and Uncle Bubba built. My heart starts to do that flippy thing it did before I had doubts about him.

56
Missy

I'm sitting here at the hospital listening to my husband tell me how scared he was that he might have lost me. "I love you, Missy." That's like the zillionth time he's said this.

Who is this man? In all the years we've been married, I don't think I've heard him say, "I love you," as much as he has in the past hour.

"I thought I lost you." His red-rimmed eyes remind me that, when I first spotted him right after the blast, he was crying. "It's all my fault that you were even in the barn. Missy, will you please forgive me for not being as good a husband as you deserve?"

I place my hands on either side of his face. "I don't want you to blame yourself."

"I have to. The only reason you were in the barn was because I was acting like such a—" He cuts himself off, letting me know he's willing to work on his language. "I'll make it up to you." He straightens up. "Starting tonight, I'll help you around the house, and you can pick the restaurant next time we eat out."

In spite of the fact that the lacerations on my face still sting like crazy, I laugh. "Have you ever vacuumed the floor?"

He chews on his lip as a thoughtful expression washes over his face. "I think I might have a time or two. I'm sure I'll mess up, but I can learn."

"Would you mind doing that for me?"

"I'll do anything for you." He gives me a tender look. "You may not realize this, Missy, but I would have done anything for you before this happened."

I blink and swallow hard. As I look my husband in the eyes, I realize how blind I've been to the love we have. I kept seeing the things that were wrong with him and ignoring his good qualities.

He might even do a terrible job at helping out around the house, but I now realize I need to let him try. It'll make him more invested in the marriage, and once he gets good at it, I'll have better feelings about him. It's clear to me now that a lot of what angered me was partly my fault because I expected him to read my mind.

"Where do you want to go tonight?" he asks as he takes my hand and kisses the back of it.

"Home. I'm exhausted."

"Are you sure you don't want me to take you someplace special?"

"Positive." I wave my hand in front of my face. "It would take more makeup than I own to get ready for dinner out."

"You look beautiful to me."

My heart melts. I think he really believes that.

"I'll buy you whatever you need."

"Please, Foster, let's just go home as soon as the doctor releases me. If you want to go back out and pick up some carryout for supper, that'll be good."

"Whatever you want, Missy."

My cell phone rings, so I glance at it. "It's Mama," I say. "I need to take this."

He backs away. "Go right ahead. I'll go talk to the nurses. Let me know when you're done."

I nod and give him a little wave as I put the phone to my ear. "Hey, Mama."

"I'm on my way to the hospital. I just wanted to make sure you're still there."

I stifle a groan. I'm not in the mood to see anyone but my husband, especially Mama, who'll go on and on about the miscreant young'uns. "They're releasing me soon, so I'll probably be gone by the time you get here."

"Then I'll go to your house."

"Can you wait until tomorrow? I'm really tired tonight."

"Then why don't I bring you some food? I know that self-centered husband of yours won't do anything."

"Mama, please don't do this. Foster is taking care of everything."

"Are you sure?" I hear the doubt in her voice, and I'm not surprised. "I'm your mama, and I have your best interests at heart, unlike your—" Mama stops herself, and I'm glad she does. I've always had to apologize for Foster with my parents, and I'm totally not in the mood for that, especially now that I've finally figured out I've always been part of the problem.

"Can you come over in the morning? I'll make a pot of coffee and we can talk then."

"Okay. I'll stop at the bakery and get some of your favorite carrot bran muffins."

After we hang up, I lean around and make eye contact with my husband. He says something to the medical people before coming back to me. One of the nurses rolls her eyes when his back is to her, so I quickly look away so she doesn't know I saw that.

He leans down to look me in the eyes. "What did your mama want?"

"She wants to come here, but I told her we'll be leaving soon."

"Do you want to invite her and your daddy to have supper with us?"

He's still trying to prove himself, and that touches my heart in a way it wouldn't have before the barn incident. He and Daddy don't get along at all. Never have and, I suspect, never will.

"No, I'm too tired tonight. I just want to relax and go to bed early."

"Then let's see about getting you outta here." He turns to go back to the nursing station, but I reach out and grab his arm.

"They'll release me when it's time. For now, I'd just like you to stay here with me."

Foster frowns and nods. He sits down beside me and we hold each other, just like we did when we first got married. I find his simple gesture comforting.

It's almost an hour before the doctor finally comes around, takes a brief look at the cuts on my face, and says I can leave. "Stay out of burning barns, Missy, and you should be just fine."

I smile at his feeble attempt at a joke. Foster scowls at him, so I yank him by the arm and pull him toward the door. I'm so not in the mood for a showdown.

Every couple of minutes on the way home, Foster glances over at me and gives me a forced smile. In the past, I would have been suspicious. But now that my eyes are open, I see how hard he's trying.

When we get home, he tells me to wait for him to help me out of the car. Okay, I like this gentlemanly gesture. But when he tries to carry me, I hold up my hand.

"I'm perfectly capable of walking."

"But—"

"Just open the door for me, and I'll be fine."

We go inside, and he rushes around, turning on lights and asking if there's anything I need. "Do you want the remote before I leave?" he asks.

"Sure." I'm not in the mood to watch TV, but he's trying so hard, I don't want to say no.

"Do you want a burger, chicken, or Mexican?" He picks up the keys and stares at me as he waits for my answer.

I'm not hungry, but I know what he likes. "Burger."

A grin tweaks the corners of his lips, but he quickly resumes his serious expression. "Are you sure? I thought you liked—"

"I'm positive." I'd like to be alone with my thoughts—and my pain—for a little while.

"I won't be long. If you need something, call me, okay?"

"Yes, of course."

Once he's out the door, I let out a deep sigh. Today is one day I'll never forget as long as I live.

"Mama."

I glance up and see my daughter standing at the door. "Hey, Wendy. I thought you were going to try to come to the family picnic."

"Things got a little crazy." She squints. "What happened to you?"

"I was in Grandpa Jay and Granny Marge's barn when it exploded."

"Their barn exploded?" She drops her handbag and comes closer. "How did that happen?"

I tell her what I know—some of it foggy, since most of what I heard came from the paramedics. "I'm sure you'll hear all about it when your daddy gets home." I pick up my phone. "Speaking of your daddy, he's getting burgers. What do you want?"

She shrugs. "I'm not hungry. I had something on the way home."

"Are you sure? How about French fries and a Coke?"

"I guess that'd be okay."

I call Foster and give him Wendy's order. When I click the Off button, Wendy is busy texting on her phone. I watch her expression go from vaguely interested to one of stunned disbelief.

She looks up at me with wide eyes. "Mama, why didn't you tell me you almost died?"

"I did. I said I was in the barn when it blew up."

"That's insane. Did Julius and Brett go to jail?"

"They're not old enough."

Wendy shakes her head, still clearly shocked. "Something needs to happen to them. Why would they do something so stupid?"

She looks down at her phone, mumbles something I can't hear well enough to understand, and does some thumb typing. What strikes me about this conversation is how, when I told her about the explosion, she didn't seem all that concerned. However, as she gets more information from her text messages, it seems more real.

"Who are you texting?" I ask.

"Hallie. She says Brett's grounded until he graduates."

I can't help but smile. When those boys came into the barn, I heard Brett telling Julius it might not be such a good idea and that maybe they should do whatever it was outside. I had no idea what they were talking about at the time. Fortunately for me, I'd made my way to the back door, so I was barely inside when they lit the firecracker fuse. After that, everything's a blur.

"Mama, why are you smiling like nothing happened? You could have died."

"But I didn't." For some strange reason, I'm not as upset about what happened as everyone else around me seems to be. Maybe the whole thing hasn't sunk in yet. Or maybe it changed me in a good way.

"I know, but ..." Wendy flinches, and her face gets all scrunched up like it did when she was a toddler about to cry. She steps closer to me and points to the spot next to me on the couch. "Mind if I sit there?"

I pat it. "Please do."

She lets out a deep breath as she lowers herself onto the cushion and leans into me. Before I have a chance to put my arm around her, she jumps back. "Did I hurt you?"

"No."

She resumes her position, and I hug her close. We haven't done this since she was a little girl. Too bad it takes something terrible to bring us close again. And too bad it took an explosion that could have killed me to realize how hard I was being on my husband.

57

Shay

Elliot has driven me home, and now we're standing on my front doorstep. He's holding my hand, and I sense he'd like to give me a kiss. But I'm not sure it's the right thing to do—at least not now. I started the day with some questions that were mostly answered, but the way it ended makes a kiss seem trivial. And I would never want my kisses trivialized.

"I like you, Shay." Elliot tugs my hand, so I'm forced to turn and face him. "I like you a lot. There's something special about you that makes me wonder how I can be so fortunate to be standing here with you right now."

I like Elliot, too. His rescue and the fact that he's still with me right now, after the craziness during the day with my family, say something about him.

Instead of telling him how I feel, I smile as I look up at him. "Thank you for what you did for Missy. It could have been tragic."

"That's why I did it. I'm glad everything turned out okay, though."

"Do you want to come inside for a few minutes?"

He purses his lips for a moment, then nods. "Yeah, if you don't mind."

I pull out my key and unlock the door. He follows me as I walk through to the kitchen, turning on lights as I go.

"Want something to drink?"

"I'll take water, if you have some."

I smile. "I'm pretty sure I have some of that."

Once I pour two glasses of ice water, I set them on the table and gesture toward the chair across from mine. "Have a seat."

He sits, takes a sip of his water, and rests his elbows on the table. I can tell he wants to talk, but he's not sure where to begin, so I start.

"What do you think of my family now?" I study his expression, hoping for a clue before he speaks.

"They're better than I thought."

"Huh?" I lean back and give him a dubious look.

He laughs. "Your family is fun and interesting. They always have been, but I never really thought about it until today. I think your grandparents are responsible for the way everyone is."

"Why would you want to blame them for all that crazy behavior?"

Elliot leans back and takes a deep breath before slowly letting it out as he shakes his head. "Blame isn't the word I'd use in this case. It's more about how they let everyone be who they are and love them anyway."

"Oh."

He leans forward again. "They remind me of how Christ loves us. He knows we're all different and flawed, yet He still loves us."

I've never seen this side of Elliot before. I know he attends church, but in Pinewood, almost everyone does, regardless of what they believe or how they act on Saturday night.

"Sounds like you've put some thought into this."

He nods. "I have. Quite a bit, actually. In fact, I think it probably contributed to my divorce."

Now I'm puzzled. "You're blaming your divorce on your faith?"

"There's that 'blame' word again." He grins then grows serious. "When I got married, my faith was there, but I'd pushed it to the back of my mind and let other things, like my hormones and physical attraction, take front and center. But that quickly faded as I realized how little her faith meant to her." He brushes something invisible on the table before looking directly at me and holding my gaze. "We never missed church until we started talking about divorce. That's when I realized her faith was more for show than about how she felt in her heart."

"Wow." I swallow hard. "I never realized—"

"I know." He drops his gaze. "I never wanted to get a divorce, but she wasn't willing to work through the problems. Money and things meant more to her than a relationship. I worked hard to keep up the lifestyle she wanted ... that I thought we both wanted. But neither of us was ever totally satisfied. I tried to talk to her about it, but she didn't agree with me, and we had a lot of arguments."

"That's really sad." I see the pensive look on his face. "But you seem to be doing okay."

"I am. I'm still paying off my debt and probably will be for a while, but I think it's time to start living again. I can't continue living with regrets."

"I agree."

He gives me a gentle smile. "Now I realize that, even though divorce isn't something the Lord wants for us, He allows it under certain circumstances. She always wanted a certain type of person, and I couldn't—and wouldn't—live up to her expectations."

"I'm so sorry, Elliot. You've had to deal with a lot more than I ever imagined."

"Even though it was a miserable thing to go through, I'm glad it happened."

"You are?"

He nods. "It's strengthened my conviction that I need to keep my faith in the forefront and not push Jesus to the back, only to pull Him forward when I need Him."

I grimace. "I think we're all guilty of that at times."

"I know you probably don't believe me, but when I look at you, I see Him." Elliot pauses. "You are not only beautiful and smart, but your faith shows in everything you do."

"Unfortunately, I'm guilty of doing exactly what you said you've done—pushing the Lord away until I need Him."

"But you catch yourself because your faith is important to you."

"Yes, it is. Very important."

"Which is one of several reasons I want to do more things with you and see where He leads us." His eyes twinkle as he smiles. "But it might be difficult to stop staring at your gorgeous face long enough to really see you."

I playfully swat at the air in front of my face as my cheeks heat up. "Oh, stop it."

"See? That's another thing I love about you." He stands. "You're humble." He gestures toward the front door. "I really need to get going now, but I'd like to see you again soon. Mind if I call?"

Be still my heart. "I'd like to see you again, too." I'm not used to coming out and saying something like that, but this feels different.

He reaches for my hand as we walk to the door. Once we stop, he places his hands on my shoulders and turns me around to face him. "I had the best time today, Shay."

"Me, too."

When he leans over to kiss me, my heart feels like someone stuck a motor in my chest. The kiss is short and sweet, but the look he gives me afterward makes my insides melt and my knees turn to rubber.

"I'll call you soon." He tweaks my nose and leaves.

I remain standing there, staring after him long after he drives away. When I finally close the door, I close my eyes and allow myself to replay the last couple of minutes we were together. Nothing in my past even comes close to comparing to this, so I'm not sure what to think. All I know is that, in spite of my exhaustion, I feel like I'm floating a foot off the floor.

58

Sally

It's been three days since my family reunion, and Tom has already called me a half dozen times. I get tickled by how our relationship is turning out.

At first, I wasn't sure how I felt about him, since he and Justin acted like high school boys. But when I called him out on it, he apologized and never ignored me again.

Even Sara has noticed that I'm not the same. "It's like someone has flipped your happy switch," she says as she makes herself comfortable in my room. "Now you know what it's like to fall in love."

"I don't know about falling in love, but I do like him a lot."

"That's how it starts." Sara flops back on my bed. "I started liking Justin back in high school, and every time I saw him, I liked him more."

I resist the urge to remind her that he could never tell us apart back then. "When did you know you loved him?"

"I'm not sure, but as soon as he told me he loved me, I said it back … and I meant it."

Her face glows, letting me know she means it from the core of her soul. I swallow hard. "I'm happy for you."

She sits up and clasps her hands together. "Do you really mean that?"

I spin around to fully face her. "Yes, I absolutely do."

Without a moment's hesitation, she jumps up and throws her arms around me. "You have no idea how much that means to me. I was beginning to wonder."

I pull away and give her an apologetic look. "Yeah, me, too. But now I think I understand."

A grin tweaks the corners of her lips. "Now that you're falling in love?"

"We'll have to see about that later. In the meantime, we have a bunch of orders to fill."

As we work, I think about what Sara said. Am I falling in love? I'm probably not at that level yet, but I do have a great big crush on Tom. The only thing that bugged me about him was when he kept chatting it up with Justin. However, I have to give him props for the fact that he stopped as soon as I let him know my feelings. That says a lot for the guy. Well, that and the fact that he's such a gentleman. And he can cook. And he looks amazing in jeans.

Our phones vibrate in unison, signaling that another order is coming in. Sara already has her hand on her phone, so I finish up the bow I'm working on while she checks. I glance over at her, and her eyes look like they might pop right out of her head.

"What's wrong?"

She slowly shakes her head as she turns to face me. "Remember how we've been talking about getting one big client that can take us to the next level?"

I point to her phone. "Is that the client?" Before she can answer, I lift my phone and see an order for more hair bows than we've made since we started in our business. "What are we going to do?"

She lets out a short giggle. "I guess we'd better start working on that order right now."

"Yeah," I agree. "And I think we need to shut down the shop until we get it filled."

We've only had to shut down our shop one time in the past, when a small chain of children's boutiques placed an order for all of their stores. They became regulars, but some of their locations were in towns that got clobbered when businesses started shutting down, causing them to scale way back on orders. They're still clients, but the orders are now much smaller.

This business is much bigger, and I suspect it'll keep us busy for the foreseeable future. "Do you think we can even make the fifty thousand bows they've ordered and have them delivered by the end of the month?" Sara asks.

"I think so." I pause to do some mental math. "We might need to bring someone in to help."

Sara folds her arms, lifts one hand to her face, and taps her chin. "How about Justin?"

"Justin?" I squint as I try to imagine my sister's husband wrapping ribbon with his calloused hands.

"Yeah. I think he'll be good."

I let out a deep sigh. "I guess we can let him try. That is, if he's willing to do it."

"He'll pretty much do anything I want him to do." Sara laughs. "Plus, I think he'd like something to do besides watch TV when he gets home after work."

I look at the breakdown of the colors they're requesting and see that it's mostly green, blue, pink, and yellow, with a much smaller number of orange, black, and white. "This order's too big to rely on the ribbon from the local craft stores, so I think we need to order it from the distributor."

Sara and I spend the next several hours comparing prices and placing orders for the ribbon we'll need. Between calls, we chat about a strategy and how we'll store the materials.

"What if this becomes a regular thing?" she asks. "We've just moved in here, and I'm afraid we might have just outgrown the place."

"Well ..." I ponder the situation for a moment before I look directly at her. "After this order, one of us can buy the other out of the condo, and we can start looking for some industrial office space to rent."

She frowns. "But I like working from home. If we have to go somewhere, I won't be able to work in my pajamas."

"That's the price we'll have to pay for success."

The sound of the front door opening and closing quiets us. I look at Sara as she slowly gets up. She turns to me and makes a goofy face. "I sure hope Justin won't mind making hair bows."

"It'll be good practice," I say. "Y'all might have children someday, and there's nothing more precious than a daddy doing his little girl's hair."

She rolls her eyes. "I'll tell him you said that."

After she leaves, I strain to hear what she tells Justin, but all I hear is a light murmur. I straighten up and pretend to be immersed in my work when I hear them walking toward our office. I glance up and see Justin grinning at me.

"You'll have to show me how to do this." He glances around the room. "Give me a second, and I'll go get another chair."

He leaves Sara and me looking at each other. "That was easy enough," she says. "He didn't even flinch when I told him what we need."

Since we don't have enough materials for our new order, Sara and I take turns teaching him how to make the styles that have been ordered. To our surprise, he catches on extremely quickly, and within a couple of hours, he's up to speed.

"You're a natural," Sara says as he attaches a bow to one of the clips. "Who'd have thought?"

"It's not that different from what I do all day. Some of the automotive work can get rather intricate."

Until now, I never realized Justin could do more than grunt single-syllable words in a conversation. Maybe I need to give him more of a chance.

I pick up the bow and inspect his work. "Good job, Justin."

I squeeze my eyes shut and say a prayer of thanks. When I open them, I see Justin staring at me. "The Lord sure has been good to us, hasn't He?" Justin asks.

All I can do is nod. Justin is not so bad, after all. In fact, I finally understand why my sister loves him.

59

Shay

A sense of dread washes over me as I walk into my office on Monday. This job that I once thought I loved now seems like a burden. It's not hard, and I'm paid well, but I'm bored to tears. The feeling has been coming on for a while, but until now, I've been able to shove it to the back of my mind because there's always so much busywork to do. Besides, until now I've had no idea what else was out there.

I know I should be appreciative of having such a sought-after position with a reputable company that is practically recession proof. But I look around and realize that I've never had much passion for it. I've always enjoyed the position more than the actual work, and the sheen from that has worn off.

The receptionist delivers a stack of envelopes to my office, and I look at them in dread. I know what they are—purchase orders—and I know that it will take almost exactly an hour and a half to go through them. Then I'll return calls until lunchtime, which will be the highlight of my day.

After a deep sigh of resignation, I rip open the first of the envelopes. I'm about halfway through them when Puddin' calls, her voice frantic.

"Shay, you gotta help me. I have to find a way to buy La Chic, or I'll be out of a job."

"Calm down, Puddin'. You and I both know that you don't need that job." I start fidgeting with the papers I still have to look at.

"You don't understand." Her voice drops. "It's not the money I need as much as what it does for me. When I come here, I feel alive."

That single word—alive—grabs my heart. My hand stills as an idea pops into my head. I've never been impulsive in my entire life, but I not only understand what my sister-in-law is saying—I feel the same way.

"What are you doing for lunch?" I ask.

"I promised Amanda I'd help wrap up the books to show the guy who wants to buy the shop, so I'll be there."

"Can you get away for an hour or so? I have an idea that might be good for both of us."

"An idea?" A momentary silence falls between us. "Can you take a late lunch, say around one thirty?"

"Sure. I'll come by the shop. Will Amanda be there?"

"I'm not sure. In fact, I never know about her anymore. Since she and her husband decided to move, it's like she's completely detached."

I totally get it. That's the way I'm feeling now about my job. "I'll see you at one thirty."

I manage to get through my paperwork quickly. Then I pull out one of my blank legal pads and start jotting down some ideas to share with Puddin'. A brief twinge of guilt flickers through me, but it quickly passes. It's not like I haven't put in the time in this job. There have been weeks when I worked sixty-plus hours.

All the phone calls I have to return are based on minor problems that any lower-level manager could handle. Every few minutes, I glance at the clock on the wall. Time drags, but that's always how it seems when there's something you're waiting for.

As soon as it's time to leave, I grab my purse and head for the door. The receptionist holds up a finger, signaling that she needs to tell me something when she's off the phone. I glance at my watch and make a face, letting her know that I'm in a hurry.

She quickly gets off the phone. "I was about to let you know that some of the home office people are stopping off this afternoon around three o'clock."

I try to remember anything being said about a meeting. "When did you find out?"

"About ten minutes ago." Her face lights up with a wide smile. "I think something major is about to go down."

A few years ago, that would have had me on edge, but now, not so much.

All I want to do is have lunch with Puddin' and share my thoughts that might solve both of our problems—or create new ones. Whatever the case, there's not an ounce of doubt in my mind that I'm due for a major change.

I nod. "I'll be back by then."

I parallel park in front of La Chic. As I walk up to the front door, my pulse quickens. If everything turns out like I think it might, I'll be parking here quite a bit very soon.

Puddin' gives me a tentative grin as I walk in. "Let me go tell Amanda you're here. She's in the back packing some of her stuff."

When she returns with Amanda, I notice the distant look in the woman's eyes. Yes, Puddin' was right when she said Amanda was detached. She's mentally somewhere else, and I'm not even sure we should trust her with her own shop for an hour.

"Where do you want to go?" I ask. "It needs to be someplace where we can have some privacy."

Puddin' gives me a strange look and nods. "Let's go to the Blossom Diner."

By the time we get there, most of the lunch crowd has dissipated. We're able to get a seat in the corner, away from the front door.

Both of us order salads and sweet tea. Once the server leaves, Puddin' puts her forearms on the table and leans toward me. "Okay, so what are you thinking?"

One of the many things I love about my sister-in-law is her directness. "How would you like to have a business partner?"

"A what?"

Since we don't have much time, I figure it's best to dive right in. "I have enough money saved up to buy La Chic. I'll work at my current job for a few more months—at least until they can find someone to replace me. Then we'll be co-managers of the shop." I pause. "What do you think?"

Her eyes have widened so big, they look like they might pop out. "Are you serious?"

I nod. "I've been bored silly with my job for a while now, but it didn't hit me that hard until I lived with the twins. I got to see two women who had some control over their daily work. I figure if they can be successful, you and I can be, too."

Puddin' shakes her head, belying the grin that takes up a large portion of her face. "You totally stunned me with this one, Shay. I never expected this from you."

"I never expected it from me either."

For the next fifteen minutes, we talk about all the things we can do with the shop, giggling like a couple of teenage girls. We nibble at our salads, but neither of us is hungry because we're so excited about what the future holds.

With the taste of excitement laced with balsamic-vinaigrette salad dressing, I drive Puddin' back to the shop, where I see Amanda standing by the door, looking out. She blinks when she sees us, but she doesn't budge from her spot.

"Looks like she's daydreaming," I say.

Puddin' nods. "She's been like that ever since she and her husband decided to move. It's like she's already gone."

"Would you mind asking her to stick around until I get off work?"

Puddin' gets out, leans over, and sticks her head in the window. "I sure hope she hasn't signed anything with that guy."

"That makes two of us."

She walks toward the door of the shop, turns to wave, and then goes inside. I pull away, praying that it's not too late to execute my plan. The more I think about it, the more I like the thought of being a co-owner of a fashion boutique.

Then I laugh. I've never been that into fashion, but I'm changing. I don't want to continue wearing what the twins have called my "harsh" look. I want to get in touch with my more feminine side. I've been wearing my hair in softer curls around my face, and several people have commented on how much better I look. That feels good. And it doesn't hurt that Elliot's appreciative gazes have increased since I've made some of these changes.

As soon as I pull into the office parking lot, I see the cars of the Southern Foods executives all lined up in the reserved spots. I was hoping for a few minutes to pull myself together and construct a letter to hand my boss before I meet with them.

The receptionist smiles and makes a gesture toward the conference room. "I told them you'd have to go to your office to prepare when you got back from lunch, but they wanted to set up."

"Thanks." I smile back at her. She's been working for me long enough to know that I hate rushing things.

It takes me about fifteen minutes to write and print my resignation letter. It is brief and to the point, without much detail. The less I put in there, the less I'll have to explain. I don't want anyone trying to talk me out of what I'm about to do.

I fold the letter neatly and stuff it into the side pocket of my briefcase before I stand up, take a deep breath, and head for the conference room. My boss greets me and points to the chair. "Have a seat, Shay."

"Hey," I say, trying to keep my voice light. All the men in there look so glum. "Is everything okay?"

My boss casts a nervous glance toward one of the other men before looking me directly in the eyes. "I'm afraid we have some bad news for you, Shay. When we agreed to this merger, we were assured everyone would be able to keep their jobs."

I narrow my eyes. "What are you saying, Dan?"

He purses his lips, visually scans the group, and then settles his gaze on me. "I'm afraid we're going to have to let you go." Before I have a chance to say anything, he continues. "I managed to negotiate a severance package that should get you through several months while you look for something else." Then he tells me the amount of the check that I'll be getting.

Once I recover from shock, the desire to jump up and give my boss—or former boss—a hug nearly overwhelms me. Now I don't have to worry about delivering my resignation letter or withdrawing any of my savings to purchase the shop.

"I'm so sorry, Shay. You've done an incredible job, but unfortunately, we can't afford to duplicate the positions." He leans forward and lowers his voice. "In all honesty, the reason we're letting you go is that you make more money—but I never said that." He grimaces. "Unfortunately, it's all about the bottom line."

I try not to show my glee as I nod. "I understand. When is this effective?"

He closes his eyes and swallows hard, letting me know this is difficult for him. "Immediately. If there is anything I can do, don't hesitate to call. I'll write you a glowing reference."

"Thank you." I stand. "Do you mind if I leave now?"

Once I get to the door, I practically run to my office. I can't wait to get everything out of my office and start my new life. As I toss things into a cardboard box, I realize that I've never really personalized my workspace.

I pause on my way out to say goodbye to the receptionist. Judging by the look of pure horror on her face, it's obvious she's as surprised as I am by the turn of events.

"I am so sorry, Shay. What are you going to do now?"

"Don't worry about me. I'll be just fine."

"Keep in touch, okay?"

60

Puddin'

Hallie's been picking Jeremy up from preschool on her way home from the high school that gets out early. That gives me more time at the shop. At first, Digger didn't like that idea, but after the first day, Jeremy seemed to have found an extra dose of love for his big sister, so Digger agreed that it's okay as long as Jeremy doesn't feel neglected. Hallie likes the extra money I give her for her gas, so it's turning out to be a win-win situation.

This morning, I gave her the party hats we never used at the reunion on account of the barn blowing up. "Can you take him to Chuck E. Cheese's?"

"Sure, but I'll need extra money for pizza."

I hand her a twenty.

She keeps her hand open. "I'll see if some of the other kids from his preschool want to join us."

I hand her another twenty.

When I hear the bells on the door, I snap out of my thoughts and walk out to the floor to see who it is. I have to do a double take when I realize it's Shay.

"Are you playing hooky from work?"

Her whole face lights up. "No. When I returned from our lunch, I got laid off. Isn't it amazing?"

"Amazing good or amazing bad?" I ask. She's acting awfully weird for someone who just lost her job.

"Southern Foods is completing the merger, and they don't need me anymore, so not only did they let me go, they gave me a severance package with enough money for the down payment on this place."

Now I'm concerned. I sure hope my boss hasn't finalized the deal with that other guy. "I haven't talked to Amanda yet."

"Can you call her?"

"Now?"

She nods. "I'd really like to talk to her before it's too late."

"Okay, wait right here. I need to go get my phone." I walk to the back room, pull my phone out of my purse, and call Amanda's cell phone.

"I'm about to go into a meeting," she says. "Can I call you back later?"

"I know it's none of my business, but if you're about to meet with that guy who wants to buy the shop, I'd like you to wait."

"Puddin', you know I can't wait. I have to sell."

I clear my throat, straighten my shoulders, and suck in a breath. "I know, and that's why I'd like to make an offer."

"*You?*" Her voice squeaks.

"Yes, me. Well, me and my sister-in-law."

"Shay? Why would she—"

"We want to be business partners." The very sound of that makes me smile. "Please don't sign anything until you at least talk to us."

"How soon can y'all do this?"

"As soon as you can get here. Shay's in the shop right now."

"Okay." Amanda pauses. "Let me tell him there's an emergency and I have to run to the shop real quick. I don't want to turn him away just yet. You know, just in case..."

"I understand." I'm so excited, I'm about to pop. This is happening so fast, I don't know if I'm coming or going.

"I'll be there in half an hour."

I walk out to the sales floor and see Shay chatting with one of our older customers. Shay pulls out one of the dresses on the rack, holds it up to the woman, and says something I can't make out. They both look over at me at the same time.

"Shay has such a good eye for fashion," the customer says before turning back to my sister-in-law. "I didn't plan on buying anything today, but this looks perfect for the ladies' lunch at the club. Let me go try it on."

As soon as she's set up in the fitting room, Shay comes out. "Well? Is it too late?"

"Almost. I think if we'd waited another hour, it would be. She was about to go into a meeting, but I told her I wanted to make an offer."

Shay grimaces. "I wish you hadn't—oh, never mind. Let's find out how much she wants, and we can work from there."

I've obviously messed up, but it's too late now. "There's so much I have to learn about business."

"You'll do fine." Shay's attention is diverted to something outside. "Here she comes."

My heart pounds out of control as Amanda walks into the shop with a curious look on her face. "Hey, Shay. I hear you and Puddin' want to buy the shop. Is this true?"

I have to force myself to keep my mouth shut as Shay extends her hand to shake Amanda's. "We'll need to get more information before we can make an offer, but we're definitely interested."

Amanda nods. "I don't have a lot of time to negotiate, so here's what Ahmad offered." She states a dollar amount that shocks me because it's so low. "Can you match that?"

I turn to see Shay's reaction, but her face is expressionless. She rubs her hands together for a few seconds before she finally nods. "Yes, and I can throw in another couple of thousand so you won't have any regrets."

Now it's Amanda's turn to look shocked. "Are you sure?"

"Positive." Shay turns to me with a questioning look, and I nod. Then she looks back at Amanda. "Is it a deal?"

Amanda smiles. "Yes, it's a deal."

Shay hesitates for a moment. "Then why don't we sign something to make it official?"

"Now?" Once again, Amanda looks confused. "Don't you want to take a look at the books to make sure everything is in order?"

"Not really. Puddin's been keeping your books, and I trust her." She glances my way and gives me a conspiratorial smile.

Now I'm beaming with pride. Shay couldn't have said anything that would have made me happier, even if she said I was her favorite sister-in-law.

Since we don't have an official contract drawn up, Shay constructs something that takes her about ten minutes. I know she's been doing stuff like this for a long time, so I completely trust her.

Once all three of us have signed the temporary agreement for Shay and me to purchase La Chic, Amanda says she has to go talk to the other guy and let him down easy. I turn to Shay as soon as Amanda is gone.

"That was fast, but I have one question. Why did you offer her more money?"

"It's only a couple thousand dollars, and I thought it might seal the deal. I didn't want to take any chances, in case he increases his offer."

Now that the reality of what just happened sets in, my nerves get ahold of me. "I sure hope we did the right thing."

"Yeah, me, too."

61
Shay

Puddin' and I have owned La Chic for almost a month now, and I don't think I've ever had so much fun working. I'm teaching her about the big-picture aspects of business, and she's helping me with some of the day-to-day details of running a boutique. Our talents complement each other, and our profits are already up by ten percent.

"I think we can do better than this," Puddin' says. "I have some ideas to bring in some younger customers."

"As long as we're careful not to neglect the regulars."

"Of course." Puddin' beams. "I love owning this place. If we keep increasing our profit like we have so far, we'll be in high cotton."

I laugh. "I don't know about you, but to me, this is better than striking oil. It's nice to actually *earn* the money."

"I agree." I see her eyes darting past me. "Don't look now, but you have a visitor."

I don't have to look. I hear the soothing tone of Elliot's voice. "I'm in the mood to have dinner with a fashion expert. Do I have any volunteers?"

Puddin' chuckles. "I would, but I promised Digger I'd fix him some pot roast tonight."

"Then you'll have to settle for me." My heart pounds as he gives me the look that makes me feel as though I'm the only woman on the planet.

He tips his head toward me. "Pick you up at seven thirty?"

I nod. "See you then."

As soon as he leaves, Puddin' sighs. "I have a good feeling about you and Elliot. Why don't you run on home now and start getting ready?"

"I don't want to leave you alone."

"I'm perfectly capable of handling this shop by myself. I want you to be relaxed for your date." She quickly glances away, making me suspicious.

"What's going on, Puddin'?"

"Oh, nothing. Just go get your purse and leave, okay? I want to be alone."

I laugh as I make my way back to the office to get my purse. On my way out, I call over my shoulder, "I don't think you'll be alone long. Here come the Junior League ladies."

"Oh, boy." Puddin' chuckles. "At least they like to spend money."

"Ain't that the truth." I've noticed that when Rita or any of her friends comes in alone, they often just window shop. However, as a group, they're very competitive. There are days when we make more money from their clique in an hour than from the rest of the day's receipts combined.

I go home and take advantage of the extra time to get ready. I pour some bubbles into the bathtub and fill it while I prepare some iced tea. Then I put on some soothing music to enjoy while I soak and sip my tea.

By the time Elliot arrives to pick me up, I'm relaxed and happy. He smiles as he takes me into his arms. "There's something I need to tell you." He leans back a little and tips my chin up so I can meet his gaze.

"What's that?"

He clears his throat. "I was going to wait until later, but I don't think I can. You look amazing, and my nerves are on the edge of my skin."

I laugh. "The way I look makes you nervous?"

He makes a goofy face as he nods. "Yes, I'm afraid so."

"Should I do something different?"

"No." He pulls me closer again. "Don't do anything different."

"Now you have my curiosity up. What do you want to tell me?"

"Promise this won't scare you away?" He lifts an eyebrow and waits.

"I don't know. Are you about to tell me something scary?"

Elliot nods. "Yeah, it's scary, all right."

"I can't promise—"

He gently presses a finger to my lips to shush me. "I love you, Shay."

My heart stops momentarily. Then it beats double time. "You do?"

"Are you surprised?"

"Yes." I think for a moment as we lock gazes. "Actually, I was more surprised when you kept coming around after the craziness at my family reunion."

"One of the things I love most about you is how much you care about your family."

"One of the things?" I tease. "You mean there are others?"

"Yes, and I'll tell you all about them, but it'll take a while." He turns me toward the door.

"I have all the time in the world."

I have to keep pinching myself throughout the evening. Who would have thought I'd own a dress boutique and be half of a couple with Elliot Stevens? Certainly not me. I keep learning new things about myself, one of them being that the scarier things get, the more exciting the outcome. Of course, not everything turns out so great, but as long as you don't give up, there's always hope.

Acknowledgments

This book is dedicated to my family, including my husband, daughters, sons-in-law, granddaughters, parents, grandparents, aunts, uncles, and cousins—especially the crazy cousins. Y'all know who I'm talking about.

About the Author

Debby Mayne writes family and faith-based romances, cozy mysteries, and women's fiction and is the author of more than 60 novels and novellas—plus more than 1,000 short stories, articles, and devotions for busy women. Debby is currently an etiquette writer for The Spruce.

Debby grew up in a military family, which meant moving every few years throughout her childhood. She was born in Alaska, and she has lived in Mississippi, Tennessee, Oregon, Florida, South Carolina, Hawaii, and Japan. Her parents were both from the Deep South, so Debby enjoys featuring characters with Southern drawls, plenty of down-home cooking, and folks with quirky mannerisms. *High Cotton* is the first book in the Bucklin Family Reunion series.

Connect with Debby!
Website: www.debbymayne.net
Facebook: www.facebook.com/DebbyMayneAuthor
Twitter: www.twitter.com/debbymayne

Coming Soon

FIT TO BE TIED

Visit us online for the latest updates:

www.debbymayne.net

www.gileadpublishing.com

GILEAD PUBLISHING

In Fall 2018, the Bucklin family is getting together again … and this family reunion is shaping up to be another hot mess!